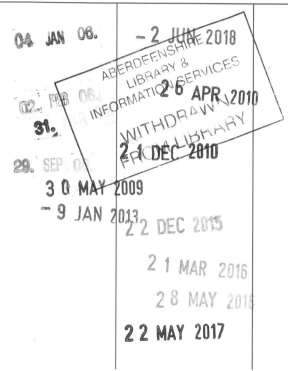

NICKOLAI
OF THE
NORTH

NICKOLAI
OF THE
NORTH

LUCY DANIEL RABY

Illustrated by Ted Dewan

Hodder
Children's
Books

A division of Hodder Headline Limited

First published in Great Britain in 2005
by Hodder Children's Books

1

ISBN 0 340 90300 7

Typeset in Bembo by Avon DataSet Ltd, Bidford on Avon,
Warwickshire

Printed and bound by
Clays Ltd, St Ives plc

Hodder Children's Books
a division of Hodder Headline Limited
338 Euston Road
London NW1 3BH

For Mum, Dad, Pete and Isabel

The Secret Kingdom

It happened one Winter Solstice Eve at the North Pole, many centuries ago.

It was the darkest end of the year. There had been no sunrise for several months and the moon shone continually on the snowy wastes. The wind howled across the vast, empty spaces. The Northern Lights danced in the sky, great shimmering curtains of rose pink and ghostly green and pale yellow, towering above the earth. They swept to and fro across the heavens in a display so majestic and so breathtaking you had to see it to believe it. But there was no one there to see it, apart from the Arctic wolves and the polar bears.

At the stroke of midnight, a deep rumbling noise came from below. The ice heaved and groaned and gave a great shudder. An ear-splitting sound tore the air and a gigantic crack opened up in the ice. If anyone had been there and looked down into it, they would have seen the strangest place on earth. Hidden beneath the surface of the North Pole, deep inside the polar ice

1

cap, lay a secret world of tunnels and caves.

They were all shapes and sizes. There were stately caverns that looked like the insides of cathedrals, with arched roofs and pillars. There were countless grottos, each one opening out into the next, and endless tunnels, twisting and turning and crisscrossing each other in a mind-boggling maze. It was the sort of place where you could get lost for ever.

The whole labyrinth was full of strange, intricate rock formations – stalagmites and stalactites which grew out of the ice floor, hung down from the roof and covered the walls. It was empty and silent, except for the slow drip drip of water. And very dark, except for a faint, eerie blue glow which filtered down from above.

Like an inquisitive animal, the Northern Lights curved down towards the earth and peered into the crack. Fascinated, they poured through the caverns, filling them with brilliant colour and finding their way into every dark corner.

For a few miraculous moments, the Northern Lights held hands with the earth's magnetic forces. There was an enormous explosion of energy. It released a swarm of tiny winged creatures, like buzzing insects.

These were the Light Fairies. They glowed so brightly and flitted around so fast you could hardly see them. They flowed through the caverns, fluttering everywhere, touching the lifeless rocks. And as they did, they brought them to life, transforming them into beautiful dainty creatures with pointed ears and ice-blue eyes full of dancing Lights.

The first elves had been born and the Elfin Kingdom had been created.

As quickly as it had opened, the ice creaked and groaned and the crack slammed shut, sealing off the secret Kingdom from the prying eyes of the world.

When the Lights Went Out

Nickolai sat on his mother's lap, shrieking with glee as her sleigh raced along the tunnels at breakneck speed. He was barely a year old, but big for his age. Like all elfin children, Nickolai had pointed ears and eyes the colour of cornflowers. His chubby cheeks were flushed with excitement and his ears twitched as the wind whistled past them, blowing his blond curls about. He was loving every minute of this rollercoaster ride.

His Light Fairy, Elvina, was not enjoying it at all. She'd tucked herself away down his front and was quivering against his chest, making agitated twittering noises. She peered out timidly at the shopfronts and houses flashing past in a blur, letting out squeaks of alarm every time they swerved round a corner. She was of a nervous disposition. Not a good thing when her elfling had all the makings of a boy racer.

It was the Winter Solstice Sleigh Race, the most important event in the elfin calendar. Its route snaked around the whole underground city as the sleighs roared down the ice streets, dived through narrow alleyways, ducked around courtyards, then soared high above the heads of the crowds.

These were no ordinary sleighs. They were colourfully decorated and hung about with millions of tiny bells which jingled loudly. Although their drivers steered them with reins, there were no huskies, horses or beasts of any kind pulling them along. They had no wheels or engines. They flew along through the air, just above the ground, at astonishing speeds.

The force that drove them came from something so mysterious, no human would have been able to understand it. The sleighs were powered by the invisible magnetic forces at the North Pole.

Over the centuries, the elves had discovered that if they moved their pointed ears around and concentrated very hard, they could link up with these magnetic forces. They could tap in to this power and use it like an electric current to drive their sleighs and all the other machines and tools they invented. A complicated transport system of 'sleigh lines' developed around the Kingdom, and it took years of practice to master the skills of navigation.

No one had practised harder than Nickolai's mother; Ella had started when she was a small girl. She was a wisp of a thing, fair and slender, with fragile looks that concealed a will of granite. She had been left a young widow with a baby when her husband was killed in an avalanche. It had been tough, but she was determined to build a better life for both of them. This meant being good at things that men usually did. No woman had ever entered the race before, so even being considered as a candidate had been an uphill task. But her steely determination had finally gained her a place.

And now she was determined to win. For ahead of them in Solstice Square lay the trophy – the Solstice Cup. And a whole year of special elfin privileges, which would come in very handy.

She tightened her grip round Nickolai's belly as they approached a sharp bend.

'Hang on tight, Nickolai! Here comes the big one!'

They swerved round the corner into Great Bear Avenue. Ahead of them they could see a crowd of other sleighs, weaving in and out of each other, jostling to get ahead. They were rushing towards the opening into Solstice Square – a circle of light showing a festive scene beyond – and the finishing line, a row of icicles strung across the gap, sparkling in the Light.

'Come on! Let's do it together!' cried Ella, and she let Nickolai hold the reins with her. She twitched her ears in small circular movements, searching for the power that crackled in the air.

There was a sudden jolt and the sleigh shot forward. Ella glanced at her son and saw with shock that he too was moving his ears, in the slow, deliberate way it took adult elves years to master.

He really was helping her!

She steered the sleigh skilfully around the others, then there was another spurt and she overtook them and zoomed into the lead. A cheer went up from the elves lining the streets as the sleigh streaked ahead at lightning speed and the finishing line rushed towards them.

Seconds later, they burst through the line of icicles. A roar rose up from the huge crowd. Ella reined in the power and drew the sleigh to a halt on the ice, where it spun round several times before coming to rest. She gazed breathlessly at the sea of cheering faces, then grabbed her son and hugged him tight. They had done it!

'We won! We won!' she cried triumphantly. She lifted him high over her head. Nickolai grinned gummily and waved his arms and legs around like a fat little string puppet. The crowd surged forward and clamoured round to congratulate the first female elf ever to win the Winter Solstice Sleigh Race.

Solstice Square was the grandest and most important of the city squares. It was in this cavern, according to legend, that the crack had opened all those years ago and the Northern Lights had created the Kingdom. The Lights still filtered down from above, through the domed ceiling, where the ice was thinnest.

Tonight, on Winter Solstice Eve, they were at their strongest, and the square at its most festive. Hundreds of elves, all of them dressed in their Solstice best, thronged the cavern and jostled each other excitedly. They wore pointed hats tipped with bells and their costumes were made of gauzy material that shimmered different colours in the Light.

Light Fairies swarmed around like insects, following their elves and buzzing in high-pitched squeaking voices. No elf was ever seen without their own Light Fairy fluttering around, somewhere nearby. They were their soul mates, constant companions throughout their lives; the moment an elf was born, a new Light Fairy would fly down from the Lights and never leave their side.

The elfin band played their strange, unearthly music and elfin dancers whirled around the floor, spinning like mad things in never-ending patterns, their coloured costumes swirling different colours.

The square was full of stalls selling traditional Solstice goodies: snow berry pies, crystal cakes, starlight syllabubs and snowball ices. Solstice gifts and toys were changing hands everywhere – Light Fairy dolls which glowed when you smiled at them, toy sleighs with their own magical built-in power supply and miniature scale models of the Kingdom, full of moving figures. It was Elfin custom to give gifts on Winter Solstice Eve, because it was the anniversary of the birth of the Kingdom and a thanksgiving celebration.

On an ice throne sat King Vilmar, watching over the festivities. Vilmar was a direct descendant of the Very First Elf, and reputed to be at least a thousand years old. He was small and wizened, with a very long white beard and twinkling blue eyes that almost disappeared behind the creases in his face. He was wearing a crown made of crystal and long, flowing white robes edged with silver. He was extremely wise and very kind, and he smiled benevolently at his subjects as they celebrated.

As midnight approached, the atmosphere began to build to a climax. A great ice bell began to chime. The crowd fell silent as the old king stood up creakily, clutching the Solstice Cup – a magnificent trophy carved from ice crystal. Only a descendant of his ancient line could perform this ritual. He held it up for all to see.

As the last stroke chimed, a shaft of brilliant Light burst through the dome and touched the Cup, making it sparkle and shimmer. A gasp of wonder went up from the elves. There was a hush, then Vilmar's cracked old voice rang out in the silence.

'It gives me great pleasure to present the Solstice Cup to this year's winners,' he announced. 'Ella Grishkin and her son Nickolai!'

A roar of approval rose up from the elves as Ella made her way towards the stage, clutching Nickolai. People cooed at him and patted her on the back as they passed. Nickolai was revelling in the attention, and Ella floated along as though she were in a dream. But she was determined not to be overcome by shyness. She was champion now.

She stepped forward and swept a deep curtsey. Then she straightened up and looked into Vilmar's misty old eyes. They crinkled as the king smiled at her fondly.

'Well done, my dear!' he whispered. 'I always knew you could do it!'

Vilmar placed the champion's robe around Ella's shoulders. It was made of red velvet lined with thick white fur, and had a red hood edged in the same. It was the greatest honour in the Kingdom to wear it and Ella was acutely aware that she was the first elfin woman to have it placed on her shoulders.

To resounding applause, Vilmar presented the Cup. Nickolai reached a pudgy hand towards it, attracted by its swirling colours. He gurgled with delight as Ella let him hold it with her and turned to face the crowd. The elves went wild, cheering themselves hoarse and throwing their hats in the air with a loud jingling sound. The music started up and they began to dance again, whirling around even faster than before.

At first the crowd didn't hear the low rumbling noise that started up from deep within the earth. But as the rumbling grew louder, the cavern began to tremble.

The music died away.

One by one, the elves stopped dancing and stared at each other in alarm. The cavern began to shudder and the rumbling grew into a roar. Black smoke poured out of the ice, billowing round the cavern and filling it with a foul stench.

There was a loud cracking sound and a hole opened in the floor like a jagged, toothless grin. It hissed and fizzled, letting out a puff of steam and another belch of

11

smoke. The elves edged forward and peered cautiously over the rim. They gasped in horror as they looked down.

Far below them lay the core of the earth. They could see the fiery glow of molten metal, heaving and gurgling. It was a terrifying sight.

Everyone fell back, shrieking, as a whirlwind of hideous creatures began to pour out of the hole. They were so vile it hurt your eyes to look at them. Snarling black wolves with white fangs and foaming jaws. Demons with grisly grins and pointed teeth, tearing at each other with their talons. Greasy goblins with glistening red skins, twisting and turning and thrashing around. The monsters howled and wailed like banshees as they burst out in a relentless stream.

And slowly out of their midst rose the most hideous creature of all. The witch to end all witches. A monstrous old crone, with matted grey hair that hung around her shoulders in clumps. Her face was haggard and covered with loose, green, putrid skin. Her red mouth was twisted into a snarl, showing the jagged stumps of rotten teeth. But the worst thing of all was her eyes. They were black holes, dark and empty and burning with hatred.

She rose up, higher and higher, until she was towering over the cavern, and glared down at the elves with a sneer on her face.

'Well well,' she rasped, in a voice that sounded like continents crunching together. 'What a cosy little scene.' A blast of foul air gusted round the cavern as she spoke and the elves recoiled in disgust.

Nickolai gaped at the monstrous spectacle. Ella noticed that his Light Fairy was nowhere to be seen, although she could hear a muffled squeaking from somewhere deep inside Nickolai's tunic. She tightened her grip on him and backed away, slipping silently amongst the crowds to hide in their sleigh, still clutching her trophy.

After the first stunned reaction, chaos broke out. The cavern filled with screams as the elves scattered in all directions, trying to escape down the tunnels that led off the square. But they found their way blocked by the wolves. The Light Fairies were making shrill, high-pitched buzzing noises and clinging to their elves.

Vilmar struggled up from his throne and shuffled forward, pointing a shaking finger at the hag. She towered over his frail old figure.

'Magda!' he cried, in a voice quivering with rage. 'Why have you returned? You were banished for ever!'

It was only then that everyone noticed the witch had pointed ears. But they were not like normal elfin ears. They were wrinkled and drooping, with charred black tips.

'I command you to leave the Kingdom immediately!' quavered Vilmar. 'Go back to where you belong! And take your vile creatures with you!'

The monster laughed, an evil, hissing sound that crackled round the cavern like a whip. 'I don't think

13

so!' she sneered. 'Not after all these centuries down there in that hellhole. Look what it's done to me!'

'It was your own fault!' cried Vilmar. 'You meddled with the forces! You were a danger to us all! You had to be banished for your sorcery!'

'And now I'm back!' spat the witch. The elves ducked as a spray of hot, steaming bile whirled round the cavern. 'Thought you'd got rid of me, didn't you? Fools! Down there I found the power I needed. To take what belongs to me. The forces are at their strongest tonight! And I want every last drop!'

A wail of terror started up from the elves. Everyone knew what she meant. She was talking about the Lights.

'No!' shouted Vilmar. 'They are not yours to take! They belong to the Kingdom!'

'Not any more!' screeched Magda. 'They're mine mine mine all mine!'

And with a loud shriek of glee, she pulled aside the folds of her charred robe to reveal a black hole where her heart should have been. It was like staring into blank, empty nothingness.

In an instant, the cavern was filled with a howling gale and a violent sucking noise. It was coming from the black hole in Magda's chest. The shaft of Light that shone down through the dome into the cavern began to quiver violently, resisting the pull. The elves' wails of terror rose to a shriek as slowly, the column of Light was drawn towards the hole. The Light Fairies set up a

*And with a loud shriek of glee, she pulled aside
the folds of her charred robe . . .*

high-pitched buzzing and clustered together in a shimmering ball of Light. Then they too were torn away and sucked into the hole, like iron filings to a magnet, until they had been swallowed up.

Outside, on the surface, the Northern Lights were whisked away, as though a curtain had been torn down. The sky darkened and the cavern was plunged into gloom.

One by one, the elves fell silent and froze on the spot like statues. Their eyes glazed over and became cold and dead. Icicles began to form on them, covering their limbs in layers of encrusted ice, blurring their shapes beyond recognition. The elves were turning back into the lifeless rocks from which they came.

Ella ran as fast as she could, stumbling along in the darkness, gasping for breath. By some miracle, she had not turned into stone. Her Light Fairy had been snatched away with the others, but Nickolai's was still with them, tucked down his front and clinging to him like a limpet. She could hear her muffled squeaks of terror. Ella had slipped away, unnoticed in all the confusion, and escaped down a narrow passageway hidden behind a rock.

All she could think of now was getting home to her little house on Ice Ridge Avenue. Nickolai was whimpering pitifully, his cries coming out jerkily as she ran along. She rounded a bend and set off down Orion Avenue. Although the whole city had been blacked out, Ella knew every corner and could find her way home by memory.

A noise behind her made her heart stop. A howling, baying sound that echoed eerily round the tunnels.

Ella glanced back and saw several pairs of yellow eyes glowing in the dark, moving towards them. The wolves! They had caught her scent! Her heart began thumping wildly as she put on a spurt and sprinted down a turning to the left. The baying sound grew louder. She stifled a cry of terror as she saw more yellow eyes coming towards her from the other direction. They were everywhere!

Nickolai began to cry more loudly. Ella hugged him tight and whispered to him soothingly.

'Don't worry! Mama won't let them get you!'

She dived into Hyperion Alley, a small winding passage that led to the left, hoping to throw them off the scent by doubling back on herself. She zigzagged through the maze, her breath coming in ragged gasps.

Slowly, the sound of the wolves faded away into the background. She had managed to lose them! Breathing a sigh of relief, she turned into Ursa Passage, feeling her way in the unfamiliar dark. Not far now and she would be back in the safety of her home.

She stopped abruptly and let out a groan of despair. Ahead of her lay a solid wall of ice. There must have been an avalanche, blocking off the alley. She heard the howling noise again. Closer now. The dark shadowy shapes appeared at the end of the alley and bounded towards them, yellow eyes glowing like brimstone in the gloom.

They were trapped.

Ella's heart felt like it was thumping its way out of her chest. Nickolai bellowed in fear and his ears began to twitch violently. There was a loud crack and the ice shifted and groaned around them. A narrow shaft had opened in the wall to their left, sloping upwards. She looked at her son in amazement. How had he done it? The shaft was just wide enough for both of them. At the end was a faint glimpse of starlight, framed in the opening.

The surface! Her only hope. It was forbidden to the elves – but this was an emergency. She lifted Nickolai on to her back, scrambled up into the shaft and began crawling along it.

'Hang on tight!' she called, and Nickolai wrapped his arms and legs round her and clung on like a baby monkey. She struggled along the shaft, using her hands and feet to brace herself. Down below the wolves growled and whined, glaring up at them. Some of them began to scrabble at the opening, trying to follow them.

After what seemed like an endless struggle, Ella reached the top of the shaft and pulled herself out on to the surface. The Arctic air hit her like a sledgehammer. She must try and keep the boy warm. She took off her Solstice Champion's robe and wrapped it round him tightly, then swept him up and

18

began to dash across the snow. Nickolai's cries were echoing around the empty silence. Ella looked round wildly, her eyes searching the horizon for shelter. The vast wilderness of snow and ice seemed to go on for ever. A pale disc of moon hung in the sky and sparkled on the snow.

She heard the terrible howling noise behind her again. She looked back and felt shock prickle her entire body. The wolves were pouring out of the crack. They had somehow managed to scramble up the shaft! With a strangled cry, she began to stumble blindly over the icy ridges.

She had no idea where she was going, but desperation drove her on. Suddenly her feet went from under her and she fell. Nickolai was flung from her arms and landed on the snow, some way from her. He sat up, reaching towards her, screaming at the top of his voice.

'Mama!'

Ella scrambled to her feet and tried to run towards him. But with each step she took, her feet became more leaden and heavy. The numbness stole over her, bringing her to a halt, paralysing her whole body. With an immense effort she reached out towards him.

'Nickolai!'

Her cry echoed into the distance and faded away. Then she became still and silent, frozen in mid-motion, leaning forward with her arms outstretched. A thick crust of icicles formed on her, blurring her shape until it was barely recognizable. Within moments she had turned into stone.

Nickolai stared at the lifeless form that had been his mother and began to howl louder than ever. The wolves bounded towards him, red tongues lolling out of their jaws, yellow eyes glowing. His screams rose high into the cold night air as the wolves reached him and circled round, growling and snarling, closing in for the kill.

Suddenly, out of nowhere, a huge shape flashed through the air. It snatched the bundle up off the ground, grabbing the red robe in its teeth and lifting him up. Nickolai's world was turned upside down as he was whisked out of the wolves' reach. The creatures yelped in surprise, their jaws hanging open. The shape picked up speed and shot off across the sky, leaving a streak of white light behind it.

A Gift from Heaven

The flying reindeer soared through the air, gripping the baby in his makeshift hammock between her teeth. Her breath made icy puffs in the cold night air and her huge, branched antlers swayed as she moved her head around, steering a course south. Below, a vast expanse of whiteness lay glistening in the moonlight, while above stretched a huge bowl of inky blackness, dotted with points of bright light.

The landscape rolled past underneath, empty and silent. After a while, a pine forest came into view, covered in a thick layer of snow. Nickolai slept on, lulled by the rocking movement, and the forest slipped past until it was left behind. She began to approach the first settlement south of the Pole. It was not much more than a large cluster of buildings with a few twinkling lights.

The reindeer began to swoop downwards, flying in circles, her head swinging this way and that, looking for something. The tops of the buildings came nearer, revealing sloping roofs and crooked chimneys, some with smoke curling out of them. On the northern edge of the town was a smaller house that looked shabbier than the rest. It had a chimney on its roof, but no sign of any smoke.

The reindeer glided down and hovered just above the chimney. Then her teeth unclenched and she let go of the bundle. Nickolai dropped like a stone. He jerked awake and screamed in shock as he plummeted into the chimney's open mouth, stayed wedged there for a moment, then slithered down into blackness.

The scuffling noise in the fireplace woke Hannah first. She and Joe had been dozing in front of a dying fire, unaware that it was now a heap of cold black ashes.

She opened her eyes and saw a chubby child sitting in the hearth, a dazed expression on his face, in a red cloak with the hood wrapped tightly round his head. He was covered in soot, but looked otherwise unharmed. He stared round the room, blinking in shock; then his blue eyes met hers. Hannah opened her mouth but no sound came out. She tugged at Joe's sleeve and he woke with a start. He saw the grubby, crumpled child in the hearth and his mouth fell open.

'Great gibbering aunts! What the . . .'

Nickolai and the old couple stared at each other in astonishment for a few moments. Joe and Hannah were at a complete loss. They were well past middle age and lived a quiet, uneventful life away from the hurly-burly of the town; they were not accustomed to surprises.

She was round and comfortable-looking, with small, inquisitive blue eyes and a kindly face. Wisps of grey hair escaped from under a well darned and well laundered white cap. He was dark and lean, with a long, puzzled, horse-like face, greying temples and thinning hair. You could tell they hadn't much money. Joe's rough working clothes were frayed at the edges and showed many signs of constant repair. Hannah's skirts and apron were covered with patches.

Hannah's ruddy cheeks wobbled slightly as she stared at the infant. She wrung her hands together, not knowing what to do. She had no experience with babies. Joe just continued to gawp and blink.

Nickolai was the first to react. His face screwed up and he began to bawl, rubbing his sooty little fists into his eyes. There was something in the tone of his cries which told Hannah he had been through a terrible ordeal. She felt her heart turn over with pity and rushed over to the howling child, sweeping him up into her arms.

'There there little duck . . . don't cry . . . it's all right . . .' she murmured in a soothing sing song voice, rocking him gently. Nickolai's sobs began to quieten.

Joe heaved himself out of the shabby old armchair and creaked over to look down at the child in his wife's arms. 'Well blow me down with a feather! Where did he come from?'

'Don't be ridiculous, Joe!' Hannah snapped. 'Can't you see?'

'See what?' he said, shaking his head in bewilderment.

Hannah fixed him with a meaningful gaze. Her eyes were shining and her cheeks were flushed. 'Well, it's obvious! This is the child we could never have!'

Joe's mouth drooped gormlessly. 'Don't be daft!' he spluttered. 'He's been dumped here by someone when we were asleep. Probably one of the village girls.'

'But how did they get in here?' protested Hannah. 'The house is locked!'

'The only way he could have got in here was down the chimney,' muttered Joe, scratching his head and peering over at the fireplace.

'Well I'm sure whoever it was did it for the best,' crooned Hannah, rocking Nickolai, 'poor little mite!'

'I wouldn't call him a mite,' said Joe, eyeing Nickolai's sturdy limbs. 'I just don't understand it. Surely if he came from round here, we would have known about it. It's a small enough town.' Suddenly he stopped scratching his head and his face cleared. 'I know – it's probably travellers!'

Hannah snorted dismissively. 'We don't get any – apart from the Inuit. And he's no Inuit. Look at him.'

Joe inspected the child. Blond hair. Blue eyes. Pink cheeks. He had to agree. Nickolai had calmed down now and his crying had settled into occasional hiccuppy sobs. He stuck his thumb in his mouth and observed them both with his steady blue gaze.

'And now I think he needs something nice and hot to eat,' said Hannah, bustling around with the child still in her arms. 'Then a warm bath. Then we'll make up a nice cosy bed for him.' With one arm still cradling the baby, she put some wood on the fire and stoked it. The flames leaped up from the glowing embers and began to lick round the logs.

'Hey, hang on, hang on,' spluttered Joe. 'Shouldn't we hand him over to the authorities? Someone may be looking for him.'

'I don't think so,' said Hannah briskly. 'Here, take him for a minute.'

She plonked Nickolai into Joe's arms. He felt like a warm sack of sugar beet and smelled of soot and baby. 'But, but –' Joe stumbled on, still bemused, 'what'll we tell people?' He glanced at Nickolai, who was staring up at him curiously.

Hannah thought for a moment. 'We'll say that he's the son of my niece, and she couldn't look after him herself so we took him in,' she said firmly, putting an iron pot over the fire to heat.

'But – but – we hardly have enough to feed ourselves, let alone a baby.' Joe looked at Nickolai's sturdy limbs and felt his weight. 'He's a sizey lad.'

'Nonsense. We can stretch things. He'll bring us luck,' Hannah said in a tone that brooked no argument. She took Nickolai from Joe and continued bustling round the room. As Nickolai wriggled round in her arms, his hood fell back and his pointed ears came into view. Hannah and Joe stopped dead and stared at them.

'Blithering bedbugs!' exclaimed Joe. 'What on earth are those?'

They inspected Nickolai's ears with wonder. They were pink and shell-like with pointed tips, not unpleasing to the eye, just a little unsettling.

'Ears, I think they're called,' replied Hannah, recovering quickly from her shock. 'A bit unusual, I admit, but I think they're rather appealing. We'll get used to them.'

She stroked Nickolai's cheek and gazed at him fondly. He gurgled back at her, then broke into an angelic smile that made his whole face light up. Suddenly, the drab little cottage seemed a brighter place. Joe and Hannah caught their breath. They were enchanted.

'Oh, he's so sweet,' sighed Hannah.

'He's certainly a fine boy,' agreed Joe.

'And he's got lovely little ears, hasn't he? Yes he has!' Hannah tickled the tip of Nickolai's ear and he flicked it, just like a cat or a dog. Joe and Hannah jumped in surprise.

'Good grief, that's strange – freakish!' Joe stammered.

'No it's not!' said Hannah sharply. 'And I don't ever want to hear you say that word again! He's just a little bit . . . different, that's all.'

Joe started babbling. 'But – but we still don't know – where on earth has he come from? He's – he's – well, he's certainly no ordinary baby!'

'Exactly!' Hannah exclaimed triumphantly. 'That's what I've been trying to tell you! He's a gift from heaven. A Yuletide gift. He's been sent to us for a reason. And he needs us! So we're keeping him, and that's that!'

The flying reindeer swooped down into the forest and began to coast along between the pine trees, brushing the snow off their branches.

She flew deep into the heart of the forest, came out into a clearing, landed gracefully and trotted quickly over to a hidden opening behind a rocky outcrop.

The cave was warm and stuffy with the hot breath of animals. A magnificent stag with a huge, weathered pair of antlers was pacing around restlessly, stamping his hoof every so often. An elderly doe sat in a circle of young reindeer, who listened in rapt attention while she told them a story in hushed tones.

They were the most beautiful creatures on earth. Their antlers were velvety smooth, branching out from their heads in delicate patterns. They had long legs; soft, thick fur coats, mottled brown and white; long elegant noses and large, liquid brown eyes. The younger ones were still gangly and not yet fully grown, and their antlers were like new saplings. The elderly doe looked rickety and frail, with a greying muzzle and misty eyes. Her antlers were gnarled and leathery and her croaky old voice quavered as she spoke.

'And then Arkfel – the great reindeer God in the sky – sent out beams of coloured light from his antlers, all across the heavens and—'

She was cut off as an elegant doe trotted into the cave.

'Comet! Where have you been?' snorted Lancer, the big stag, stamping his foot on the earth floor. 'You've been gone since moonrise! We were worried!'

'It's a long story,' sighed Comet. 'I've had quite an adventure.'

'Tell us, Mamoosh, please!' cried one of the young reindeer.

'Not now, Rudy. We must do the Passing of the Power ceremony first. Then I have something very important to tell you. Come on now, trot trot. Form the sacred circle.'

The young reindeer stood up and began to shuffle around the cave. Comet began calling out their names. 'Rudolph, Dancer, Prancer, Dasher, Blitzen, Cupid, Vixen – and Donder.' Once the youngsters had organized themselves, Velvet, the old doe, heaved herself up and trotted creakily over to the circle. Then Lancer and Comet took their places.

They all knelt down and kept as still as statues, antlers touching to form an unbroken circle. There was a hush, then a current began fizzling round the circle of antlers, passing from one to the other, like a ring of coloured lightning. After a few moments, Comet stepped back, breaking the circle. The current stopped. The other reindeer stared at her.

'That'll do for now,' said Comet firmly.

There was a loud chorus of protest.

'But Mother! That's not nearly enough!' spluttered Rudolph.

'Yes. It won't even last a full moon cycle!' added Blitzen.

The fur on Comet's back quivered. She looked at them all gravely. 'I have some very disturbing news. The Lights in the sky have gone. Arkfel has vanished!' Cries of horror greeted this announcement. The reindeer shook their heads and pawed the ground anxiously. Comet continued. 'Something terrible has happened up at the North Pole. I was just drawing in the power from the Lights, when they suddenly went out. Disappeared, just like that.' She puffed out her cheeks and blew through her muzzle to demonstrate her point. 'The sky went dark. Then I heard wolves, howling.' A shudder ran round the ring of reindeer. She paused for effect. 'And I found a Two Legs!' she finished dramatically.

A gasp of astonishment ran round the cave. 'A Two Legs!' chorused the reindeer.

'I hope he didn't see you!' growled Lancer. 'You know it is forbid—'

'He was only a baby, Lancer!' Comet cut in crossly. 'So he will not remember. He was abandoned in the snow. The wolves were about to get him. I rescued him and took him to the Two-Legs town. I left him with some people. That's why I was late.'

There was an astonished silence, filled with heavy reindeer breathing, as they took in this alarming new information.

Lancer pawed the ground and shook his great head. 'So how are we going to fly if the Lights are gone?' he muttered. 'It happens on this night, every twelvemoon, in the darkest time, when Arkfel shines at his strongest, when you pass it on to us, to give us our flying power. How are we going to survive without it? How will we keep ourselves safe from the beasts of the forest?'

Comet sighed and swung her head. 'We shall have to preserve it very carefully. I have enough to last a few twelvemoons if we use it sparingly. So that means flying times must be strictly limited. And for the deerlings, under adult supervision only.'

This was the worst news ever for a group of adventurous young reindeer who were dying to get outside as soon as the spring came and practise their flying skills. Their cries of dismay echoed round the cave and out into the stillness of the forest.

'A bird of prey? What kind of bird of prey?' screeched Magda at the sinister-looking man beside her. The heavy black veil she had put over her face puffed out as she spat the words.

Her companion's hooded eyes shifted uneasily. 'We

couldn't really see much, Majesty. It all happened so fast.' He spoke in an oily voice meant to appease her, but his head was hunched defensively into his bony shoulders and his hands twitched nervously under his cloak. He was constantly on his guard when he was with his mistress. She was the only person in the world he feared, because her powers were even greater than his.

Volpo's appearance was disturbing, whatever species you were from. Even as an elf, he had not been good-looking. And after he had been banished to the Vortex as one of Magda's disciples, the incredible magnetic pressures had emphasized his worst points and brought out his true nature.

His heavy brows concealed eyes that would make your blood run cold: a dark, sulphur yellow with vertical slits instead of pupils and the dangerous glint of a wild beast. His spiked black hair, long angular face and scrawny body added to the impression of a prowling animal, as did his disconcerting habit of appearing and disappearing like a shadow. When he smiled, his thin lips pulled back to reveal a row of sharp pointed teeth.

Volpo could see through the wolves' eyes and hear through their ears. He had complete power over them. Now he was Magda's Chief Advisor, his wolfish powers of cunning second only to her incredible powers of sorcery.

'Well, it's not good enough!' stormed Magda,

twitching at the veil. 'No one was supposed to escape! How could you have let him go?'

'But I saw his mother turn to stone through the eyes of my children,' replied Volpo smoothly. 'And he will have done so too. The bird of prey must have had a nasty shock when he turned into a dead weight. He's probably just another little boulder in the snow now.' He sniggered nastily, showing his pointed teeth.

Magda grunted, satisfied for the time being. She had other, more pressing matters on her mind. She turned to look around the cavern and her eyes gleamed. Solstice Square had now been turned into a fiery inferno. The Vortex still gaped open, belching fire and smoke. A hellish red glow lit up the whole place, making flickering shadows on the walls.

All around, the lifeless figures of the frozen elves stood still and silent, as goblins lumbered back and forth from the Vortex, bringing armfuls of red hot coal and piling it up on the floor. Two voices boomed out conflicting orders from the hole.

'That's enough!' Magda commanded. 'Now let me put my powers to the test!'

She hobbled towards the pile of smoking coals and pointed a clawed hand towards it. A huge bolt of Light shot out from her fingertip. At once, the coal began to transform. The dense black lumps began to glow from within. Then they began to change colour, from black, to brown, to dirty yellow.

The colour deepened and began to gleam luridly.

After a few minutes the whole pile of coal had transformed into glittering gold, heaped up like a treasure haul. Any pawnbroker would have known at a glance that it was Fool's Gold, an artificial creation brought about by alchemy of the worst kind. But at first sight, it was impressive.

The goblins stood transfixed, grunting and gaping, their ape-like arms hanging by their sides. Magda let out a long rattling sigh of satisfaction and turned to Volpo.

He smiled back, his eyes glowing in the gloom. 'See? What did I tell you, Majesty? Your powers are astonishing. It has worked.'

'Yes!' she whispered. 'Now there is no stopping me! Will it really bewitch every human on earth?'

Volpo made a growling noise in his throat that would have been a chuckle from anyone else. 'Oh yes, Majesty. They will find it irresistible. Phase One of the Masterplan is complete. I shall order the Head Goblin to start work immediately.' He snapped his fingers and called over to the Vortex. 'Skank! Skism! Come forward and receive your orders!'

The two bickering voices stopped. There was a horrible grunting noise from the pit and two heads emerged above the rim, panting and gasping. As they clambered over the edge, it became apparent that they were attached to the same body, which struggled upright and lumbered heavily towards them.

The Head Goblin was, in fact, the Head Goblins. He

looked like all the other goblins – beefy, red-skinned and extremely ugly. But the two heads were like bald, shiny, bulbous potatoes growing on two separate, bullish necks out of his massive shoulders. They had coarse cauliflower ears and piggy red eyes. The two faces wore completely different expressions. The one belonging to Skank wore a surly, aggressive scowl, like someone about to pick a fight. The one belonging to Skism wore the bemused expression of someone who can barely string two thoughts together.

Like all Magda's followers, this creature had originally been an elf. But under the incredible pressures of the Vortex, his true nature had emerged, turning him into one of her many goblins. His original self had always been in two minds about whether or not to follow Magda. Now this uncertainty had come out in his physical form. He had literally split into two personalities, which were always at war with each other.

'Are you ready to start work on construction?' boomed Magda.

'Your hevery wish is my command, Most Gracious and Royal Majesty!' replied Skank.

'*Our* command,' corrected Skism, glaring at him resentfully. 'Remember I'm 'ere too.'

Skank's head swivelled round and glowered at Skism. 'Shut it, meathead, and let me do the talking. I'm the one with the brains.'

* * *

Hannah was peeling the layers of clothing off Nickolai, getting him ready for a bath. She had fed him some warm bread and milk, which he had gulped down like a ravenous puppy, straight from the bowl. She set aside the thick red robe and hung it to warm by the fire.

'Nice bit of cloth . . .' murmured Joe, fingering it thoughtfully. 'He obviously comes from a good home.'

Hannah was trying to remove the fleecy green babysuit that encased Nickolai from neck to toes, but he was wriggling, giggling and kicking his arms and legs about. 'Never mind that!' she gasped. 'Help me get these things off him. Now come on, young man, behave!'

Joe shuffled over to help her and began fumbling ineptly. Nickolai had a strength beyond his tender age. After much kicking and screaming, Hannah finally tugged off the tunic. A small, glowing creature, about as big as a butterfly, flew out with an indignant squeak and buzzed around the cottage in dizzy circles, whirring its tiny wings. It seemed to light up the whole room.

Hannah and Joe stared at it in astonishment. Hannah gave a gasp of shock and began shrieking hysterically. 'An insect! Catch it, Joe! I hate insects! Quick quick, get rid of it!'

Joe picked up a broom and began chasing the Light Fairy round the room, trying to swat her. Nickolai uttered a cry of distress as Elvina buzzed round in loops, avoiding the swipes. She flitted away from Joe's thrashing broom, diving out of the way until he tripped and landed in a heap on the floor, gasping for breath. Then the creature streaked across the room and settled on Nickolai's shoulder. He rubbed his cheek against her and gurgled fondly. She warbled back in answer.

'Seems to be some sort of – pet . . .' muttered Joe, 'although it don't look like anything I've ever seen before!'

The old couple shuffled forward and squinted at the Light Fairy. It was impossible to tell its exact shape and form, because the halo of light around it made it difficult to see. But if you narrowed your eyes you could just make out a small rounded body with two legs, a tiny cherub face and a blur of wings.

'Maybe it's not an insect,' said Hannah nervously.

'If I didn't know better I'd say it was some sort of fairy.'

'Oh, don't be ridiculous, Joe!'

Suddenly the creature took off again and began to fly in loopy circles above the baby's head, making a long, joined-up row of shapes. The old couple goggled as she repeated the process several times. The baby chuckled and tried to catch her.

'Well blow me down!' gasped Joe at last. 'I think she's trying to spell out a word!'

They stared closely as the glowing shape whizzed round and round, over and over again, squeaking at them impatiently, until the row of shapes became clear.

'Ni . . .'

'. . . ck . . .'

'ol . . .'

'. . . ai!'

They looked at each other in amazement.

'She's telling us his name. Nickolai!'

Growing Pains

Nickolai squirmed out of Hannah's grasp and dashed out of the door into the snow. He was seven now, but nearly as tall as Hannah and much too strong for her.

'Come back here at once, Nickolai!' she yelled crossly, her temper rising.

Nick ignored her and tumbled over and over in the snow until he was at a safe distance, then rolled on to his knees and glared at her challengingly.

'No way! I'm not wearing *that* thing!'

He would rather die than be seen in the horrible, limp brown thing with the earflaps that Hannah was holding out. Elvina fluttered after him, landed on his shoulder and blew a raspberry at Hannah in a show of solidarity.

Hannah pursed her mouth, put her hands on her plump hips and glared at them both. 'That's enough of your cheek, young lady! Now do as you're told, my boy, and put this on! And a proper coat!' She held out a grey woollen greatcoat of Joe's that she'd cut down.

Nickolai shook his head defiantly and set his mouth

in a stubborn line. 'No! I'm wearing this.' The red velvet cloak he'd arrived in as a baby was now an improvised tunic wrapped round him and tied with a cord, adapted to his growing frame. It still looked as good as new. Despite the passing years, it had never become worn or shabby. And Nickolai wouldn't be parted from it.

Hannah sighed with frustration and decided to try another tack. 'Look, dear, I really think it's time you started wearing normal clothes. You don't want to stand out from the other children at school, do you?'

Nickolai shot a look of pure scorn at the clothes. 'And you think they won't tease me in that lot?' He felt an immediate pang of guilt as a hurt look crossed Hannah's face. Even at seven, he knew that they were much poorer than the other people in the town and that his parents were much older than everyone else's. He was filled with sudden remorse and ran across to the doorway, flinging himself into her arms.

'Sorry, Mother! I didn't mean to be rude! Please let me keep my special outfit on. It's the only thing that keeps me warm. And I need the hood.'

Hannah's heart wrenched with pity; she put her arms round him and kissed the top of his curly blond head. Of course. He wanted to hide his ears. No other child in town had pointed ears that moved uncontrollably, like a dog's. Although Nickolai pretended not to care, he was extremely ashamed of them. She relented. 'All right then love, have it your way.'

They both turned at the sound of bells and panting husky dogs as Joe rounded the corner from the back of the house on his delivery sledge. It was an old, ramshackle structure but very serviceable, painted and re-painted many times in bright red and hung with heavy bells that made a loud clonking sound, so that everyone knew the postman was coming. Joe pulled the sledge to a halt and the dogs strained at their leashes, yelping and whining as they tried to leap towards Nick.

'Come on lad! Hop up! Don't want to be late for your first day at school! I've still got my rounds to do an' all!' Joe jerked his head at a pile of parcels and letters stacked in the carrying compartment at the back of the sledge.

Nick ran over to the sledge and stopped to pet the dogs. They calmed down immediately, and rolled over on their backs as Nick stroked their furry coats and whispered strange crooning sounds to them. He flicked his ears and mimicked their movements.

Joe and Hannah exchanged glances; this strange child had an uncanny power to communicate with animals. And then there was the glowing creature who never left his side. Nickolai was an oddity, but they loved him.

Nickolai dragged his attention away from the dogs and leaped nimbly on to the sledge beside his father.

He leaned down to kiss Hannah goodbye and the sledge shot off before she had a chance to wish him good luck.

As they sped along the track at the edge of town, Nick stared at the forest in the distance. The sun was shining brightly today and the snow was sparkling on the treetops, a jagged line of dark green and dazzling white against the azure blue of the horizon. It looked so beautiful and mysterious. But no one ever seemed to go there and Hannah and Joe refused even to talk about it. He'd heard strange rumours about magical beasts who lived there, flying reindeer. But they were all dismissed as fairy tales.

'Looking forward to school then?' said Joe conversationally.

Nick jerked himself out of his reverie. School. He was dreading it. All those kids from town who giggled and stared at him. But he mustn't let on to Joe. He tried to think of the pleasanter possibilities of school. 'Yeah!' he said enthusiastically. 'It'll be great. I can make things!'

Joe laughed indulgently. 'You won't be able to do much of that, lad. They make you do things like 'rithmetic and writing and reading, so you can get a good job when you grow up.'

Nick thought this all sounded very boring. 'Not me,' he declared confidently, 'I'm going to be a sleigh driver when I grow up. A racing one! I think it's a grand job!'

Joe laughed again, and they continued in companionable silence.

Soon the sledge was weaving its way into the jumbled maze of streets that crisscrossed the little town called Norsk. The school house was a large, friendly-looking building just off the main street in the middle of town, with a sloping, snow-covered roof and green-shuttered windows. It had a fenced-off area which served as a playground, now full of noisy children running around throwing snowballs at each other. Nick felt a pang of nervousness, which he tried hard to conceal. He said a hurried goodbye to Joe, jumped down and ran towards the entrance.

As he entered the yard, everyone stopped playing and stared at him. Whispers and giggles ran round the playground. He strode forward boldly, then found his way barred by a row of boys standing in front of him. At their head stood a tall, tough-looking, dark-haired boy with piercing blue eyes, who stared at him nastily.

'Come on, then! Show us your ears!'

Nick glared back at him. 'No. Mind your own business!'

Suddenly a large snowball hit him in the side of the head and knocked his hood down. His ears were exposed and he felt snow dribbling icily down his neck.

There was a stunned silence. Then the whole playground burst into loud, brazen laughter. To Nick's horrified shame, his ears twitched. He tried as hard as he could to control them, but he couldn't stop them flicking. The laughter faltered for a moment, then the children erupted again, more raucously than ever. Nick looked at the sea of faces crowding round him and felt a hot rush of anger.

'There they are!' jeered the dark-haired boy. 'Pointy ears, just like a dog. Woof woof! Shouldn't you be at home in the kennels, Dog Boy?'

The laughter grew louder as the boys closed in, hurling snowballs at him.

'Woof woof!' they chorused. 'Go on Dog Boy! Back to the kennels!'

As the jeering faces loomed at him and the laughter echoed in his ears, Nick felt something snap inside him. How dare they speak to him like that? He was as good as any of them! With one swift, bear-like movement he lunged towards the dark-haired boy and wrestled him to the ground. A clamour rose as the children gathered round in a ring, watching eagerly. Nick and the dark-haired boy rolled over and over, screaming, punching and kicking each other, with the others cheering and shouting.

The air was pierced by a shrill whistle. Silence fell. The children drew back and an earnest young woman with pebble glasses strode into the ring.

'Stop it! Stop it at once, boys!'

The combatants wrenched themselves apart and staggered to their feet, glaring at each other breathlessly. The teacher glowered at them both. Her eyes swept over Nick's ears and a look of understanding crossed her face. She fixed the dark-haired boy with a stern gaze.

'I've had just about enough of your behaviour, Finn Stark!' she bellowed. 'And it's only the first day of term! Now get inside at once. Double detention at the end of the day. I will not tolerate teasing, bullying or prejudice of any kind in my school!'

Finn gave Nick a nasty look. 'Thanks a lot, Dog Boy!' he hissed. 'You'll pay for that later!' And he and his gang swaggered off, muttering amongst themselves and throwing resentful glances back at him.

The teacher turned to Nickolai and smiled. Her face suddenly looked very different. 'Don't worry, I know he's the one who started it.' She sighed heavily and looked at his ears. 'Some people are very ignorant, you know. Can't understand when people are a bit different.'

'It's all right,' said Nick as casually as he could. 'I don't care.'

The teacher looked momentarily chastened. 'Of course not. Now go inside and try and keep out of his way. You're in class eight.'

She strode off and the other children, bored now the show was over, began to drift in to the school. Only one child lingered behind, looking at Nick curiously. She was a pretty girl about his age.

'You all right?'

Nick nodded bravely, taking in her appearance. She had silky blonde hair in two braids. Her eyes were pale blue and her gaze direct and searching. She had a perfect oval face and a very determined, pointed chin. To him she looked like an angel.

'Don't take any notice of that Finn. He's an ignorant oaf. And a bully. My name's Anneka by the way. I'm seven and eleven twelfths. Eight next month. Here, have a toffee.' And she handed him a rather squashed-looking sweet from her pocket. Nick took it and crammed it in his mouth gratefully. It tasted chewy and sweet and it stuck his teeth together.

'Fhanksh,' he mumbled.

'Well, how was it?' asked Joe when he came in from his rounds.

Nick was sitting in front of the fire, whittling away at a piece of wood, carving a crude figure of a husky dog. He shrugged vaguely. 'Oh, not too bad. You know, school is school.' He noticed that his parents were gazing at him expectantly and felt obliged to offer more information. 'They've got lots of nice stuff to make things with. And Madame is quite nice. And there was a nice girl there called Anneka, and . . . er . . .' he trailed off.

Hannah knelt down beside him and looked at the carving. For a child of seven, it wasn't at all bad. 'That's very good. Did you do it at school?'

'No.'

'So – everything all right then, was it lad?' ventured Joe.

Nick knew what they were getting at. 'Well – er – I got into a bit of a fight. But I didn't get into trouble about it, because – this boy was . . .' He left the sentence hanging in the air.

'Teasing you?' enquired Hannah in an anxious voice.

'Yes. About my ears. But I don't care!' Nick said fiercely. 'I'm not ashamed of them!'

Jo and Hannah exchanged uncertain smiles. Hannah swept Nick into a motherly embrace. 'Quite right too! You're perfect just the way you are!'

The Rise of Doransk

The gleaming golden spires had begun to thrust above the horizon. As the long daylight hours of the Arctic summer wore on, they rose silently and stealthily, glinting in the midnight sun, reflecting beams of light across the snowy wastes like beacons.

The Inuit were nomadic peoples who wandered continually across the lands of the far north, following the animal herds they hunted, so it was only a matter of time before they spotted the new city. Word spread quickly and soon tribes of stocky, dark-skinned, almond-eyed people began to gather at the Pole and gaze in awe at this strange new sight. They travelled from all over the Arctic Circle, trekking many miles with their sleds and their teams of huskies. They stared at the eerie gold towers glinting in the distance and whispered uneasily amongst themselves. Their dogs whined restlessly, sensing something unnatural.

One morning Zakurak crested a ridge with his father and grandfather, and stared in disbelief at the mysterious city mushrooming out of the ice.

'This can't be right,' muttered his grandfather in his thick leathery voice. 'Who are these new gods building this city? How could anyone but our people survive up here?'

Zakurak was only eight, but already he knew that his were the only people who had learned how to carve an existence from this harsh place. He had hunted and fished with his father, watched his family cleaning skins, drying meat and using every part of the animals they killed. Only they had learned to live with the land.

'This must be bad magic!' concluded his grandfather, shaking his head. 'No good will come of it. It will upset nature's balance. We will be driven away.'

If the Inuit had seen what was going on beneath the surface, they would have wanted to migrate off the planet altogether. It was a scene from hell. Solstice Square was now an underground forge, filled with an unbearable heat and a deafening din. Teams of greasy goblins slaved round the clock, hammering molten gold on their anvils. Their massive muscles shone in the fiery glow of the furnace as they toiled, goaded on by cackling demons who prodded them with their sharp claws. Unearthly grunts and shrieks rose above the clamour. Skank and Skism prowled around the rows of sweating bodies, bellowing at the goblins to work harder. Their two heads swivelled this way and that, frequently squabbling and glaring at each other.

'Come on, you 'orrible little gobbos!' roared Skank. 'No slacking!'

He lashed his long-tailed whip at a goblin who had just heaved a lump of gold on to an anvil and was pausing to wipe the sweat out of his lumpy, furrowed brow.

'Give 'im a chance!' protested Skism. ' 'E's only just got it on the block.'

Skank's head yanked round and glared at Skism, his piggy eyes gleaming fiercely. 'It'll be your 'ead on the block in a minute. What kind of wimp are you? You 'ave to keep 'em on their toes! Ain't that right, your Royal Majesty?'

'What?' said Magda irritably. She had been pacing restlessly back and forth, watching the proceedings through her cobwebby veil, followed by Volpo who was consulting sheaves of paper scrawled with complicated plans and diagrams.

'You gotta keep 'em on their toes!'

'Yes yes yes, carry on,' she muttered. 'And stop quarrelling, you two. It's wasting time.' She lurched off with Volpo in her wake.

Skank's fat lips curled into a triumphant sneer and he looked Skism in the eye. 'See? You're wasting goblin time. Now shut it, twerp face, and let me run the show.'

Skism blinked, wobbled his head in a disgruntled manner and looked away.

Volpo prowled along at Magda's heels amongst the anvils and the workbenches. She stopped to watch the diamond demons setting fake gemstones into some golden building blocks. Their talons hissed as they dug deep holes into the metal and pressed in the stones.

'The master plan is going well, is it not, Majesty?' Volpo whispered obsequiously, tapping a bony finger at the papers he was holding.

'It's not moving fast enough!' Magda snapped. 'We're already well behind schedule!'

Volpo's eyes slid around uneasily and he suppressed a weary sigh. Couldn't she see how much work was required for a project of this scale? She always had been impatient. 'Great cities take time, Majesty,' he replied evenly. 'The goblins have been working twenty-four hours a day for several years now.' He jerked his head at his papers. 'The layout of the city is proceeding as planned. We are making good progress.'

'Not good enough!' roared Magda, twitching her veil. 'I want the city ready so I can move on to the next stage!'

'Majesty, if we are to attract people from all over the globe, we must create a city of such extraordinary beauty and magnificence that word will spread like wildfire. No human who hears of it will be able to resist its lure!' Volpo gazed into the middle distance and gestured grandly with a scrawny arm. 'Doransk, the Golden City! Where the streets are paved with gold, where everyone's dreams can come true and fortunes can be made! And the good Queen Magda—'

'Yes yes yes, I know all that!' Magda cut in impatiently. 'But production is slowing down!'

'Then we must make more gold!' announced Volpo. 'Come, Majesty. To the Vortex!'

He nudged Magda towards the gaping hole, where goblins were heaving out great lumps of steaming coal and piling them up. 'Stand back!' he commanded. 'Her Majesty is about to perform the rites!'

The goblins lumbered out of the way. Magda pointed a clawed finger and a bolt of Light shot out and struck the steaming black mound. The top of the pile turned into sparkling gold, but the coal beneath it changed only to a dull, greenish yellow colour. Volpo felt a shiver of alarm run along his spine. Magda snorted impatiently and sent out another bolt of Light. The coal underneath turned yellow and glowed faintly, but it still didn't have the sparkle of the gold on top.

'I'm losing my touch!' hissed Magda.

'Not at all, Majesty!' soothed Volpo, stroking her arm. 'Even the greatest of sorceresses have limits. You have been overstretching your powers. You must pace yourself, learn to be patient!'

Magda threw his hand off her arm and whirled on him in fury. 'There's something you're not telling me, isn't there?' she screeched. 'Something is weakening my powers! Tell me!'

A low whine of fear escaped from Volpo. 'Well, now you come to mention it, Majesty, there is something that has been nagging away at the back of my mind. You remember the elfin mother who escaped?'

'She turned to stone!' roared Magda. She went still for a minute, then jerked her head in fury. 'It's the elfin brat, isn't it? He got away, didn't he?'

Volpo steeled himself. 'W . . . well no one can say for sure, Majesty . . .'

'I knew it!' screamed Magda. 'I knew there was something strange about that incident! Why did they not turn to stone straight away, like all the others? Because there was still a ray of Light with them. One of those beastly little Light Fairies!'

Volpo shuddered and the spiky black hair stood out on his head. 'Yes, Majesty. It is indeed possible that one of them escaped with the child and is keeping him alive.' He looked away furtively, then mumbled, 'The truth is, there is one tiny ray of Light left in the world that is not under your control. And without total possession, you may find your powers diminished slightly. For the time being things can proceed, er, more or less according to plan. But for our long-term projects to succeed, your power matrix must be complete.'

There was a nasty silence, then Magda erupted in fury. Her veil puffed out and her whole body quivered with rage; her shrieks tore round the cavern. The goblins gaped as Magda hurled a thunderbolt at Volpo, sending him sprawling on the floor. He lay curled up in a ball with his hands tucked under his chin, whining.

'Idiot!' she roared. 'Your stupid mistake could ruin all my plans! Find him for me!'

Volpo scrambled up and bowed low. 'Yes, Majesty,' he said submissively. 'But do please bear in mind that you will only be able to take the Fairy from him at midnight on Winter Solstice Eve.'

Magda quivered under the veil and her voice rose to an ear-splitting screech. 'Why?'

Volpo shrugged and spread his hands. 'The universe has its own rules, Majesty, which even you have to obey. You can only draw in particles of Light with your magnetic powers when *all* the forces are at their strongest, at midnight on Winter Solstice Eve. You must wait again for the right moment to scoop up this last remaining ray.'

Magda was silent as she struggled to control her impotent rage. 'Fine!' she snapped. 'Just get him up here!'

'He will have grown, Majesty,' said Volpo carefully. 'How will we recognize him?'

Magda screamed in frustration. 'Just look out for a child with pointed ears, you fool! He must be somewhere! Search high and low!'

Volpo bowed, then whistled softly. In moments, the cavern was full of dark swirling shapes as the wolves materialized from all sides. He spoke to them in a low guttural whisper and they disappeared like shadows in a dream.

Without Anneka, Nick's first few months at school would have been very lonely. He was still an object of

53

scorn and derision; Finn and his gang tormented him constantly at school and around the town. But Anneka didn't care what people thought and had been his staunchest ally. Nick followed her around everywhere. They made a comical sight, a graceful young princess and her burly minder. Anneka persuaded her little gang of girlfriends to accept him and he was soon adopted as their mascot. The jibes and taunts from the boys continued, but Nick didn't care. At least somebody liked him.

It was one early winter evening, as they walked home from school through the sodium-lamplit streets, that Anneka first became aware of Elvina. A faint whistling sound came from inside Nick's tunic. He coughed in embarrassment. Elvina was snoring.

'What's that noise?' said Anneka sharply, looking round at the region of his chest.

Nick coughed more loudly to cover up the noise. 'Nothing. I've just got a bit of a wheezy chest, that's all.'

Anneka was not fooled. 'Rubbish! You never get ill! What is it?'

Nick blushed and pulled his hood tighter. 'It's nothing.'

Anneka stopped dead, folded her arms and fixed him with a challenging stare. 'I know you've got something down there. It's making a buzzing noise. Is it an insect?'

'She is not an insect!' said Nick hotly.

'Oh. So she's a she, is she? What kind of a she?' Anneka cocked her head on one side, waiting for an answer.

Nick shook his head. 'I don't know, she's just always been with me. She's – some kind of – fairy-type thing. But she's very shy. She doesn't like coming out.'

Anneka's eyes had gone wide with astonishment. 'No! A fairy? You're kidding! I've always wanted to see one! Why haven't you shown her to me before?' She began tugging at his front. 'Come on! If we're friends we shouldn't have any secrets, should we?'

Nick broke away awkwardly and hurried ahead. 'She'll come out and talk to you one day. It takes a long time for her to trust anyone. You'll meet her, I promise.'

It was at Anneka's house that Elvina finally made her appearance. Nick was invited back for tea.

'Dad's a builder,' explained Anneka, chattering non-stop as they walked through the narrow cobbled streets to her home. 'He does all the roofs in town. Then there's Mum – she makes some money baking bread and cakes. She's really good at it. She's a bit of a fusspot and she's always nagging Dad to work harder and make more money, but she's very nice really. And there's my little sister Louisa. She's, well – she's Louisa. You'll see.'

Anneka led Nick into a small cottage in a narrow backstreet. It was sparsely furnished, but warm and cosy. A fire crackled in the grate and the delicious smell of baking wafted out from the kitchen. A chubby baby with blond curls was sitting on the floor, playing with a set of worn-out wooden blocks, a look of intense concentration on her face. She glanced up as soon as Anneka entered and her face lit up. She scrambled up and began to toddle towards her sister, holding out her arms.

'Neeka!' she cried. Anneka picked her up and the child hugged her tightly round the neck, gazing curiously at Nick.

'This is my friend Nickolai.'

'Klai!' announced Louisa proudly.

Anneka's mother Lotta came out of the kitchen, wiping her hands on her apron, carrying a hot platter of something that smelled delicious. She was a pretty woman, still young, but careworn and thin, with wisps of blond hair around her pale face.

'Oh hello, Annie! You've brought your friend home for tea. How nice. I've just baked some of my berry pies. Would you like to try one?' and she held the platter out to Nick. It was full of small round pastries.

'Thank you,' he said shyly. He took one and bit into it. A mixture of different flavours exploded in his mouth. It was delicious. He saw that Lotta was watching him anxiously. 'Very nice,' he said with his mouth full.

'Yummy, aren't they?' said Anneka. Nick nodded with bulging cheeks. 'Berry pies are Mum's new speciality. They've got nuts in them too.'

'I'm planning to sell them in the marketplace if

enough people like them. Do you want to take your coat off now, Nick? It's warm in here.'

Nick shook his head. This was the moment he'd been dreading. He kept his cloak and hood on all the time, except when he was at home. 'No, I think I'll keep it on if that's all right.'

'Don't be shy, Nick,' coaxed Anneka.

Nick went hot and cold all over, but he felt it would be rude to refuse. Slowly he lowered his hood, untied his cords and took the cloak off. Lotta's eyes flicked over his ears for a brief second, then she smiled. 'There! That's better.'

To Nick's acute embarrassment, his ears twitched. Anneka and her mother exchanged glances and Louisa squealed in delight.

'Babbit!' she chortled, pointing at them.

'I'll go and get the tea,' said Lotta tactfully. 'Your father'll be home soon, Anneka.'

She bustled off into the kitchen. Louisa toddled up to Nick and held her arms up. Nick picked her up and twitched his ears deliberately. Louisa burst into peals of delighted laughter. Within minutes the three of them were sitting on the floor playing with the bricks. Which was when Elvina decided to make her entrance. There was a muffled squeak and she shot out of Nick's tunic and flew around the room, lighting it up. The two girls gasped in astonishment.

Louisa's eyes went like round blue saucers as she watched the glowing blur of Light darting around the room. The fairy did a few crazy loops, then flew up to Louisa and flitted around her playfully, making her turn her head as she followed the fairy's darting movements. Louisa giggled and shrieked, trying to swipe at Elvina, but the fairy dived out of her way every time.

Anneka for once was speechless. She stared at the fairy with an expression of awe on her face. At last she let out a long slow breath. 'So. Fairies do exist. I always knew it. What's her name?'

Nick thought for a minute. 'Elvina,' he said. 'I don't know how I know that but I just do.'

They all jumped as they heard the rattle of the latch and Anneka's father came in through the front door. Joachim, a burly, handsome man with a bushy beard and tousled hair, strode into the room, bringing in the smell of fresh air and woodsmoke. Nick warmed to him immediately.

Joachim beamed at his two daughters. 'How are my best girls then?'

Anneka looked round, but Elvina was nowhere to be seen. Nick could feel her back in her usual hiding place.

One night not long after that, wolves began to prowl around the town.

Nickolai was sitting cross-legged by the fire, making a moving model of a reindeer, trying to carve the antlers. Hannah stopped knitting and watched him for a moment. The arrival of a child in her life had prompted a flurry of handicrafts. She had started with warm baby clothes, but now she had built up her trade and the whole town was wearing her brightly coloured socks, hats and scarves, which Joe delivered along with the post. The family income was boosted. She had been right when she said that the child would bring them luck.

'You and your reindeer!' she sighed, shaking her head.

'I hope you've not been listening to any of those daft fairy tales about flying beasts in the forest,' muttered Joe from his chair by the fire. He shot Nick a warning look.

Nickolai said nothing. They had no idea that he gazed out of his window every night, hoping to see a flying shape above the line of fir trees in the distance. The fire crackled in the silence that followed. Then, suddenly, a low howl came from the distance. First one, then another, until a chorus filled the emptiness beyond the town.

Hannah stiffened and Nickolai's ears began to flick involuntarily. Elvina squeaked and delved down Nickolai's tunic, quaking with fear.

'Wolves!' whispered Hannah fearfully. 'Come on, Joe! Check the doors and windows!' She got up and started scurrying around the room, securing the locks on the windows. Joe heaved himself up and began to put great bars across the door.

Throughout the long, dark winter of endless nights, the howling continued. Children were collected from the school gates by anxious parents and hurried home. Doors were firmly locked and bolted. Community festivities were stopped and no one was allowed outside the town limits. Then the wolves began to prowl around the town itself, loping along the streets and sniffing in dark corners. People lay awake in their beds, listening in terror to the sounds of snuffling and whining outside their windows. Elvina was in a state of high anxiety at these times, and for some reason began to whizz round in circles, squeaking at Nick to pull up the hood on his cloak, even when he was in bed.

As spring approached, the howling noises began to lessen.

It was one night towards the end of March that Nick awoke with a start. Something felt different. Elvina was not there, nestled on his pillow in her usual place. He heard a squeak and saw her buzzing excitedly at the window, beckoning him.

He got out of bed and went to look. The forest was outlined in the moonlight and there, clearly etched against the sky, were eight flying shapes soaring over the treetops. Definitely not birds, for even from that distance he could see they had antlered heads and four legs tucked underneath their bellies.

Nickolai's heart began to thump wildly and his stomach somersaulted in excitement. Flying reindeer!

The stories were true! They must live somewhere in the forest, hidden away from the world!

He *had* to go and investigate. Nothing on earth would have stopped him. He tiptoed to the bed and wrapped his cloak tightly around him. With a satisfied squeak, Elvina dived down his front. As he opened his door, the latch clicked. It sounded deafening in the silence. He stopped, waiting to hear if he had disturbed Joe and Hannah, but their steady breathing continued from the next room.

He began to creep downstairs, trying to avoid the creaky floorboards. As one of them groaned unexpectedly he stopped, holding his breath. No sounds from the room above. They were still asleep. The clock ticked loudly in the quiet, moonlit room. He glanced round, looking for a way out.

How on earth would he do it? The doors and windows were bolted and locked. Hannah kept the keys on a belt round her waist, which she wore even in bed.

Panic rose in him. He had to get to the forest quickly, seize the moment, before the reindeer went away. His gaze swept the room – and came to rest on the fireplace. The fire had died some hours ago and the logs were now cold. The chimney! A perfect way to leave the house undetected.

He tiptoed over to the fireplace, crouched down and ducked his head into the shaft. He squeezed himself into the opening and eased himself upright. To his delight, despite his broad shoulders, the chimney was just wide enough for him. He began to scramble up, bracing himself with his hands and knees and ignoring the soot as it shook loose and tumbled round him.

After a few struggling moments, he emerged at the top of the chimney stack and looked around. All was silent and empty. The town slept and no wolves howled. He slid down the sloping roof through the thick layer of snow and plopped on to the ground.

Once down, he suddenly felt foolish and exposed. How would he get to the forest? He couldn't possibly walk, it was too far. Then he remembered the sledge. Of course! The dogs would help him.

He crept round the back of the house to the kennels and quietly opened the door. The huskies were rolled up into tight balls of white fur. He made a soft whistling noise and they raised their heads and looked at him sleepily. It was vital that they didn't make a sound.

He dropped on to his haunches and squirmed towards them on his belly, whispering and crooning to them in the private language they shared. The dogs blinked, yawned, stood up and stretched. He turned and crawled out of the kennels on all fours and the dogs padded obediently after him.

He led them to the sledge and harnessed them up quickly, remembering to remove the bells. Then he climbed on, shook the reins, whistled softly, and the dogs set off with a gentle panting.

Within moments they were heading for the forest. A feeling of exhilaration swept through Nickolai as the sledge sped across the ridges and furrows, its blades hissing softly in the snow, the cold night air blowing against his face. He felt as if he would burst with joy. Joe had let him hold the reins many times, but this was different. He was driving the sledge, all on his own!

Slowly the forest drew closer and closer, until he could see into its shadowy depths. He pulled the sledge to a halt, whispered to the dogs to be quiet and ran the short distance to the edge of the forest. He gazed up at the towering pines above him, and was about to plunge into their midst when he heard an unmistakable, spine-chilling sound behind him.

A low, crooning yowl, followed by another. Nickolai turned and saw several wolves loping towards him, their yellow eyes smouldering in the gloom.

Four-legged Friends

Nickolai's heart seemed to have stopped beating. Even Elvina was too frightened to make any noise. The wolves crept forward on their bellies, their yellow eyes fixed on him. Low growling noises came from their throats and their tongues dripped horribly out of their jaws. The hairs on the back of Nickolai's neck prickled. He had seen this before, somewhere, some time in the past. Memories stirred, half-forgotten flashbacks of dark, shadowy shapes leaping towards him while he sat small and helpless in the snow.

He shuddered and pulled himself together, looking round wildly for a way of escape. The wolves were closer now, creeping up on him silently, forming a menacing circle around him. An idea came to him.

He dropped to his haunches and moved towards them on all fours, echoing their noises and mimicking their movements. This seemed to have some effect. The wolves stopped in their tracks and stared at him intently. Nick held his breath, hoping he had won them over. If he could only get to the woods, he might be able to shin up a tree and get out of their reach. But quick as a flash, without warning, the wolves moved as one, leaping through the air towards him.

In the split second that followed, Nick saw a gap in the trees. Was it his imagination or had they actually moved? He sprang into action and sprinted towards the gap. The wolves were taken by surprise for a moment, then switched course in mid air, twisting their bodies round and bounding after him, snarling ferociously.

Nick dived into the trees, flinging himself at the nearest trunk and scrambling up it, hauling himself higher and higher, careless of the twigs and branches scratching at his face. After a few moments he stopped to catch his breath. The wolves were swarming into the forest, swift as running water, weaving in and out of the trunks until they all stood in a circle at the foot of Nick's tree, glaring up at him.

Now what? If he called for help no one would hear him. He was stuck up a fir tree in a deserted forest, with a pack of wild beasts below him, baying for his blood.

Elvina crawled up under his hood, staying hidden, and gave his ear a sharp and meaningful tug, before diving back down his front again. The message was pretty clear. He listened intently, straining to hear above the growling of the wolves. He searched for sounds in the night air.

Voices. Hushed, whispering voices in the

background. 'Over here . . . oooover here . . .' they seemed to be saying.

Who could be making those sounds? There was nobody there. Then suddenly Nickolai understood, and a tingle of surprise ran up his spine. The trees themselves were talking to him.

'Over heeeere . . . ffffollow us . . .'

There was a loud rustling noise and his tree moved underneath him. The whole thing. Not like a tree swaying in the wind, for there was not a breath of it in the still night air. It shifted sideways across the ground – and all the others followed in perfect formation, like fabric rippling into a new shape. A new track opened up, inviting him forward.

The wolves yelped. Nickolai looked down and saw a wall of trees, their great roots joined up like clasped hands and their trunks pressed together, blocking the creatures' path. The wolves hurled themselves against the line of trunks, howling in fury. Nick took a flying leap and landed on the soft white ground, picked himself up and raced along the track.

The wolves tore along beside him on the other side of the wall of trunks, their shapes glimpsed in flashes between the gaps. Nick ran like lightning, his heart hammering, terrified that a space would open up and let them through. Then he heard a louder whispering to his left.

'Dooowwwnnnn heeeere now!'

The track ahead twisted and turned like a

rollercoaster ride and veered sharply to the left. Nick swerved and followed the path. More voices, this time on his right. The trees ahead of him closed into a dead end and a new path opened up, curving round into infinity. He turned down it and sped along, his feet kicking up sprays of snow.

Back at the North Pole, Volpo prowled back and forth, his shoulders hunched and his hooded eyes staring sightlessly into space.

'Where's the brat now?' hissed Magda.

'Still running along on the other side of the trees,' murmured Volpo. 'I fear he may be getting away, Majesty.'

'No!' shrieked Magda. 'Send them in after him!'

'We cannot get through,' whispered Volpo hoarsely, seeing an image in his mind's eye of flashing tree trunks. 'The trees won't let us in.'

'Damnation!' screamed Magda. 'Why isn't the forest on my side? Make it obey you!'

'I'll do my best, Majesty.' Volpo went into a deep trance; his eyes went blank and the vertical slits of his pupils narrowed until all you could see was the streaked, sulphur yellow of his irises. His scrawny body undulated as his mind raced along with the wolves in the forest, following their every move.

Magda's voice was low and deadly. 'Can you see the child?'

'No,' replied Volpo distractedly, concentrating hard.

'He escaped before we could get a good look at him.'

'So we still don't know if it's the elfin brat?'

'No, Majesty, but it may have been.'

'I must find out! Send the wolves in!' she roared. 'Now!'

Volpo closed his eyes and issued a silent command. In his mind's eye he leaped towards a tiny gap between two trees. Then he cried out; two solid trunks closed in, trapping him. He yelped and fell to the floor, twisting in agony. He thrashed around, lashing out at nothing, then let out a long and horrible howl. His yellow eyes shut as he fell into a faint.

Nickolai slowed to a trot and listened. He seemed to have left the wolves behind. Animal howls rang out faintly from behind him, echoing eerily round the forest. The place must be full of wild beasts. He must have been mad even to think of coming here. He had to find a way out and get back to the sledge and the dogs.

He stumbled on, his legs shaky and numb. The trees were more relaxed now, idly shifting around in a slow dance. Their voices had quietened to a low background hum and the paths opened lazily, making soft swishing noises in the snow. Nick followed them uncertainly.

He stopped. 'Where do I go now?' he said aloud, as politely as he could. 'I would like to go home, if that's all right with you all. Can you please show me the way out?'

He felt a tremor of unease at the faint echo of laughter that came in reply. The trees carried on lulling and sighing. Then suddenly they began to bristle and stir. They drew away from him and fell back into a wide avenue, hushed and expectant, standing to attention like a row of soldiers.

'This way, then?' Nickolai asked hesitantly. He heard a low chuckle from the trees, as though they knew something he didn't.

Suddenly there was a loud whooshing noise from behind him and he ducked as something roared past overhead, with incredible speed and force. Then another. And another. He lifted his head carefully and looked. Seven gangly, four-legged shapes soared through the air ahead of him, flying along the avenue in formation. Snorts of delight and laughter rang out as they whooped and dived and wove in and out of each other.

Nickolai's mouth fell open. His heart pounded with joy until he thought it would explode. Tears sprang into his eyes.

The reindeer. The flying reindeer. He had not imagined it.

The trees ahead shifted and curved round to the right. The reindeer cornered the bend and disappeared in a flash, leaving a faint trail of light behind them.

Nick straightened up, shaking all over. There another whoosh, and four dangling hooves clunked him on the head. He passed out.

The reindeer. The flying reindeer. He had not imagined it.

Nick struggled to surface, his mind swimming through darkness.

'It's a Two Legs!' he heard a voice say, in a strange, whistling language.

'If you hadn't been so far behind, Donder, we wouldn't have noticed him.'

'You're so clumsy, Donder,' said another, 'you could have killed him! I keep telling you to tuck your hooves up under your belly.'

'Shhooossh, Vixen,' said another voice. 'What are we going to do?'

'Mamoosh will go berserk if she finds out we were out flying on our own.'

'*And* we're not allowed to let a Two Legs see us.'

'We'll have to leave him.'

'No. We will do no such thing, Blitzen,' said another voice.

Nick wondered if he was back at home in his bed, dreaming. But he could feel the snow underneath him, and a wet nose nudging his cheek. He opened his eyes. Eight worried faces stared down at him, covered in soft downy fur. Eight beautifully sculpted heads with long elegant noses, dark brown eyes and velvety antlers. The reindeer stood round him in a ring, gazing at him in concern. He could feel their hot breath as they snorted gently through their soft muzzles, making clouds in the frosty air.

'He's alive, at least,' said the biggest reindeer. 'Now what?'

Nick decided to try speaking to them. He cleared his throat and his voice came out in a hoarse whisper. 'Jish Nicklaish . . .' he tried, uncertainly.

As one, the reindeer jumped and leaped back in surprise.

'He can speak!'

'Of course he can speak!' said Vixen scornfully. 'All Two Legs can speak. But . . . not usually in our language.'

The biggest reindeer trotted forward and nudged Nick's shoulder gently. 'I'm Rudolph. I'm the oldest. Are you all right? We haven't injured you?'

Nick scrambled to his feet and faced the reindeer. They backed away hesitantly.

'Don't be afraid. I don't want to hurt you.'

The reindeer's eyes were wide and watchful and their ears twitched nervously. They held themselves poised, ready for flight. 'Don't go!' Nickolai pleaded.

'I think we should skirmoosh back to the cave now,' muttered Blitzen.

'No!' snuddered Rudolph. 'He might need our help.'

An Arctic fox let out a distant cry and Nick's ears twitched alertly at the sound. The reindeer jumped, gasped and shook their antlered heads.

'Akfaskoosh! He's got ears like us!' Vixen spluttered.

'Maybe Two Legs aren't so different from us?' suggested Cupid, who was the gentlest and shyest of the young does.

'Smoosh! Try telling that to Lancer,' Blitzen snorted sourly.

Nick decided to get to the point. 'I'm lost,' he announced. 'I saw you flying above the forest and I came to look for you. I've heard all these stories, but no one believes them except for me. I wanted to meet you. But then I got chased by wolves and the forest took me down all these paths and now I don't know where I am.' Tears of bewilderment filled his eyes. 'Can you help me?'

The reindeer stared at him for a few moments, their big brown eyes full of sympathy. A sigh escaped them in a low whiffling sound. They moved forward again and gathered round, nudging him affectionately.

'So, Two Legs. Your elders don't know you're out here?' said Rudolph.

'No. I disobeyed orders. No one is allowed to leave the town after dark because of the wolves.'

A murmur of approval ran round the reindeer.

'Kushtoosh! We're disobeying orders too!' said Rudolph proudly. 'We've been forbidden to come out flying on our own. That's why we come out at night when the elders are asleep.'

'Comet says we must not fritter away our flying powers,' said Vixen.

'Who's Comet?' Nick asked.

'The Head Doe of our Tribe,' said Blitzen. 'She is the Holder of the Power. She flies up to the North Pole every year to gather it from the Lights in the sky.'

'Except she doesn't any more, 'cos they're not there,' added Donder. 'They disappeared one night, many years ago. No one knows why.'

'But we're not going to let something like that stop us flying!' declared Vixen defiantly. 'It is our birthright!' She stamped her dainty foot to reinforce her point.

Rudolph shook his head at the others. 'Smoosh, you lot. Slow down! Don't you think it's time we introduced ourselves?'

One by one, the reindeer stepped forward, nodded their graceful heads at Nickolai and told him their names.

'Dancer.'

'Prancer.'

'Dasher.'

'Donder.'

'Blitzen.'

'Cupid.'

'Vixen.'

'Rudolph. I'm the oldest.'

'You already told him that, Rudolph,' snapped Blitzen. 'And you're only older by one moonset and half a sunrise.'

Rudolph chose to ignore Blitzen and nudged Nick again. 'Can you ride, Two Legs?'

Nick stared at him. 'My father put me on our horse's back once, but I only stayed on for a few minutes while it walked around the yard.'

Without a word, Rudolph sat down on his

haunches and swung his beautiful head round to nod at his own back. 'Climb on,' he told Nick. 'And we'll take you home.'

Nick hesitated. Inside his tunic he could feel Elvina shaking her head. Maybe she was right. It could be dangerous.

'Do hurry up, Nickolai,' snorted Rudolph. 'You're in trouble. We're in trouble. We have to get back soon – but I don't want to leave you here on your own.'

Fear held Nick back. What if he fell off? This was all so strange and new and utterly incredible. He walked uncertainly over to Rudolph and climbed on his back. It felt warm and soft and comfortable like an armchair, a perfect fit.

'Now grab my antlers,' instructed Rudolph, 'and hold on tight!'

Nick clung on to Rudolph's soft velvety antlers and lurched as the young stag rose into a standing position. The reindeer lined up in a row, Rudolph slightly in front.

'Ready everyone?' said Rudolph.

They all nodded and their bodies began to quiver in preparation for take-off. They pawed the ground with their hooves and began to canter forward, building up speed, then after what seemed like an eternity, they kicked off and rose smoothly into the air.

Nick wrapped his legs round Rudolph's body as they flew higher and higher, keeping below the line of the trees. The wind whistled past his ears and the cold air stung his cheeks. He had never felt so exhilarated in his life. Tree trunks flashed past at dizzying speed, whispering loudly, urging the reindeer on.

'Right, right!' snorted Rudolph to the others. The reindeer swerved and cornered the bend. Nick hung on tight, clinging to Rudolph's antlers and lying low along his neck.

'Bank to the left!'

A new path opened up abruptly and they veered into it on a racing turn.

'I said left, Donder!' Rudolph roared.

Nick glanced back and saw that Donder had barely missed crashing into the line of trees, turning in the nick of time. His gangly legs scrabbled in the air to regain control before he shot forward again. The ride continued through the forest, along the ever moving paths. Nick clung on to Rudolph, leaning into every bend, revelling in the sensation of speed. He began to shout for joy, all his senses alive.

Suddenly the trees opened out. They had reached the edge of the forest. The reindeer climbed higher and the view stretched out below. In the distance, the huddled dwellings of Norsk nestled under a ridge.

Nickolai saw his sledge, left abandoned and forgotten from what seemed a lifetime ago, the dogs sitting on the ground nearby, waiting patiently for him. The wolves were nowhere to be seen.

'Down there!' he whispered in Rudolph's ear. 'That's the sledge I came in.'

Rudolph began to bank round in circles, slowly moving down towards the sledge. He landed gracefully, his hooves making skid marks in the snow. The dogs looked up and blinked as Nickolai slid off Rudolph's back. He whistled softly to tell them not to be alarmed and they stood up and shook themselves.

'Can I come and see you again?' Nick asked Rudolph, his eyes shining with hope.

Rudolph looked doubtful. 'It is dangerous out here, with the wolves and bears. But if you tell me where you live I could come and get you.'

'The house on the north edge of the town, all on its own, with a red roof and one chimney. This red sledge will be outside it. I could meet you up on the roof.'

Rudolph nodded. 'All right. Tomorrow night at midnight. But remember – no one else must see us. And you must not tell anyone about us, do you understand? No Two Legs must know of us – except for you. You're different from the rest. It is the reindeer code of secrecy. If you break it you will endanger us.'

Nick nodded solemnly. 'I promise.'

The next morning Nickolai woke up with the early spring sun streaming into his room. He wondered if it had all been a dream. He leaped out of bed and ran across to the window. The sun sparkled on the snow-covered tree tops in the distance. He thrust his hands into the pockets of his red robe, and found a fir cone. He had not dreamed it. It was real.

All that day Nickolai hugged his secret knowledge to himself, no longer caring about the familiar taunts and jeers of the children at school. He had done something that none of them had ever done, or ever would. Something so special it was better than anything else in the world. Only one person noticed a difference. As they walked home from school, Anneka tackled him.

'OK. What have you been up to?'

Nickolai suppressed a smile. 'Nothing,' he said, the picture of innocence.

'I know there's something you're not telling me,' said Anneka suspiciously, 'you look too pleased with yourself.'

Nick was bursting to tell her. But he'd been sworn to secrecy, he'd made a solemn oath. 'It's just that a toy I'm making is coming on very well,' he replied carefully. 'It's a reindeer. I'm thinking of putting wings on it.'

Anneka scuffed her fur boots along a stale ridge of blackened snow, kicking it into the verge where the tundra was beginning to show through. Her forehead was furrowed with a thoughtful frown. 'Funny you should say that. We were talking about flying reindeer only the other night. Me and Louisa.'

Nick felt a tremor of alarm. 'What do you mean?'

'Oh nothing really. It's just that, you know, there've always been these fairy tales and rumours about flying reindeer in the forest. The grown-ups always get all huffy when we talk about it. None of them believe in the flying reindeer of course. But there have been sightings. I believe it. I mean, why not? Anything can happen.'

Nick felt alarm bells ringing in every part of his body. Had he given anything away? He would have loved more than anything in the world to share this with Anneka, but he couldn't. 'It's a load of nonsense!' he declared, rather more forcefully than was necessary. 'You're a fool if you believe fairy tales like that.'

Anneka glanced round at him in surprise, as though someone else had spoken.

As winter slowly melted into spring and the waking tundra began to green the landscape, Nick continued his nightly escapades. He began to learn the ways of the forest and anticipate with the reindeer where the trees would move next. He began to feel more confident and soon he was doing circus acts, standing on Rudolph's back, swinging athletically down underneath him and sometimes even leaping off into the trees and swinging along the branches. It was blissful.

One night, he and the young reindeer had stopped for a rest by a stream that sparkled and gurgled as it ran through a gulley. They were all drinking from the ice-cold water, Nick with his head dunked right into it, when they heard a stern voice nearby.

'And what do you think you are doing?'

The reindeer's heads jerked up guiltily. There, standing on the other side of the stream, was a fully grown doe with magnificent antlers. Her brown eyes gazed from one reindeer to the next.

'I'm very disappointed in you all.'

The young reindeer shook their heads and pawed the ground, muttering and snorting.

'Sorry, Mamoosh!' muttered Rudolph meekly. The other reindeer murmured a chorus of sorrys.

Comet suddenly stiffened as she saw Nickolai. 'A Two Legs!' she spluttered furiously. 'How could you? Not only have you been disobeying the curfew and flying on your own, squandering our powers, but you have broken the reindeer code of secrecy!'

Rudolph took a running leap and landed beside his mother. 'We can explain! We found him in the forest. He was lost and would have been killed by wolves if we hadn't rescued him. So we took him back. Surely it's part of the reindeer code also to be kind and helpful to others? Isn't that what we do for all the creatures of the forest?'

Comet snorted. She was still too furious to speak.

'And he's not like other Two Legs. He's different. He can—'

'Enough!' roared Comet, cutting him off. 'Follow me at once. We return to the cave immediately. And bring the Two Legs! Lancer will decide what is to be done with him!'

* * *

The reindeer's cave was warm and stuffy. In the tense silence, all Nick could hear was the gentle snorting of the reindeer and the scuffling of their hooves on the hard earth floor. Shafts of moonlight found their way inside, filling the cave with a faint silvery glow.

Nick stood facing Lancer, who towered over him, his huge antlers casting shadows across his face. The other reindeer of the tribe huddled around in a circle, nodding nervously.

'What are we to do with him?' boomed Lancer. 'This is an outrage!'

'I'm sorry . . .' began Nick.

Lancer jumped in shock and stared at him, flabbergasted.

'See?' said Rudolph. 'He can speak our language. I said he was different!'

'I have not told anyone about you!' babbled Nick. 'And I promise I won't!'

Rudolph cut in. 'He is no ordinary Two Legs, Papoosh! He's special. Nickolai, show them your ears.'

Nick had no qualms about showing his ears to these creatures. Slowly he let his hood fall down and flicked them around. A gasp ran round the reindeer and they stared at him in astonishment. Comet gazed at him thoughtfully, as though seeing him in a different light. Velvet, the oldest of the tribe, creaked forward, her misty old eyes ablaze with emotion.

'This Two Legs child has been sent to us for a

reason. It is the will of Arkfel!' she whispered dramatically.

Lancer snorted and stamped on the ground, making the whole cave shake. 'Enough of your mumblick jumblick, Mamoosh! It is no excuse for disobedience. Because of this thoughtless behaviour, we may have to consider migrating further south, to another forest!'

A stunned silence filled the cave. Nick felt Elvina trembling under his tunic and knew she was going to make one of her rare appearances. With a triumphant squeak and a flurry of blurred wings, the fairy shot out of the top of Nick's front and buzzed around, lighting up the whole cave with her strange unearthly glow. The reindeer flinched and snorted in disbelief.

Elvina began buzzing round the cave excitedly, making patterns in the air. The reindeer backed away in alarm as she came near them. Then she began bouncing gaily around on the reindeer's antlers like a naughty child, squeaking with glee as she landed on each velvety tip. Round and round she went, whizzing faster and faster in an endless circle, until she seemed to be creating a ring of light.

The reindeer's heads swung this way and that, following her movements, flinching slightly as she came towards them. Their antlers began to spark and an electric current fizzled and crackled around the ring, joining them up. The fur along the reindeer's backs rose in a ridge and their bodies quivered with a new energy. Nick felt an answering tremor of excitement run up his spine.

'The power!' cried Comet. 'She has brought us back the flying power! She must have come from the Lights!'

From then on, Nickolai was fully accepted amongst the tribe of the flying reindeer. But now it was Comet who came to pick him up from the roof of the little cottage every night, because the Elders felt that only an adult could safely ferry him around without being seen.

She would take him back to the cave and Elvina would perform her ritual, renewing the reindeer's powers until they had several years of flying time stored away inside them. Then Nick and the young reindeer would be allowed to go off on their nightly jaunts through the forest, until the moon began to sink in the sky. Nick was so quiet and careful when he crept out of the house, and Comet was so deft and graceful with her landings and take-offs, that his nocturnal adventures were never suspected.

One night Comet brought him home as usual and gently set him down on the roof. She had to be extra careful now, for there was less snow to muffle her hooves. Instead of shooting off as she usually did, she lingered uneasily and gave him a long searching look.

'There is something I must tell you,' she said at last. 'It has been troubling me for some time. But I feel you must know.'

Nick held his breath. She was going to tell him his nightly visits must stop. He waited anxiously while Comet blew some air through her muzzle and continued, 'It is about your origins. Why are you so different from other Two Legs?'

Nick breathed a sigh of relief. He shrugged. 'I don't know. Just a freak, I suppose. That's what they all call me round here.'

'You are not from round here,' Comet said gently. 'You are from the north. I rescued you, many years ago when you were a baby. I recognize you from your red coat. I found you alone, abandoned in the snow, surrounded by wolves. And I brought you to this very house and dropped you down that chimney.'

A cold feeling descended from Nick's heart into his stomach. The shock hit him like a thunderbolt and he lost his balance. He landed heavily on the roof and let out a sharp cry of surprise.

'You mean – Joe and Hannah are not my real parents?' he said thickly.

Comet shook her head gravely. 'No. I'm afraid not, Nickolai.'

The Gold Rush

Nickolai felt numb with shock. He had never questioned who he was or where he came from. Now he'd discovered that he knew nothing about himself, except that he was from the north, abandoned as a baby. His eyes filled with tears and a lump rose in his throat. He felt cut adrift, as though he had become a stranger to himself. He flung his arms round Comet's neck and buried his face in her fur.

'I want to come and live with you in the forest! I feel like you're my family now!'

Comet shook her head sadly. 'You know that's not possible, Nickolai.' She glanced round nervously and her ears flicked. 'I must go now, before I'm seen.' She turned and took off elegantly into the night. Nick tried to call her back. He wanted to ask her more, but she was gone.

He climbed into the chimney with a heavy heart and slid down into its familiar dark sootiness. When he landed in the fireplace, he found Joe and Hannah standing in front of him, stony-faced.

'What on earth do you think you've been doing?' exploded Hannah. 'We heard a thumping noise on the roof. Then we found you missing!'

Nick stared at the people he had thought were his parents: Hannah with her hands on her hips and her little blue eyes flaring with anger, Joe scratching his thinning head, like he always did when he was flummoxed. Suddenly they looked very old. A hard lump of doubt and mistrust formed in Nick's chest.

'Where have you been, lad?' Joe asked.

Nick thought quickly. He had to protect the reindeer. 'I went for a ride,' he said defiantly.

Joe made a sharp intake of breath and Hannah went white around the mouth.

'You mean – you borrowed your father's sleigh?'

Nick felt a hot rush of anger. 'He's not my father!' he shouted. 'I know he's not! And you're not my mother! You lied to me! I hate you both!'

There was a stunned silence. Nick stood facing them, hunched with misery, clenching and unclenching his fists. Hannah and Joe gaped at him.

'How did you find out?' whispered Hannah. 'Who told you?'

Nick bit his lip. He couldn't tell them the truth. 'I just worked it out for myself. Why didn't you tell me?'

'We were going to, dear,' said Hannah, wringing her hands. 'We were just waiting for the right time.'

'But who am I? Who are my real parents? Where do I come from?'

Joe and Hannah exchanged uncomfortable glances.

'We don't know, lad.'

'We – found you, abandoned, in the fireplace. We took you in.'

Nick let out a long breath. So Comet had told him the truth. But where exactly had she found him? Where in the north? Who lived up there? Nick felt a rising anger at Joe and Hannah's dishonesty. They should have found out more. They shouldn't have just kept him, like someone's lost property.

There was a long and awkward silence. No one knew quite what to say.

'Why did you go out, lad?' said Joe. 'What were you looking for?' His face dropped in sudden alarm. 'It's that forest, isn't it? Did you try and go there?'

Nick shrugged mutinously. 'Might have done.'

'You and your silly fancies about flying reindeer!' spluttered Joe. 'No one ever comes back out of that forest! Don't you ever do anything like this again!'

Nick glared at them both. 'You can't tell me what to do!' he burst out. 'You're not my real parents.'

Joe looked mortified. Hannah's cheeks flamed. 'Well, we've looked after you ever since you were a baby!' she rallied, her voice rising in hurt indignation. 'We took you in, fed you and clothed you, even though we hardly had enough for ourselves! And what thanks do we get for it? Whoever your real parents are, we are responsible for you now! Joe, you're to block that chimney up every night as soon as the fire's gone out.

And put a lock on Nick's bedroom door and window. From now on, Nickolai, you're to be confined to the house at all times!'

'Why won't you tell me what's wrong, Nick?' Anneka's pale blue eyes bored into him. 'You've had a face like a donkey's backside for ages.'

They were walking home from school together. The days were getting longer and lighter now, and watery sunlight washed across the landscape. Tufts of coarse grass pushed their way through the snow and Arctic flowers nodded in the breeze. The threat of the wolves had faded away and the children were allowed out and about again. Even Joe and Hannah had relented and begun to relax Nick's curfew.

'Oh it's nothing,' said Nick, shrugging. He still wasn't ready to talk about it, even to Anneka. He preferred not to think about it too much either; during the long evenings when he was still grounded, he had distracted himself by making more and more toys, surrounded by odds and ends that he had scavenged from Joe's toolshed and Hannah's workbasket.

Cleverly crafted things began to take shape: dolls with arms and legs that moved, fairies with wings that flapped, toy houses with windows and doors, working models of sledges and dogs. He began to carve miniature models of people who looked like him, with pointed ears that moved. Whole families emerged: children, men and women, little babies, until he had built up a whole collection. It was as though he was trying to re-create his lost people. He was jerked out of his reverie when he and Anneka turned a corner and came face to face with Finn and his gang.

'Just ignore them,' said Anneka, grabbing Nick's hand and marching ahead. But suddenly Nick felt rough hands from behind, pushing something over his head, pulling down his hood. He was jerked violently backwards.

'Time to put you on a lead, Dog Boy! Come on, walkies!'

Finn laughed nastily and ran ahead, dragging Nick along like an animal by the lead and collar he'd put over his head. Nick stumbled and pulled back, clutching at his neck, trying not to fall. Jeers of laughter rang out.

Anneka let out a roar of rage and flew at Finn like a wildcat. 'Leave him alone, you brute!' she screamed and leaped on Finn's back. He threw her off roughly and she fell to the ground in a sprawling heap.

Nick felt something inside him snap. He could feel a force coming from within him, brought about by his fear and anger. His ears began to twitch violently.

'Oh, look at the doggy's ears!' shouted Finn. 'Come on, doggy! Walkies!'

There was a rumbling noise and the ground underneath Finn began to shake. At first it was just a tremor directly below his feet. The tremors increased so that Finn began to lose his balance. He yelped in shock and let go of the rope, trying to keep his footing. Several tiles fell off the roof above and landed around him, narrowly missing his head. The rumbling stopped as quickly as it had begun. Everyone stared, white-faced with shock.

Finn pointed a trembling finger at Nick. 'Did you do that?'

Nick looked bewildered. 'No, of course not!' he stammered. 'It just happened!'

'It'd better not have been you, else you're dead, Dog Boy!' Finn shouted.

He and his gang ran off down the street in disarray, their feet slithering in the spring mud.

Anneka stared at Nick as though she was seeing him for the first time. 'Nick!' she whispered breathlessly. '*Was* it you?'

Nick pulled his hood up over his ears. 'I don't know,' he mumbled.

'Well, I don't think you'll have much more trouble from them from now on, anyway,' she said, staring after the bullies with contempt.

Anneka was right. Finn and his gang didn't bother Nick again. But he was still an outcast. His only real friend was Elvina. And of course Anneka. Her home was the only one where he was accepted, and he spent many happy hours there, making toys for Louisa and eating Lotta's berry pies.

But nothing could keep away the empty feeling that had lodged itself in his heart. He didn't belong here, in this town, with these people. He missed his reindeer friends terribly; Comet had returned only once since that momentous night. Nick had watched helplessly through his bedroom window as she hovered overhead looking for him, then finally flew away.

Now he could only gaze with longing at the outline of the forest on the horizon. Were they wondering what had become of him? Did they miss him as much as he missed them? Sometimes he felt as though those happy times in the forest had all been a dream.

It was during the summer, when the sun shone late into the night, that the strangers began to drift through Norsk. They came in a small trickle at first, straggling groups of weary travellers, trailing fretful children, their horses and carts laden with all their worldly possessions. Sometimes they were accompanied by Inuit guides. As the Summer Solstice approached and the sun was still shining at midnight, the trickle turned into a constant stream, and they started to pour through the outskirts of the town in droves.

They had come from all the lands south of the Arctic Circle. Most of them were fair-haired and pale-skinned. Some had flat, Slavic faces, and high cheekbones. Some had red hair and pale, milky complexions. And some were dark and swarthy, with almond eyes: people from the nomadic tribes of the Mongolian plains. The town children took to standing by the roadside to watch them pass.

Soon the travellers grew bolder and began to ride right through the centre of town, looking for shelter. This was the last settlement before the landscape opened out into the desolate wastes of the Pole. Now the travellers were amongst them, the children could get closer. One evening Nick and Anneka were eavesdropping on a whole gaggle of people camped out in a barn. Nick's ears flicked as he listened intently, picking up every word.

'What are they saying?' whispered Anneka, agog.

'They're talking about a Golden City,' Nick murmured, still listening. 'At the North Pole. A place called Doransk. They're saying that it has turrets and spires of gold, towering up into the sky. And the streets are paved with gold, and everyone who goes there can make their fortune and have a better life.'

'A golden city? At the North Pole?' said Anneka sceptically. 'That's impossible. There's nothing up there except ice and snow!'

'Well there's obviously something up there now,' said Nickolai. 'Else why is everyone . . .' He stopped suddenly, as a massive insight struck him. He looked at Anneka, his eyes shining with excitement, his heart swelling with a new and thrilling possibility. 'Anneka, I think that's where I come from! The North Pole.'

Anneka frowned. 'What on earth are you talking about? You're from round here, aren't you?'

Suddenly Nick felt ready to tell her about his

unknown origins. 'No. Hannah and Joe found me abandoned, as a baby.'

Anneka stared at him in astonishment. 'But – but how . . . who . . . I mean – you can't be an Inuit. They're the only people who go that far north. You don't look a thing like them. Who are your real parents? Where did they live?'

'That's the whole point,' Nick said impatiently. 'I don't know! But I feel I come from the north. Maybe it's something to do with this Golden City everyone's talking about.' A look of sudden determination crossed his face. 'And I'm going to find out! But don't tell anybody what I've just told you. Promise?'

That night at home, Nick started to make a city, carving the spires and turrets out of old blocks of wood and painting them yellow. It was his way of broaching the subject.

'What are you making now, lad?' enquired Joe, knocking his pipe out on the hearth.

'A Golden City like the one at the North Pole,' replied Nick casually. 'The one that all these travellers are going to.'

Hannah tutted sceptically. 'Cuh! That's just a pipe dream. I've heard all the rumours. A place like that can't possibly exist. The Pole is not fit for human habitation.'

'They'll be back, starving and exhausted, by Yuletide, mark my words,' muttered Joe.

'If they don't perish first,' added Hannah darkly.

93

'Well I think there is something up there!' retorted Nick. 'And what's more, I think that's where I come from.' He was about to say: 'Because that's where Comet says she found me,' but he stopped himself just in time.

Joe and Hannah glanced at each other uncomfortably. The matter of Nick's origins had not been discussed since that fateful night.

'Don't be silly,' sighed Hannah, putting down her knitting. 'You can't be from up there.'

Nick was bursting to tell them they were wrong, that he knew more than they did. And the urge to go and find out more was pressing in on him like water behind a dam. 'Well, I want to go up there and find out for myself,' he declared. 'I feel sure that I will find my real family up there.'

'Certainly not,' said Hannah shortly. 'You're too young to go on your own.'

'Well, let's go together then!' said Nick. 'Some of the townspeople are already talking about going up there to see what all the fuss is about.'

'No. We're too old for that kind of caper. It's out of the question.'

Nick slumped in defeat. It was no use arguing.

'Now why don't you make more of an effort to fit in round here instead?' continued Hannah in a gentler tone. 'After all, you're nearly eight now.'

'I *do* make an effort!' Nick protested. 'But I'm so different from all of them. Anneka's the only one who likes me. Finn has turned everyone else against me!'

Hannah's face darkened. 'That boy's a heap of trouble. He'll come to no good in the end. Take no notice of him.'

Nick stared moodily into the fire, pondering the hopelessness of the situation. Maybe Hannah was right; maybe he'd have to wait until he was older. And in the meantime, he should try to make the best of things.

Suddenly a new and entirely different thought struck him. Finn was the leader of all the town kids. If Nick invented something that Finn liked, a game that all the children in the town could play . . . if Nick could win Finn over, everyone else might start liking him too.

He pushed the thought around in his mind for a while, then hit on an idea.

'Joe?' he began casually. 'Have you got any spare wood in your shed?'

'Yeee-eees,' Joe answered.

'Good. I've had an idea. Only thing is . . .' Nick paused, knowing he was asking a lot. 'Could I borrow the dogs?'

Joe gave a start of surprise. 'What?'

Nick held his breath, waiting. Hannah looked up at him enquiringly. 'Well now, that depends, dear. What do you want them for?'

The Snowball Effect

Winter had come to Norsk again. The whole town lay under perpetual twilight and a blanket of snow. Tonight, all its inhabitants were gathered around the race course just outside the town. The sledge teams were lined up in a row at the starting post, their bright colours standing out against the white backdrop. The dogs harnessed to them yelped and crooned, straining at their leashes. Each sledge was lightweight and streamlined, needing only two dogs to pull it along. They were neat little racing craft, built for speed.

Nick gazed round at the scene and felt like pinching himself. He still couldn't believe it. Four years on, his plan had succeeded beyond his wildest dreams.

All the town children were ranged beside him in their sledges, poised and ready at the reins. The drivers carried their own hurling devices: something like a hockey stick with a carved wooden cup at the end, designed to scoop up snow from the ground as the sledge sped along and hurl snowballs at the racers on either side to distract them and drive them off course.

The finishing line was a row of painted logs at the far end. The sledge lanes were marked out with black lines. There was a row of posts down the centre of each lane, bendy young saplings that the drivers had to weave through before they could complete the race.

All around them were cheering crowds of supporters, gathered around the piece of land that had been flattened and cleared to be the official racetrack. It had come to be known as Splodging; a riotous and messy game which every child in town had taken up with enthusiasm. It was great fun to watch and even more fun to take part in.

And it was all because of Nick. He'd never thought this game he'd invented would become so popular. It was a regular sporting event in Norsk now, and every child over the age of ten had built their own sledge and trained their own team of huskies.

'Are we ready then, Nicko?' said a voice beside him.

Nick glanced over at the boy who was now his best friend. Finn called him 'Nicko' now. The days of 'Dog Boy' were long gone. Finn was jiggling with anticipation, his face alight with excitement as he held his reins ready.

'Yeah, come on, Nick!' called Anneka from his other side. 'My dogs are getting restless.'

Nick nodded at Joachim, waiting on the sidelines, who grinned, strode forward and blew his whistle.

Mayhem broke out at once; the crowd erupted into roars as the huskies shot forward, yelping and baying, pulling the sledges at enormous speed. The crowd screamed themselves hoarse, the younger ones jumping up and down, urging on their brothers and sisters.

Nick shook his reins and whistled at his dogs. They bounded forward, putting on an extra spurt of speed. His sledge went into the lead and he began scooping up snowballs and hurling them at the other drivers. There was a soft thunk and a spray of snow blurred his vision as Finn landed a big one right on his face.

'Ha ha! Got you, Nicko!' shouted Finn.

Nick laughed and dug his hurler into the snow as he raced along. He lobbed it over his head and aimed it at Finn. It landed on the back of Finn's neck with a splat.

Roars of laughter and screams broke out on either side as cold white spray flew in all directions. They were heading towards the first post. Nick clicked his teeth at the dogs and pulled the reins. He leaned to the right and the sledge swerved neatly round the post. The next one was already rushing towards him.

Suddenly there was a commotion from his left. Anneka and Finn's sledges had collided, the reins hopelessly tangled up, and Anneka's sledge had overturned. The dogs were barking hysterically and wheeling about in a frenzy. Joachim blew the whistle and the race ground to a halt as the drivers reined in. Nick leaped off his sledge and ran over.

'What happened?' he cried. Finn and Anneka were glaring daggers at each other, their chests heaving.

'He drove straight into me!' gasped Anneka, trying to pull her sledge upright.

'Did not!' shouted Finn. 'You didn't keep to your lane! You were too far over my way! You girls are useless drivers!'

Anneka's pale eyes glowed with fury and she looked ready to explode. 'That's total rubbish and you know it. You could see I was getting in front of you and you missed with a snowball so you deliberately swerved towards me and—'

Joachim strode on to the scene.

'He fouled me, Dad!' shouted Anneka.

'No I didn't! You fouled me!'

Joachim rolled his eyes. This was a common dispute in Splodging races, where it was difficult to keep track of everyone's movements with all the snow being hurled around. 'Calm down, everyone. Let's look at the tracks.' He examined the furrows that the sledge blades had left in the snow. They crisscrossed each other over the black line that separated the two lanes.

'You should disqualify him from the race!' Anneka prompted him hopefully.

Joachim was still inspecting the ground. 'Hmmm . . . borderline, I'm afraid.'

Anneka glared at her father, expecting his support. Joachim shrugged and glanced at Nick. 'Well, you invented this game, Nickolai. What do you think?'

Nick felt he should come up with a compromise. He didn't want his two best friends quarrelling again.

They were always finding excuses to get at each other, and sometimes he felt like knocking their heads together. Such were the problems of the most popular boy in town.

It was a big responsibility.

'I think we should start the race again,' he said finally. A loud groan went up. 'It's the only fair way!' he cried. 'And everyone has to be more careful about keeping to their lanes, OK?'

The racers grumbled and turned their sledges round towards the touchline. Anneka brought her sledge up alongside Nick's.

'I still don't trust him, Nick,' she whispered. 'He definitely drove into me. He hates losing. Especially to girls. I know he's your friend these days – but once a bully, always a bully.'

The Inuit boy watched the travellers trekking towards the Golden City from his usual lookout post on the ridge. The steady stream of pilgrims had been passing through since he was nine, gathering speed and volume as the years rolled by. Now he was twelve and they showed no signs of diminishing.

From the start, it had been obvious they weren't the usual whalers, or explorers. These people looked like ordinary citizens from the lands further south. During the summer months they came in droves, taking advantage of the long days to make some progress. Zakurak and his family had crossed paths with them many times on their hunting expeditions: a constant flow of colourful, bedraggled people on horses and wagons loaded with clanking possessions. When they reached the shores of the Arctic Sea they would abandon their former transport and take kayaks with the Inuit across the water, if it hadn't frozen over yet. As they headed further north into the land of eternal snow and ice, they would trade their goods for sledges and teams of huskies bought at the Inuit trading posts.

Zakurak would never forgive whoever had built this city. It had killed his grandfather. Nanuk had been right. It had upset the balance of nature here, driving away the animal herds, making them more difficult to hunt and track. Even the fish had been affected. The Inuit people had been forced to travel further and further.

When supplies had begun to run short, Zakurak's family had followed the tribe for better hunting down south. Nanuk was too old to travel and said he would be one fewer mouth to feed. He had stayed on, and Zakurak had refused to leave him. He was old enough to fend for himself and his grandfather now, and he had already killed his first seal.

But the spirit seemed to have gone out of Nanuk. One night, he died. Zakurak had been forced to bury him through a hole in the ice, since it was too far above the tundra to cover him with a cairn of rocks.

Now Zakurak was completely alone in the igloo, hunting and fishing every day and cooking his catch over the fire. He fingered the talisman that hung on a leather thong round his neck, making sure it was still there. He dreaded losing it. He'd done well today, caught several Arctic char through a hole in the ice. He had enough seal meat to last several weeks and soon the chamois would be passing through. And he'd stored up enough dried meat to see him through winter. He would survive. But it was very lonely.

All he could do now was keep an eye on the city. Because one day his people were going to come back and reclaim their territory.

'Some of it's going to have to go!' declared Hannah, looking round the tiny cramped cottage. There was now only a small circle left free in the middle of the floor. The rest was occupied by Nick's toys and models, which he'd continued making whenever he was at home. His collection had grown over the years and it was now crammed everywhere – in every corner and on every surface.

'If you'd only let me sell some of them in the market, along with my knitwear . . .' Hannah suggested.

'No!' said Nick sharply. 'I will not sell them.' He looked round at his inventions with pride. Each one was slightly different.

'Well you're going to have to do something, if you're going to keep making more,' said Hannah firmly, folding her arms across her chest.

'She's right, lad. Out with the old, in with the new. I'm running out of space in the shed,' agreed Joe.

Nick sighed. He hated letting go of anything. But Hannah had a point. Now the days were long and dark, he was at home more and making more things.

The Winter Solstice was approaching. The sun had gone from the sky altogether and time had merged into one long dark endless night. Bonfires were lit in the streets to remind everyone of the sun that had deserted them and to reassure them that it would return in the spring. Fairs, festivities and wild hog roasts took place in the town square, to cheer the continual darkness.

The celebrations were gathering pace, leading up to the high point of the season – the festival of Yuletide that marked the depth of the Winter Solstice, when gifts were given and feasting took place in every home.

Yuletide.

Yes!

With a blinding flash, Nick realized what he was going to do.

Just before midnight on Winter Solstice Eve, all the older children of the town gathered outside the school, each with their racing sledge and huskies and a large sack. They had crept out of their homes secretly, many of them climbing out of their bedroom windows and sliding down the sloping roofs to the ground. None of them had asked permission. It was a

Secret Mission. Parental consent would have spoiled all the fun. Nick was adamant that it should be a mystery.

The children stayed quietly in the shadows of the old schoolhouse, watching and waiting, unaware that Madame was smiling as she peered down from behind the curtains of her bedroom window. A huge disc of moon hung in the sky, spreading a silvery light everywhere and sparkling on the snow-covered roofs.

'D'you think he's coming?' whispered Johan, the youngest of the racers.

'Hope he hasn't been found out and grounded!' muttered Finn.

'Nah. He won't let us down,' said Anneka quietly.

A few seconds later, there was a gentle panting noise from the huskies and Nick's familiar blue and red racing sledge hissed across the snow towards them. His red cloak was wrapped tightly round him and his hood was pulled close round his ears.

A huge, bulging sack was perched precariously on another sledge towed behind his, wobbling slightly as it bumped along. He whistled at his dogs and drew the sledge to a halt.

'OK? Everyone ready?' he whispered. The other children nodded. 'Come and have a look at this lot.'

Nick leaped off his sledge and opened the huge sack. The children crowded round and peered in.

'Blimey! Where d'you get all those?' asked Finn. 'Did you nick 'em?'

'Certainly not!' snorted Anneka. 'He made them. Didn't you, Nick?'

Nick nodded. The other children stared at him in astonishment.

'You mean you made those, all on your own?' said Finn incredulously.

'Course! He makes things all the time. Didn't you know?' said Anneka nonchalantly. She never missed a chance to get one over on Finn.

'Come on, we'd better get this lot delivered,' said Nick, pulling toys out of the sack. 'Remember the plan? Half of you do the south side, the other half the north side. OK?'

When all the toys had been divided, the children climbed on their sledges, each with a full sack. They whistled at their dogs and set off, fanning out across the town in all directions, speeding silently through the snow-covered streets.

The next morning, young children all over the town woke up to find toys mysteriously left on their doorsteps overnight. Squeals of delight rang through the streets. Where had they come from? Their older siblings simply shrugged and looked innocent. Every one of them kept a straight face and nobody gave the secret away.

But quite a few parents exchanged conspiratorial smiles and said nothing.

The Trek North

'Please can I go?' begged Nick. His eyes were blazing so blue they seemed to dazzle the room.

Joe and Hannah were both sitting very still by the fire, concentrating on their tasks: Hannah with her knitting and Joe cleaning some harnesses.

'All my best friends are leaving me,' continued Nick plaintively. 'I miss them. I'm lonely again!'

Now spring was here, more townspeople had started going north to investigate the mysterious Golden City, spurred on by travellers' gossip. It had been bad enough when Finn and his family had set off, but now Anneka had announced that she and her family were going too. Nick couldn't bear it.

There was a tense silence, during which Hannah's nimble fingers flew over her knitting and Joe scrubbed extra hard on his leather harnesses.

'Well, it all sounds too good to be true if you ask me,' said Hannah tartly. 'I mean, really, streets paved with gold, dreams coming true, magical climate . . . load of piffle in my opinion. I'm surprised people are taken in by it.' She clicked her teeth and shook her head at the folly of it all.

Nick saw the sadness in their faces and the slump of their old, defeated shoulders and felt as though he was being torn in two. He knew how much he meant to them. But he had to go to this place, he just had to. And he *was* old enough now.

The fire crackled in the silence.

Hannah finished a row, sighed and looked up at Nick with a wan smile. She glanced at Joe. 'Well, Joe, I've thought about this long and hard. I'm sure he's on a hiding to nowhere, but he'd be with Lotta and Joachim and their girls, responsible people we know. He's nearly twelve now. And he'll never rest until he's satisfied his curiosity. You'll come back and see us, won't you, Nick?'

Nick stared at Hannah, then Joe, in amazement. 'You mean — you're letting me go?'

They both nodded and smiled sadly. Nick let out a shout of joy and rushed towards Hannah, flinging himself into her arms and sending her knitting flying across the room.

A week later, the little party was ready to set off. Nick had been hovering expectantly at the window since the early hours of the morning. Finally he heard the creaking of wheels, the clip clop of hooves and the sound of excited voices as the wagon hove into view along the muddy track. The horse plodded along in front, pulling the swaying caravan, with its rounded roof made of heavy canvas, bulging with belongings and waving people. Nick's heart leaped at the promise of adventure that lay ahead.

Louisa, now five and full of herself, was jiggling about, waving her dolly at him. She'd had to be restrained from bringing her entire collection of toys. 'Hello, Nick! We're all going to Doransk! Yay!' she shouted gaily.

The wagon creaked to a halt outside the cottage and the horse snorted and stamped his shaggy hooves, which were easily the size of dinner plates. He was a massive, gentle creature with a huge head and kind eyes, bought from the local blacksmith.

Joe and Hannah came out of the cottage with Nick and handed him his rucksack. They stood side by side, arms round each other, a childless old couple again.

'Look after yourself, lad. And remember, all that glitters is not gold,' said Joe solemnly.

Hannah was too full of emotion to speak and just held out her plump arms. Nick hugged them both in a bear-like embrace and kissed Hannah's apple cheeks. After a heart-wrenching last hug and kiss, he climbed into the wagon next to Anneka.

'Don't worry. We'll look after him,' said Lotta, trying to disguise her excitement.

'I'll come back, I promise,' said Nick, biting his lip.

'Come on then, you lot, let's go and see what it's all

108

about. Just hope this Golden City lives up to your expectations,' said Joachim to his wife. He grinned at Joe and Hannah, whistled and shook the reins.

The horse heaved forward. Cries of goodbye rang out as the wagon creaked off down the rutted lane towards the open tundra.

Nick looked back and waved to the forlorn-looking old couple standing on the track. They grew smaller and smaller, until they were only tiny specks in the distance. As the wagon lurched along, passing the distant forest, Nick gave it one last glance, hoping as always to see a fleeting glimpse of a flying form above the tree tops. He was leaving his childhood behind.

'Are we there yet?' enquired Louisa, for the fifth time that day.

'Not yet, sweetheart,' said Lotta soothingly. 'It'll be a while yet.'

They had been trekking north for some weeks now. The rolling plains of tundra had gradually given way to a barren landscape fringed with jagged mountain ranges, remote and distant on the horizon. They had passed through vast, eerie graveyards on the tundra, where Inuit bones were buried under cairns of rock.

By the end of the second month they were crossing a frozen plain that stretched towards a low range of white-capped mountains. They were approaching the northern rim, where ice and snow ruled all year round.

Nick, who was walking ahead of the cart on foot with Anneka, stopped and concentrated hard, twitching his ears in tiny rotating movements.

'Over that way,' he said, pointing in a two o'clock direction.

'Righto.' Joachim clicked his teeth and turned the horse round.

Ever since they'd set off for the city, Nick had been feeling a gravitational pull inside him. Now it was stronger than ever. It had turned him into a walking compass, the guiding force of the expedition. He seemed to have a natural sense of direction buried deep inside him. Whenever high ridges or deep clefts in the land took them off course, his ears picked up the magnetic vibrations and pointed the party due north again. Every step of the way he had a growing sense that fate was leading him on. It was almost like going home.

Their journey was full of encounters with animals moving through the landscape: herds of caribou drifting across the plains like smoke; flocks of birds rising into the air from an icy lake shore; Arctic foxes prowling and barking in the wild, empty silence. Although the place looked like a desolate wilderness, it was heaving with life – ground squirrels scurrying into the undergrowth, musk oxen grazing on the rough grassland, golden plovers rising suddenly out of the scrub in front of them and vanishing into the sky with a loud beating of wings.

Apart from the food supplies which Lotta had packed, it was hunting that kept the party alive. They stopped at an Inuit trading post and picked up some sealskin furs and hunting equipment. Nick seemed to have a natural skill in tracking and stalking, using nets and spears to catch mammals and harpoons to catch fish from sparkling streams that ran through boggy ground. While Anneka and Nick were off hunting, Lotta would forage amongst the tough vegetation of the tundra, collecting a variety of sharp-tasting plants and berries which she used to flavour the food they caught.

As autumn came on, the sun began to dip over the horizon for hours at a time. The sky grew inky dark and stars winked overhead. The nights were back and time was divided up into logical patterns again. Nick began navigating by the stars, keeping his eyes fixed on the Pole Star. It lies directly over the North Pole, linked to the seven-star constellation of the Great Bear.

Some hours after dark, they would stop and make camp, huddling together round a fire and cooking whatever they had managed to catch. The campfire evenings became the high point of the day. Elvina would flit around like a firefly, lighting up the darkness and amusing everyone with her antics, especially Louisa. The child had turned out to be tough and surprisingly hardy for one so young. She was cheerful most of the time but became fretful and peevish towards evening, when she would settle down on Nick's lap, sucking a piece of dried meat and clutching her doll, until her eyelids drooped and she was tucked up in her nest in the wagon.

Every night they could see the campfires of other travellers scattered across the distant hillsides.

'How come we never see any of these people in the daytime?' wondered Anneka one night as she and Nick sat together, a little apart from the others.

'This is a big place,' said Nick, spearing another piece of cooked squirrel.

'How come you know where you're going, Nick?' said Anneka. 'Do you really feel like you're heading home, where you first came from?'

Nick nodded.

'But how do you know? Where did you get all these ideas from?' Anneka persisted.

Nick would have loved to tell her, but he couldn't. 'Just a feeling. I'm sure there are other people like me up there. And I'm going to find them.'

As they travelled further north the sun began to slip over the side of the earth in ever smaller arcs, until it seemed to roll over on the horizon like a whale. It rose and set in almost the same place, casting only a faint light for a few hours. The borders between day and night were becoming blurred.

Winter had at last come upon them, creeping up like a stalking animal. They were entering the True

North, a desolate, icy wilderness of haunting beauty. It was going to be harder to catch food; they would have to hunt seals and catch fish through holes in the ice. And the horse and cart were becoming increasingly difficult to steer through the snow.

They passed though the last Inuit village, a small settlement of hide tents, where they traded in the horse and cart for a large sledge and team of strong husky dogs. Their journey became tougher; the party was obliged to take it in turns to walk alongside, since the sledge was too small to take all of them. Nick continued navigating by the stars, and the charcoal lamps they'd brought lit their way.

One afternoon, on a day without a sunrise, under a moon that had not set for six days, they found themselves on the edge of a great frozen ocean. It stretched to infinity, a sea suspended in motion. Huge ridges of snow and ice that had once been waves threw themselves up into jagged edges, then plunged into deep ravines. Icebergs the size of whole cities beckoned from the distance and vast ice floes jostled each other in a heaving mass of ghostly grey against a moonlit sky.

The party began to cross the uneven ridges and the huskies panted and heaved as they dragged the sledge along. After a few hours, it was time to strike camp.

Nick was walking ahead, using poles to feel his way on the rough terrain. Suddenly he stopped in his tracks, stifling a cry of terror.

Towering above him, at least four times his height, was a massive polar bear.

The Golden City

The beast let out a roar and lumbered towards him, growling threateningly. She bared her teeth and lashed out with her huge paws, ready to strike. Behind her in a hollow huddled two furry white cubs. Nick felt his blood freeze in his veins. Slowly, a step at a time, he began to back away.

'Don't move!' said a quiet voice.

Nick turned his head and saw an Inuit boy about his age, crouched nearby. He looked like a snow lion. His lean frame was clad from head to foot in furs and skins: furry white bearskin trousers, a bunchy coat made from caribou and sealskin boots tied with leather thongs. On his head was a bulky hood, also made from polar bear fur, which framed his brown face, and he held a long spear, poised and ready to aim. His eyes were jet black and almond shaped, and they darted around taking in everything at once. He looked tough and resourceful, but there was an air of wariness about him that reminded Nick of a wild animal.

'Stay where you are, chavuk,' ordered the boy. He

'Don't move!' said a quiet voice.

brought a crossbow from behind his back and took aim. 'I've got her.'

The bear was angry and restless; she began to wheel around, unsure which intruder to attack first. Then she growled and continued lumbering towards Nick. She was getting closer; she would be on him in seconds.

Quick quick quick.

Without pausing to think, Nick dropped to his haunches and began to creep towards her on all fours, making low whining noises. The bear stopped growling and fell still. The Inuit boy lowered his crossbow, unable to shoot a target so close to Nick. He watched in astonishment as Nick rolled over on his back and began to make whimpering noises under his breath. The bear stared, a puzzled expression on her long face. Then Nick rolled back on to all fours and began to circle round her warily, like a half grown cub in the moonlight.

The mother bear hesitated as the rest of the party watched in an agony of suspense. Even Louisa was quiet. Nick loped around the polar bear, bobbing his head and sniffing at the ground. Then, in a move so daring the others had to suppress squeals of terror, he padded up to her on all fours and rubbed his head tentatively against her legs. She began to growl again.

For one terrible moment, the great beast seemed about to pounce. With a massive effort of will, Nick kept his nerve and curled into a ball at her feet. Then suddenly, she relaxed. Grunting dismissively, she swung

117

around and shambled up to her cubs. She nudged them and set off across the snow. The cubs picked themselves up and lolloped after her. As their white shapes disappeared into the silvery gloom, the whole party let out one long, collective sigh of relief.

The Inuk boy glared at Nick angrily. 'You ruined my hunt!'

There was a cry of horror from the others at the thought of orphaning two helpless cubs. The boy cast a scornful glance in their direction.

'Er, excuse me, but I just saved your life,' said Nick.

'I can fend for myself!' said the Inuk curtly. 'What do you know about surviving up here? You chavuk – you come blundering along with your interfering ways. I haven't eaten for three days!'

There was an awkward silence as the two boys glared at each other. Joachim strode up to them, holding up his hands in a peace gesture.

'I am Joachim,' he said. He waved his arm to indicate Nick. 'And this is Nickolai. Sorry if we disturbed your hunt.'

Nick was about to protest, but Joachim silenced him with a look. They had to be respectful to the people of the Arctic. It was their territory, after all.

Lotta came struggling across the ice and smiled warmly at the boy. 'We have plenty of food if you would care to join us,' she said. 'We were just about to set up camp.'

Suddenly the boy relented, as all the weariness and

loneliness of the past year caught up with him. His lean brown face looked sad and vulnerable for a minute, then creased into a smile, which made his eyes almost disappear.

'Thank you,' he said. 'My name is Zakurak, but you can call me Zak.'

Elvina was the one that finally won the boy over.

Zak had been subjected to Anneka's usual interrogations and had revealed his sad story. They had been horrified to hear how the arrival of the Golden City had shattered his life. They all murmured sympathetically when he told them of the death of his beloved grandfather and how he had been living alone in his igloo, fending for himself, for over a year.

As the evening progressed, the ice began to melt between the two boys. Nick liked Zak's directness and his tough, down-to-earth attitude. Zak was a survivor, forced to rely on his own resources.

Anneka seemed to find Zak endlessly fascinating.

After supper Zak, Anneka and Nick settled down on a ridge to look at the stars. Occasionally a meteorite would streak across the sky, leaving a trail of light, reminding Nick of the last time he saw Comet. Zak sighed, his dark eyes scanning the northern horizon.

'What are you looking for?' asked Anneka.

'The Lights in the sky,' Zak murmured. 'There, above the Pole. All my life I've longed to see them.

Every night I watch, hoping there'll be a miracle and they'll come back.'

Nick felt as though someone had lit a flame inside him. The famous Lights that the reindeer had always talked about! The most important thing in the world to them. 'Does anyone you know remember them?' he asked eagerly. 'We live too far south.'

'Oh yes. My paptik – grandfather – used to tell me about them. He said they were a wonderful, magical sight. They were said to contain the souls of unborn children, but that's just folklore. They went out one night, when I was a baby. One day they will come back and I'll see them.'

'What happened? Why did they go?' demanded Anneka.

'Nobody knows,' said Zak mysteriously, 'but everyone felt it was a bad omen. And I think it was something to do with that Golden City up there. That's why I carved this.'

He pulled a thong from round his neck and brought out a small carved wooden pendant. Nick and Anneka inspected it closely. It was only the size of a thumb, but it made them shudder. Zak had carved a terrifying monster with a jagged, snarling mouth. He had inserted chips of stone into the eyes, which made them glint dangerously in the moonlight, and painted the ugly face green. Strands of fox fur were stuck with fish glue on to the head to mimic the appearance of grizzled grey hair.

'What is it?' asked Anneka, astonished. 'Some sort of talisman?'

'Yeah. It's a Tupilak. A charm to ward off evil spirits. I carry this with me everywhere for protection.'

It was at this moment that Elvina decided to make her nightly appearance. She flitted out of Nick's furs and flashed around in the dark, lighting up the backdrop of icy ridges. No one took any notice except Zak, whose mouth dropped open into an O.

'Sedna's toenails! That's a tuktik!'

'A what?' said Nick and Anneka together.

'A Light Fairy!' Zak gasped. 'It's part of our folklore. They're the handmaidens of Sedna, our supreme Goddess. The Lights are supposed to be her hair, streaming across the heavens, and her tuktiks tend to it. I can't believe I'm actually seeing one!'

Zak watched Elvina swooping and diving around his face with a mixture of wonder and disbelief. 'How did you find her? Where has she come from?'

'She's always been with me.'

Zak stared at Nickolai with awe and new respect. 'Then you come from up there?' he nodded at the northern horizon, where the Great Bear constellation lay over the Pole. 'From the North Pole?'

Nick glanced at Anneka with a triumphant smile. 'Yes, I believe I do. That's why I'm going up there, to find my people.' He slowly lowered his hood and revealed his ears.

Zak gasped. 'You're no ordinary chavuk!'

Anneka, practical as always, made a suggestion. 'Zak,' she said, laying a hand on his arm. 'This Golden City has affected your life so much, I reckon you should come there with us and find out more.'

Zak looked wary. 'No, I don't think—'

'You could satisfy your curiosity and then leave,' Anneka cut in. 'Things are going to be more difficult for us as we get further north. Your skills could be very useful to us. We'd be really grateful for your help. You'd be with us and you can share our food.' She paused for effect. 'And you wouldn't be alone any more.'

Zak thought for a minute, then beamed at them both. 'OK, I'll come. I should go and investigate.' He looked at Nick. 'And I think that somehow, you're a part of it all, Nicku; you hold the key. Together we'll find out.'

The two boys clasped their palms together and Anneka placed her hand over theirs. The three of them stayed like that for a minute, making a silent pact.

And so they travelled on, grimly crossing the snowy ridges, occasionally seeing the great rolling tail of a whale flipping over in the distance.

It was towards the end of the sixth week that they first saw the golden glow in the sky ahead. They had been in continual darkness for some time now. After several hours spent cresting a great icy ridge, hauling the sledge, the dogs and the supplies up the slippery slope, they finally reached the top and stopped to catch their breath. Then they all let out a gasp of surprise and wonder.

On the horizon rose the Golden City, outlined against the curve of the earth. It was surrounded by a halo, a bubble of yellow light, its gleaming spires and domes twinkling unnaturally in the haze.

'Doransk!' breathed Lotta. 'The Land of Promise! We've reached it at last!'

The area outside the great golden gates of the City was thronging with hundreds of people, all waiting their turn to pass through. Camps had sprouted up everywhere and their fires glowed in the dark. Stray husky dogs ran around, barking and playing with ragged children. Mixed smells of cooking floated on the air. Everywhere you looked were weary families, all their worldly goods heaped on sledges, taking shelter in makeshift tents. They had formed into a long and straggling line which stretched back from the gates.

Over the City walls hung a strange aura, enclosing the City in a massive dome of light and warmth.

Zak stared at it suspiciously. 'What is that?' he said. 'Is it a fire?'

'No, Zak,' said Lotta excitedly. 'It's a big magic bubble enclosing the city and sealing it off from the outside world, so it's always warm.'

Zak shook his head doubtfully. 'I don't like it,' he muttered. 'What's it cost to make something like that? It's too good to be true.'

They made their way through the crowds, looking for a place to pitch their camp. Enticing sounds from within the City walls drifted across the air – festivity, music and the babble of many voices. As they neared the camps, Nick felt Elvina quaking against his chest. She peeped out of his front and squeaked.

Looming towards them were the dark shadowy shapes of wolves, exactly like the ones Nick had encountered outside the forest all those years ago. He shivered at the sight of them. The phantom-like creatures were everywhere, prowling amongst the crowds, their yellow eyes darting and watchful.

'Must be patrol dogs,' said Joachim nervously.

In one split-second movement, Elvina shot out of Nick's front, yanked his hood firmly round his head, pulled the cords tightly under his chin and dived back down his tunic, where she continued to make agitated twittering noises.

They took their place in the queue and set up a temporary camp for the night. The noise and babble of the crowds made it impossible to sleep.

Hour after hour, the same thing happened. The gates swung open silently, revealing two inner gates, designed to create a sealed vacuum between the two. An excited buzz rose from the people at the front of the crowd and they surged into the space, herded by the wolves, leaving their carts and tents behind. The gates swung shut with a clang. Those still in the queue began to uproot themselves and re-camp, not much further than before. The process was repeated every few hours, round the clock. It was very unsettling.

Finally, after two weeks, Nick and his party reached the gates. They could hear a commotion from inside the City and a stir of excitement passed through the people around them. Lotta, Nick, Joachim, Anneka, Louisa and Zak clung together, hemmed in by the crowd. The atmosphere of hushed excitement grew as the first set of gates swung open. The people shuffled into the space between the gates, which clanged shut with a heavy thud that sounded horribly final. The crowd jostled restlessly, pressed uncomfortably together.

A silky, disembodied voice oozed out from some hidden source, accompanied by tinny violin music. 'Welcome to Doransk, my new citizens! This is your Queen speaking. You are about to enter the magic zone of the Golden City, where all your dreams can come true!'

There was a gasp of anticipation, then a drumroll and a fanfare of trumpets – and the inner gates swung open to reveal a dazzling scene.

The streets were bathed in bright sunshine, in contrast to the continuous darkness of the Arctic winter outside, and lined with stalls crammed with merchandise of all kinds. Music blared out from every quarter. People in rich clothing strolled around, and garishly dressed clowns and jesters, pedlars, street performers and minstrels cavorted amongst the crowds. The steamy air hit them like a blast from an oven, assaulting their nostrils with a rank, sweaty smell.

The source of the smell soon became apparent. Standing in front of them was a row of goblins, the ugliest creatures they had ever seen. Lotta and Joachim stepped forward tentatively and Nick, Anneka, Zak and Louisa peered between them, gawping at the spectacle.

'Aktuk!' murmured Zak. 'I knew there were evil spirits here.'

Nick's eyes swept along the row of gruesome goblins. They stood like gormless Neanderthals, their long, beefy arms swinging loosely at their sides, and their beady red eyes staring straight ahead. They looked as though someone had stopped making them halfway through – lumpen and curiously unfinished, like chunks of raw ham. Their greasy red skin and bald heads shone in the glare of the sunlight. They were clad in identical black chainmail uniforms, through which could be glimpsed huge muscles.

At their head stood the most appalling specimen of all. A monstrous, two-headed goblin: one face gormless and dull-eyed, the other suspicious and aggressive, with piggy eyes that roved over the new intake. Everyone stared aghast at this vision, too shocked to speak.

'Right, you lucky people!' boomed the aggressive-looking head. 'My name is Skank, and I'm your Chief of Police!'

The other head twisted round and glared at him. 'You keep doing this! It's givin' me the 'ump.' He looked back at the intake. 'I'm Skism and I'm—'

'My assistant!' boomed Skank. Skism looked furious, and opened his mouth to speak, but Skank stamped brutally on his foot and made him gasp in pain. This looked very strange indeed, because, since they shared the same body, Skank had really stamped on his own foot. But this creature functioned in a perfectly logical way – Skank's head was on the right, so he felt everything down the right-hand side of the body, and Skism's head was on the left, so he felt everything down the left-hand side.

'Welcome to Doransk!' roared Skank. 'Follow me to your accommodation! Please stay in file.'

'Thank you! Have a nice day!' added Skism, not to be outdone.

Skank threw him a scowl and turned to the other goblins. There was a lot of stamping and clinking of armour as he bawled out instructions and the goblin guard formed up. The creatures flanked the new intake, ready to escort them through the city.

'They're er – not exactly easy on the eye, are they?' muttered Joachim, as they began to move forward. 'And they could do with a wash.' He wrinkled his nose as a stinking gust hit him from a nearby goblin.

'Well, this is a *magic* city,' said Lotta tentatively. 'You have to be prepared for all sorts of strange things.'

Nick, Anneka and Zak glanced at each other with growing unease. Nick felt a wave of nausea stealing over him, but he scarcely had time to reflect on it, for the next moment the newcomers were chivvied forward by the goblins and hustled along the narrow streets through the crowded marketplace.

Nick searched anxiously amongst the crowds for people who looked like him. Not a pointed ear in sight. Maybe his type were privileged people who lived in a special part of the city.

They passed through the thronging marketplace, the din of stallholders shouting their wares ringing from all sides. The stalls were groaning with goods of all kinds: steaming slabs of freshly cooked meat, roast chickens and pies, luridly coloured fruit piled high. Other stalls were festooned with brightly coloured flags, all bearing the same emblem of a woman's head in profile, and displays of garish dolls, all identical, with long black hair, gold robes and brightly painted faces.

'Get your Queen Magda dolls here!' shouted a stallholder. 'Only two gold maggots!'

'I want one!' cried Louisa excitedly, pointing at the dolls.

'Not now, darling,' said her mother. 'Maybe tomorrow.'

'Gold maggots! That must be the local currency!' exclaimed Joachim.

'Fool's gold,' remarked Zak sourly.

Throughout the crowded marketplace, gold coins, all stamped with the same woman's profile, clinked as they changed hands. Everything else in the City seemed to be made of gold. Gold streets, gold pavements, gold walls, all glittering in the eerie sunshine.

And everywhere you looked there were solid gold statues, standing on every street corner, every one an effigy of the woman on the coins. The heads of the statues swivelled constantly, and their eyes, made of some black stone, glittered as they followed the moving crowds.

'Who are all these statues of?' Nick wondered aloud.

'Queen Magda, the Great and Glorious One,' said Lotta. 'She's supposed to be very, very beautiful, and good and kind and bountiful. According to the pamphlets.'

Zak suppressed a loud snort of disbelief and Anneka shuddered. 'They're weird, Mum! I don't like them.'

'Don't be silly,' said Lotta brightly. 'They're lovely statues!'

The warmth was becoming stifling, and Nick was feeling increasingly uncomfortable. Everyone began to take their furs off and carry them as they straggled along. Nick tried to loosen his hood, but once again Elvina climbed on to his head, burrowed into his curls and gripped his hood firmly in place.

Suddenly there was a commotion as one of the goblins spotted some pies that had fallen from a stall. He made a dive for the food, throwing himself down and gobbling the pies greedily off the ground.

Mayhem was let loose as the other goblins broke ranks and joined in. Within moments they were all scrabbling like stray dogs, fighting over the food. Skank roared at them in fury and there was a loud crack as he lashed his whip over them.

'Get back in line, you animals!' he bellowed.

The whole marketplace stopped and stared as the two-headed goblin roared out commands, until order was restored and the goblins fell back into line.

'They're very rude people, aren't they, Mummy?' observed Louisa.

'Animals,' muttered Anneka.

'Don't insult the animals,' said Zak indignantly.

'Shhh!' said Lotta.

Nick said nothing.

Their dawdling progress continued until they left the market and came out into the main part of the City. They gawped in amazement as they passed down sweeping avenues lined with magnificent buildings, all glittering and glowing with precious stones. They gasped, pointed and stared as they saw the majestic golden castle on the hill overlooking the City, its turrets and domes gleaming in the sunlight.

Everywhere they looked, richly dressed people paraded around; they swept past in grand carriages, strolled along the banks of the silvery river that snaked its way through the City, sauntered across the grand bridges, or wandered in the stately parks, which were full of trees in brilliant blossom, vivid tropical plants and exotic-looking birds. Every corner revealed a new and astonishing vista.

'Isn't it wonderful!' breathed Lotta as she gazed at the scenes unfolding before them. Louisa for once was silenced, gawping at the splendour around her, her mouth open and her eyes popping.

They came to what Skank proudly announced as Golden Square – the largest and grandest in the City, right at its centre. It tinkled with fountains that sparkled like jewels. Glittering golden façades flanked it on all sides. In stark contrast, a sinister-looking building made of some kind of dull black metal stood hulkingly in one corner, looming over them. This was the Goblin High Command, the headquarters of the elite police force that ran the City. Right in the middle of the square stood another golden statue of the woman, the tallest in the City and the height of ten men.

'Look!' exclaimed Joachim. 'The best effigy yet of the great Queen herself!'

'She must be very beautiful!' gasped Lotta. 'I can't wait to see her in the flesh.'

They all jumped as a great clock tower on the Doransk City Hall, an imposing building with a domed gold roof, began to boom out the hour of noon. Everyone in the square stopped and the goblins stood to attention in a salute. The procession ground to a halt. When the heavy chimes of the bell had finished, the breathy female voice began to ooze out of the statues all over the City.

'It is noon in our glorious realm of Doransk, my loyal people! Once more give praise and thanks that you are here, in the land of Promise, ruled over by me, Queen Magda, the Good and Beautiful Queen who will make all your dreams come true.'

Everyone in the square bowed low to the statue. 'Hail Queen Magda, O Great and Glorious One!' they all chanted in unison. Then the citizens went about their business again and the procession moved forward.

Zak shuddered. 'This place is full of evil.'

'I don't like it either,' agreed Anneka. 'And have you noticed, there are no children around? There's something very strange going on. Can we go home now, Mother?'

Lotta looked flustered. 'But we've only just got here. Give it a chance.'

Nick felt overwhelmed; hope, fear and curiosity all tussled with each other in his mind. There was no way he could turn back now, after so long. And the urge to find his family was stronger than ever. 'I have to stay, however weird it is,' he whispered to Anneka. 'I've come all this way to find my people.'

Anneka glanced at him sceptically. 'Wake up, Nick. If your people are worth knowing, they wouldn't want to live in a place like this.'

Nick was going to answer her, but he stopped dead and stared at something. 'That's strange. It looks out of place . . . I wonder what it is?'

The others followed his gaze and saw a rock formation standing in a corner of the square. Unlike the gold statues, it was of dark, natural-looking rock, shaped almost like a human figure. It seemed frozen in mid motion, leaning forward. A shiver ran through Nick, and a woman's voice crying 'Nickolai' echoed faintly though the back of his mind, like some dim wisp of memory.

'Come on! Get a move on!' shouted a goblin, shoving at Nick.

'What is that please?' asked Nick, pointing at the rock formation.

'Blimmin' nuisance,' grunted the goblin. ' 'Er Majesty wasn't able to destroy it when she built the City. Wouldn't budge. Come on now. Move!'

Nick continued staring at the strange rock as they passed out of Golden Square and shuffled through the glittering streets, following the straggling procession. In every square and on every street corner stood more gold statues of Queen Magda, all watching over the City. Their eyes swivelled constantly, following passers-by, and their smiling mouths issued regular, echoey proclamations. Nick began to wonder what sort of woman would want her image stamped on everything in sight.

They passed out of the main part of the City and slowly things began to change. The buildings became dark and dingy, and finally they reached a grim and shabby area, surrounded by a tall perimeter fence.

'So. This is the other side of Doransk. The side they don't tell you about,' muttered Joachim. 'I thought it was all too good to be true.'

'Well, every city has its down side,' replied Lotta uncertainly, her enthusiasm beginning to waver.

They were led up to tall iron gates, which swung open silently to reveal a depressing sight, in stark contrast to their first impressions of the City. It was like an army camp; a collection of tin huts in regimented rows. Families sat listlessly outside the front doors. Children of all ages walked around in orderly groups. Some of them stopped to stare at the new intake, then walked on silently. None of them were playing, and there was no sound of laughter in the whole place. Nick searched in vain for a glimpse of some of their friends from Norsk.

'I don't like this place!' piped Louisa. 'Can we go back to the nice part? I want to play in the park.'

'I think this is our accommodation,' said Lotta in a faltering voice. 'It's probably only temporary.'

Once inside the compound, the immigrants were divided into groups. Nick's group was sectioned off and led along a narrow alley to a hut marked '21'. One of the goblins wrenched the door open to reveal a bare and shabby interior, with flimsy partition walls and pallet beds on the floor. There was a bucket in the corner and a row of tin mugs hanging on pegs.

'Your accommodation. Dinner served at six o'clock in Central Compound Square. Queue for tickets at the entrance. Curfew at eight o'clock, when your doors will be locked. Goodnight.'

And he lumbered off, leaving them gaping at each other in dismay.

The Rules of the Game

Dinner was a few lumps of gristly meat in what looked like warm dishwater and a hunk of stale bread, washed down with weak tea. They had queued for some time for their meal tokens – flat metal discs – handed out by a fat, surly goblin picking shreds of meat from his teeth. Coming into Central Compound Square, they had found row upon row of long metal tables and benches, full of people munching mechanically on the unappetizing food. You could tell how long they had been there by the state of their clothes, which were all in varying stages of shabbiness and disrepair; some were literally hanging off them.

The catering goblins, ranged behind long counters and dressed in greasy leather aprons and caps, ladled the slop on to tin plates from great steaming vats.

Nick's eyes still constantly scanned the crowd, looking for people with pointed ears. But there was no sign of anyone who looked anything like him. Or anyone from Norsk either. Disappointment crept over him.

They found spaces at one of the tables and sat down to eat their first meal in Doransk. All of them were quiet and gloomy, too embarrassed to admit their disillusion and despair.

'Aktuk! This isn't fit to feed a tundra rat!' spluttered Zak as he took his first mouthful.

'Never mind, I've got plenty of supplies. We'll have some when we get back to the hut,' said Lotta with forced cheerfulness. She was trying to keep everyone's spirits up, and Nick had to admire her courage.

'I want to go home now,' whined Louisa.

'This *is* our home, sweetheart. Our new home.'

Louisa looked at the surroundings with an expression of deep disgust. There was awkward silence, during which everyone avoided each other's eyes. Joachim coughed.

'I'm sure this is only temporary,' said Lotta at last.

No one had the heart to contradict her. Nick began to feel hot and loosened his hood. Elvina immediately let out a squeak of alarm and started pulling it forward from the inside.

'Let me take it off, Elvina. I'm boiling!'

A volley of frantic high-pitched noises sounded from inside Nick's hood, just as a goblin was passing. He stopped and glared at Nick.

'You talkin' to me?' he demanded aggressively.

Nick stammered and averted his gaze. 'N-no. It's just the soup was a bit hot.' This was patently untrue; there wasn't a whisper of steam coming off it. The goblin curled his lip, spat on the ground and lumbered off.

'What charming hosts,' remarked Anneka.

'They're only doing their job,' said Lotta. 'They have so many people to look after.' Suddenly her hand flew to her mouth. 'Oh, look! There's Kristoff and Rosa!'

Everyone followed her gaze. Further down the table, eating quietly, were a thin, reedy-looking man and his plump wife. A boy of about ten was sitting with them. Nick felt a tingle of recognition. At last, someone from Norsk.

'Johan!' Anneka cried, recognizing Norsk's youngest Splodging racer.

'How wonderful!' cried Lotta, relieved at the distraction. 'Let's go and join them.'

After much greeting and handshaking, watched suspiciously by the goblins, they all sat down and began to eat together. But Anneka and Nick were dismayed to see the change in Johan. He was a shadow of his former self, subdued and downcast.

'What's happened to you?' hissed Anneka. 'You look all droopy.'

'It's a long story. Listen to my parents and you'll get an idea,' said Johan glumly.

Joachim began quizzing Kristoff, while everyone listened avidly.

Kristoff lowered his voice to a whisper, keeping a furtive lookout for any passing goblins. 'The general idea seems to be to get out of the compounds and move up in the world. It's important you play the game. A lot of worshipping and swearing allegiance to the great Queen Magda seems to go down well. No hint of doubt or criticism, even in private. The statues have eyes and ears. If you obey the rules and work hard, you eventually get out of the compound to better homes and jobs.'

'And then,' added Rosa, her eyes shining, 'maybe a place at court, mixing with the grand people. Balls and banquets – glittering events where you get to meet the Queen herself and rub shoulders with the inner circle. And if you're lucky, you may get your picture in the *Doransk Daily Echo*, in the celebrity columns!' she finished triumphantly, as if this was the pinnacle of achievement.

Lotta's cheeks glowed at the thought of mixing with the cream of Doransk society, but Joachim looked sceptical.

'And the catch?' he enquired grimly. 'There always is one.'

Kristoff's face darkened. 'Yes. There is. You have to send your children to one of the Queen's special welcome parties. At the grand castle. You can't even start on the road to a better life until then.'

'Oh, for heaven's sake!' exploded Rosa, looking at Johan and Kristoff. 'I can't understand why you two are so negative about it!' She turned back to the others. 'They're great, apparently. The kiddies have a wonderful time. Lots of nice things to eat, and clowns and jesters and party games. And they all get given free Queen Magda dolls and a special storybook. They come back very happy and very well behaved. The good Queen loves children.'

'Well, that's very kind of her,' said Lotta. 'What a nice idea.'

'I want to go!' shouted Louisa, jiggling excitedly. This news had cheered her up no end.

Nick's heartbeat had quickened and his mind raced. If he went to the castle, he might be able to find out more about his people. Maybe they were these grand folk Rosa was talking about: the inner circle. He was just about to ask more when Rosa cut in.

'Unfortunately,' she said loudly and with heavy emphasis, glaring with reproach at her son, 'Johan is ruining all our plans. He refuses to go.'

Johan looked down at his plate. Nick caught a passing glance between the boy and his father.

'Why?' enquired Anneka.

Johan glanced meaningfully at the other children in the square. Anneka, Nick and Zak followed his gaze and took in the rows of unnaturally docile youngsters. Nick realized with shock that they were all sitting so quietly they'd mistaken them for adults.

'There's nothing wrong with them!' said Rosa defensively. 'They're very nice and well mannered.'

'Exactly,' murmured Johan under his breath.

Suddenly Nick spotted another familiar face. He let out a cry of surprise and pointed. 'Look! Look who it is!'

On the far side of the square, where there were slightly better tables laid with cloths and proper cutlery, was Finn with his parents and brother. He was sitting bolt upright, eating very daintily with a knife and fork, talking quietly and dabbing his mouth with a napkin.

'That's not the Finn I know,' muttered Anneka. Nick shook his head, confused.

After they'd finished their meal, Kristoff and Johan went back to their hut for a game of chess. Nick, Zak and Anneka excused themselves and went up to Finn's table. Nick had to restrain himself from dashing up to Finn and giving him a playful punch. Somehow he thought it wouldn't go down too well with the goblins.

'Finn!' cried Nick heartily. 'Great to see you!' He noticed that Finn had a large silver badge on his front, saying 'Street Monitor'.

Finn looked up and his face was blank. 'Sorry? I don't recall . . . ?'

'Finn! For heaven's sake! It's only been a few months. Surely you can't have forgotten us?' Anneka exploded.

Finn continued to look puzzled for a few moments. 'I'm sorry, I do not remember you.'

Anneka and Nick exchanged astonished glances.

'However, I am very pleased to meet you,' continued Finn formally, 'and welcome to Doransk. I trust it is to your liking?'

Nick was stunned. Where was the boisterous, rebellious boy he remembered from Norsk? Why didn't Finn remember them?

'He's a changed boy now,' said his mother, smiling. She was a thin elegant woman who had been a leading light in Norsk, arranging local events. 'So mature for his age. And sensible. Aren't you, Finn dear?'

'Yes, Mother. Rules are there for a good reason,' said Finn.

'D'you fancy meeting up later?' said Nick hopefully. 'Have a game of something?'

Finn gave him a supercilious smile. 'No, I've put all childish things behind me now. I'm a Street Monitor for the new arrivals.' He tapped his badge, looking smug. 'Making sure everyone behaves in an orderly and decorous fashion.'

'Quite right too,' said his mother fondly. She beamed at them, evidently very proud of her son. But Finn's father – a dark taciturn man – didn't look too sure about it.

'We are all very lucky to be here!' announced Finn. 'Queen Magda is a great and good Queen. Her beauty is matchless and her bounty knows no bounds.'

'Did you swallow a text book or something?' said Anneka with a look of pure scorn.

Finn ignored her. 'Soon we shall be reaping the rewards for our loyalty. We are nearly at the top of the waiting list for the Orion Quarter.'

'A very pleasant part of town,' added his mother, with a self-satisfied smile, 'with a better class of people. You know you've arrived when you move there.'

'Yes, well, right, we'd better be going,' said Anneka.

They beat a hasty retreat. 'Don't say that was a friend of yours?' said Zak incredulously.

'What's got into him?' spluttered Anneka. 'Why doesn't he remember us? It's like he's been brainwashed or something.'

'I know. It's weird,' agreed Nick, thinking wistfully of the boy with whom he used to rampage round the streets of Norsk, hurling snowballs at passers-by and tobogganing crazily round corners.

'I preferred him when he was a bully; at least you knew where you stood,' Anneka grumbled on. 'Anything's better than this creepy grown-up politeness. I said you shouldn't trust him, Nick.'

Nick nodded uncomfortably, trying not to notice the subdued manner of the children around him as they helped clear away plates, then followed their parents meekly out of the square.

'I mean, what is going ON?' Anneka insisted. 'It isn't natural.'

They returned to their hut and arranged their belongings as best they could around the stark interior. Then they sat outside on hard chairs, chatting and drinking Lotta's crowberry tea. Louisa fell asleep on Nick's lap. The atmosphere was peaceful and relaxed at last, a family group settling into their new surroundings after a long journey. The golden sky inside the dome of the bubble began to turn pink at the edges.

'Isn't this lovely?' mused Lotta.

'I think it stinks,' snorted Anneka. 'I prefer fresh air.'

Lotta gave her a shocked and disapproving look. 'Ungrateful girl! If we play our cards right, we'll get to the top of the waiting list and move to a nice part of town.' She patted Joachim on the arm. He smiled uncertainly.

'If you think I'm going to one of those parties, Mum, you've got anoth—'

Anneka was cut off as the bell rang out from Golden Square, chiming out the hour of eight o'clock. The light began to fade and romantic, sentimental music started up.

'Well I never! It's an artificial sunset!' exclaimed Joachim.

A lurid orange glow filled the sky. Then streaks of purple, pink and gold appeared on its huge canvas in great swirling strokes, a picture being painted before their eyes. As darkness fell, the music from the statue tannoy system faded up.

'And so another glorious day draws to a close in Doransk,' rang out the silky female voice against the background music. 'Another day of noble toil and worthy effort, my loyal people, all to the greater glory of the Golden State! Remember, we are all working together here to realize our great dream! Freedom!

Wealth! Prosperity! Harmony! A golden future lies ahead for us all. Goodnight, my people!'

Slowly the light faded to black, with only the faint gleam from the sodium streetlamps casting a glow over the compound. In the distance they could see the lights of the City twinkling and the castle standing on the hill in floodlit splendour. A lurid, artificial moon rose in the sky, and stars began to twinkle garishly like jewels studded on a dark cloth.

The ground began to shake as a posse of goblins came marching down the alley towards them.

'Lights out! Into your homes. Off to bed! Doors locked!'

Everyone was hustled into their huts and locked in. All around, Nickolai could hear the sounds of doors being slammed and the muffled noises of families settling down for the night. He lay down on his pallet bed, too exhausted to talk, wondering uneasily what the next day would bring.

The next morning they were rudely awoken by a klaxon horn echoing across the compound. In the background the bell tower chimed the hour of six. There was a fanfare of trumpets from the Tannoy system and Magda's voice rang out again.

'Good morning, my loyal people! And it's another lovely day here in Doransk, where the sun always shines! Wake up, rise and shine, ready for another day's glorious work in my glorious realm! But first – today, remember, is another procession day, when you will have a chance to throng the streets to see me in the flesh and to pay homage to my greatness! I look forward to greeting you all!'

The voice finished and their door was wrenched open by a goblin, letting in a flood of glaring sunshine.

'Up you get! Chop chop!' he roared. 'Breakfast in Central Compound Square in five minutes.'

Breakfast was no better than dinner – half-cold lumpy porridge and some bread that tasted like mashed cardboard. They scarcely had time to eat their breakfast before they were hustled out of the compound and herded along the glittering streets towards the main part of the City.

The roads had been roped off with golden tasselled cords, keeping the main highway clear for the procession. Jesters and clowns frolicked around, handing out royal flags. Nick felt a stab of alarm as he looked at them. They were cavorting about like maniacs, crowing with wild laughter. Despite their colourful costumes, there was something not quite right about them, a glint behind their masks that sent a shiver down his spine.

Everyone jostled forward on to the pavement, jam-packed against the cordons. Goblins patrolled the edges to keep the crowds under control, whips twitching at their sides. An air of expectancy and excitement hung in the air.

Nick craned his neck to see up the road. Suddenly

there was a stir and the crowd further along the street began to cheer and wave their flags. Excitement rippled around them and Nick's heart beat faster as the procession made its stately progress towards them.

First came the goblins, thumping along heavily. This was Magda's home guard, decked out in black and red leather pantaloons and gold waistcoats. Heavy gold helmets were jammed on their lumpy heads, pressing their cauliflower ears down so they stuck out in a ridiculous manner. If they hadn't been so scary, they would have looked comical.

Then came a band of minstrels in brightly coloured clothes, marching in time to a blaring fanfare of trumpets and horns. After them tumbled a company of masked clowns and jesters in extreme fancy dress, doing somersaults and cartwheels.

Then finally, the high point of the procession arrived – a magnificent carriage, made entirely of gold. It was very ornate, heavily carved and studded with stones which glittered blindingly in the sunshine. It was drawn by a team of huge black wolves, dark and shadowy in the bright daylight, pulling the carriage along with a supernatural strength. As it drew near, the cheering rose to a deafening roar and the air became a forest of waving flags.

Nick glimpsed the woman sitting inside the carriage, waving graciously and flashing a brilliant white smile. She was the most stunningly beautiful creature he had ever seen. Her face was a perfect oval.

Her skin was like ivory. Her red lips curved in a gracious smile, revealing a row of perfect pearly teeth. Her dark, lustrous eyes seemed to send out beams of light. Her flowing black hair gleamed in the sunlight. She was dressed in a gown of pure gold, with a tight bodice studded with pearls and rubies that showed off her tiny waist. An elaborate lace collar framed her face, and over her shoulders was a cloak made of green velvet and sewn with gold thread. On her head was an ornate gold crown, made to resemble the spires and towers of her City skyline, covered with brightly coloured gems that flashed in the sun.

She was a goddess. Even from this distance, Nick was spellbound. No wonder her people worshipped her.

Next to Magda in the carriage sat a dark, sinister-looking man, clad in purple robes edged with gold. His hands were hidden under the folds of his cloak and his shoulders were hunched and bony. He had a thin, sallow face with a long nose and black hair that seemed to stand out like the scraggy fur on an animal's back. His hooded eyes, almost concealed under heavy black eyebrows, flicked from side to side, raking across the crowd, never missing a thing. Occasionally he would lean across to Magda and whisper in her ear.

As the carriage drew near, Nick felt Elvina quaking more violently than ever. She tugged sharply on his hood then crawled behind his ear to hide. Nick's heart began to thump as the golden wheels hissed louder on

The high point of the procession arrived —
a magnificent carriage, made entirely of gold.

the ground. Closer and closer she came, the radiant goddess. As the carriage swept past and the cheering roared in his ears, he gasped in shock. His head began to swim and he felt as though he was going to faint.

The Queen had beautiful, dainty, pointed ears, just like him.

Goblin Daycare

Nick tingled from head to foot. At last! Someone who looked like him! And she was no less than the Queen herself! Without even thinking, he began to pull his hood down, hoping she would catch a glimpse of him. But Elvina held his hood in a vice-like grip.

He turned feverishly to Anneka. 'Did you see her ears?'

Anneka looked at him blankly. 'No. I didn't notice. Why?'

Nick was about to answer when a horrible image flashed into his mind. A green, putrid face, hung with rotting flesh; a snarling red mouth with jagged broken teeth; a halo of grizzled, matted grey hair. He shook his head and the image vanished. He was shaking all over and everyone was staring at him.

'Are you all right, Nickolai? You look as though you've seen a ghost,' said Lotta, feeling his forehead.

'It's the heat,' he mumbled. 'Hallucinations or something.' He brushed the creepy feeling aside. All that mattered was that this beautiful woman, the

Queen, had pointed ears like him. He had found his kind. Now he wanted more than ever to get close to her and reveal his ears with pride. Surely she would clasp him to her bosom like a long lost son?

'So? What does the ear thing mean?' said Anneka, as they were marched along in crocodile formation towards the Goblin Daycare centre. Louisa skipped along beside her.

Nick looked at Anneka with irritation. 'It means I'm closer to finding out who I am, where I come from, who my people are!'

'Next thing you know, we'll find out he's royalty,' said Zak. 'Hail, your Majesty!' He swept a mock bow and was immediately reprimanded by a goblin.

'Well, anyway, she's very beautiful,' continued Nick sulkily, 'and anyone that beautiful can't be bad.'

Zak shot him a withering glance. 'Idiot! Beauty comes from inside. You chavuks are always taken in by outward appearances.'

They rounded a corner and Johan joined them as they filed ahead, obviously relieved to have their company. A long, low building, painted in glaring neon colours, loomed ahead. They were marched through the doors and down a long corridor lined with children's pictures. All of them were of Magda. Underneath were written slogans like 'The Good Queen Magda' and 'Our Lovely Monarch' in shaky handwriting.

Louisa was herded into a room marked: 'Really Young Brats'. It was full of quiet children playing methodically with construction toys. Louisa bounded in with a yelp of glee and began creating chaos.

Zak, Anneka, Johan and Nick were led into a large classroom marked 'Sub Teenage Brats'. They were greeted by a fat, pompous goblin with several double chins and a large wart on his bulbous nose.

'Good morning, young citizens!' he boomed. 'I am your Director of Youth, Mr Spong. And this is my esteemed and worthy classroom assistant, Mr Flange.' He indicated a self-satisfied little goblin who looked like a peeled shrimp. Both of them were wearing scholarly blue robes and strange clerical-looking hats with earflaps.

It was much like the classroom back in Norsk, except everything in it was about Doransk and Queen Magda. There were maps on the walls of Doransk, and the only pictures and drawings were views of Doransk, or portraits of Queen Magda.

There were books on the building of Doransk, a visitors' guide to Doransk, and an official biography of Queen Magda. The history books were all about the history of Doransk, and the geography books all about the geography of Doransk. The biggest book of all was the *Book of Lore According to our Great and Glorious Queen, the Most Illustrious Queen Magda*, a huge black leather volume stamped in gold. Beneath the title was the name of the author – Volpo Volterammerdung.

153

Nick leafed through to the back cover and saw an engraved image of the dark man he had seen sitting in the carriage next to Queen Magda. He looked even more sinister as an engraving.

'Haven't they heard of anywhere else in the world?' Zak demanded as he stared round.

'Maybe they feel that this world is enough,' murmured Nick.

The class was called to attention by Spong. 'Welcome to those of you who are newcomers. I trust you have all settled into your dwellings and are now ready to become useful members of our Glorious Golden State!'

'Hail Queen Magda, O Great and Glorious One!' came a droning monotone from the other children. Nick noticed with alarm that Johan had joined in.

'They don't expect us to do that, do they?' whispered Zak in outrage.

'Just do it, it's much easier,' warned Johan.

Nick saw Spong glaring at them. 'Please repeat the daily chant, children. After me. Hail Queen Magda, O Great and Glorious One!'

'Hail Queen Magda, O Great and Glorious One!' mumbled everyone except Zak.

Spong strode up to Zak and glared at him. 'Please repeat the daily chant!'

Zak glared back at him mutinously. 'I'm an Inuit. We don't worship false gods.'

Spong went white around the mouth. 'How dare you speak so blasphemously of our Glorious Monarch? Do as I say, or you will be put in solitary confinement until you come to your senses!'

Zak continued to gaze steadily back at Spong, his black eyes glinting in rebellion. Spong towered over him in a column of silent rage. There was a long and nasty pause, then Spong blew a whistle and several burly goblins strode into the room and stood over Zak, twitching their whips. Zak's eyes flickered in alarm, then his shoulders slumped and he gave in.

'OK hailqueenmagdaogreatandgloriousone!' he mumbled very fast. Nick noticed he was holding his talisman, his Tupilak. Spong appeared to be satisfied with this and the goblins departed.

'Now I want to introduce a most exemplary young man,' he announced. 'He is head of Youth Activities here at the Daycare centre and will give you a short introductory speech on the history and principles of Doransk.'

The door was flung open and in marched Finn, puffed up with self importance, his badge glinting on his lapel. Nick's stomach lurched.

'Why am I not surprised?' muttered Anneka.

'The history of Doransk is a long and fascinating one,' Finn began pompously. 'It was built after the old Elfin Kingdom was reduced to ruins. This is of course where our great Queen came from originally, many centuries ago. Because she is so good and wise and bountiful, she was given the gift of immortality from the Great Spirit of the Light in the sky. She was Queen of the old Elfin Kingdom, but alas, an evil power rose up and tried to usurp her. The Great Spirit of Light in the sky came to her rescue and she fled the Kingdom in fear of her life. When the Kingdom was destroyed by its own evil, she returned in triumph and, with the help of her loyal supporters, she built this glorious City!'

He stopped as he saw Nick with his hand up. 'Please? Could you tell me what kind of people Queen Magda comes from?'

Finn looked momentarily perplexed. Then Spong cut in.

'Why, she is an elf, of course. From a once great and glorious people, who died out when they were corrupted by evil. As far as we know there were no other survivors.'

A huge wave of understanding and relief flooded through Nick. *He was an elf!* He was about to pull down his hood and shout, 'Well you're wrong! I am another survivor!' when Elvina stopped him, digging her tiny nails into his scalp. He decided instead to ask another question. 'And please, could you tell me where the old Elfin Kingdom was?'

A deathly hush fell over the room. Finn glared at him stonily and Spong's face went purple. He was shaking with rage and his wart looked ready to explode.

'It is not your place to ask impudent questions like that!' he erupted finally, his chins wobbling like jellies. 'That is a state secret! And you only speak when spoken to. Remember that!'

'I am an elf!' said Nick solemnly, as they were marched back to the compound at the end of the day. 'I am an elf!'

'I wouldn't shout about it if I were you,' muttered Anneka. 'You heard what they said. You wouldn't be welcome, as a descendant of those who were supposed to have betrayed her.'

'That's not my fault!' protested Nick. 'Maybe my family escaped, migrated somewhere. Maybe they weren't in on the plot. I just have to find out! And she might be able to help me.'

'I don't reckon she wants to help anybody but herself, Nicku,' said Zak grimly.

'Nick, you have to face up to it,' said Anneka as gently as she could. 'They said the whole Kingdom was destroyed. Your home and your family are probably gone for ever.'

'How was your day?' asked Lotta brightly when they arrived back at the hut. Louisa hurled herself into her mother's arms and showed her a scribbled cardboard plate with a rather unflattering picture of Magda on it.

'We had a lot of very long boring lectures,' Anneka told her. 'What about you?'

Lotta had been put into a large bakery making sky-high cakes for the Queen's banquets and Joachim had been employed on a building site on the edge of the City, where expansion plans were under way. If they worked hard, they would eventually be promoted. Both of them looked grey with exhaustion, but Lotta's enthusiasm for Doransk was unflagging.

'We were all given a newcomers' presentation in a great hall,' she gushed. 'And they showed us pictures of some of the smart areas of the city and the sorts of houses we could live in. They were wonderful! Buildings made of gold and studded with gems! Courtyards and balconies and sweeping staircases! And huge gardens with these peacock birds wandering around on the lawns and exotic blooms in the flowerbeds!'

Anneka looked at her mother with pity. She jerked her head at Nick and Zak and they all sloped off out of the hut.

Outside, they found Johan loafing listlessly on the corner, bouncing a ball on the ground. His face lit up when he saw them. In no time the four of them were kicking the ball around the alleys between the huts. Children passed by, looking vaguely shocked, and veered out of the way to avoid them.

'Come on!' Nick called out to them. 'Join in!' But the children just stared dumbly and walked on. Annoyed at their refusal, Nick gave the ball a mighty kick. It bounced off the side of a hut and tumbled along the alley.

Suddenly a whistle rang out shrilly, and three figures approached round a corner. One of them put his foot out and stopped the ball as it rolled towards them. It was Finn.

'What on earth do you think you're doing? No street games allowed. And this ball is confiscated.' Finn picked the ball up and handed it to one of the two goblins he was with.

'Hey!' shouted Johan. 'You can't do that. It's my ball!'

'Not any more, it isn't,' said Finn, smiling thinly. 'I would advise you once more that I am Street Monitor of Compound Eleven and it is my job to keep order in the alleyways. I'll thank you to remember that. Now please keep the noise down and behave in a seemly manner.'

He turned and marched away, the goblins on either side of him. Nick and the others stared after him in stunned silence.

'Please, children! Do it for us!' pleaded Lotta.

'It'll be good for all of us. We can't even begin to make our way up the ladder until you've all been to the first children's party,' said Joachim.

'No!' said Zak and Anneka together.

Nick said nothing. He had never felt so torn and wretched in his life. He desperately wanted to go to the next party, which was scheduled for the following night. But his friends were adamant he shouldn't. They had been arguing about it for two days.

'Well, I want to go!' piped up Louisa. 'It sounds like fun.'

'Over my dead body!' exploded Anneka. 'She's not going anywhere near that castle!'

'But why?' pleaded Lotta. 'All you have to do is go, just once. It's not much to ask, is it? Then we can all get out of this compound!'

Zak stood up, shaking with frustration and rage. His dark eyes were glowing with passion. 'Can't you see what's happening? Look at the children round here! All the ones that have been to the castle! They're like little grown-ups! It's not natural!'

'Well, their parents seem quite happy, with them being so well behaved,' remarked Lotta sulkily.

Zak snorted with disgust.

'No, Mother! We're not going! Are we, Nick?'

Nick looked round at them all. 'Well, actually I *am* going.'

There was a gasp from Zak and Anneka. Elvina flew out of Nick's front and buzzed against his face in a frenzy of anxiety, releasing a long volley of angry and frightened squeaks.

'See?' said Zak. 'She doesn't want you to go, and she's your guide. She must know something you don't.'

'I don't care. I have to go,' protested Nick. 'It's the only way I can find out what happened to my family. It's why I came here!'

'There you see, he's got the right idea!' cried Lotta triumphantly. 'He knows what's good for him, for all of us. I think you others are being very selfish.'

Zak and Anneka glared at Nick reproachfully.

'How could you?' whispered Anneka. 'I thought you felt the same as us?'

'I wasn't sure. But now I know. I have to go,' Nick said, the words like poison on his lips.

Anneka exploded. 'You're crazy! If you go, I won't want to know you any more. You'll come back like all the others.'

Nick felt a surge of anger. 'It's all right for you!' he shouted hotly. 'You've got your families, you've got your parents! Even you Zak, you know your parents are somewhere down in their new hunting grounds and you'll see them again one day. But I haven't a clue who I am! And now I'm getting closer to finding out. You don't know what it's like, not knowing who you are, where you came from. Feeling left out all the time. Not having parents of your own. And I'm going to go up to that castle to try and find mine!'

And he stormed over to his corner and threw himself down on his bed.

The Hostess from Hell

Nick spent a sleepless night, tossing and turning, listening to Zak's steady breathing on the pallet bed next to his. His friends had been ignoring him. Even Elvina didn't come out to sleep next to him on the pillow as usual.

The next morning Anneka and Zak hardly spoke to Nick, studiously avoiding his eyes. Lotta kept smiling at Nick and patting him approvingly, at which Zak and Anneka would scowl and turn away.

'See what's happening to us already?' whispered Zak to Anneka as they all filed down to Central Compound Square. 'This place is bad news. We're at each other like seals fighting over a fish.'

The atmosphere was very tense at breakfast and everyone spooned their sloppy porridge in silence. They were relieved when they heard Rosa's chirpy voice behind them as she bustled up with her family.

'Morning all! Guess what – Johan's agreed to go to the party tonight!' She looked triumphantly at them all, hands clasped under her generous bosom, beaming from ear to ear. 'Isn't that grand?'

Johan wore an expression of weary resignation and his father looked uneasy. 'Are you absolutely sure you want to go, Johan?' he asked in a low voice.

'Yes, if it'll make things easier for everyone,' said Johan with a sigh.

Lotta shot a meaningful glance at Anneka. 'See? Someone round here has got their head screwed on the right way.'

'S'not fair!' grumbled Louisa, with her lower lip stuck out. 'Can't I go with Nick?'

'No, darling,' said Lotta, 'I can't let you go without Anneka.' She looked at Anneka accusingly. 'See? You're really letting your little sister down. She was so looking forward to going.'

Anneka lifted her chin stubbornly and said nothing.

Johan shot Nick a swift glance. 'So you're going too?'

'Yup,' said Nick. He felt himself blushing to the roots and his hood felt hotter than ever. He couldn't even look at Zak and Anneka.

The false sunset was beginning to play across the sky and Magda's usual sickly evening broadcast oozed through the air when the children assembled at the compound gates to be escorted to the castle. As they marched through, flanked by goblins, Nick glanced back at his friends. Anneka and Zak were watching with stony faces. Louisa was glowering at him. They didn't even wave goodbye.

The little procession was frogmarched through the City streets, flanked by goblins. Clowns and jesters cavorted along beside them, whipping up a sense of anticipation. They passed through Golden Square and Nick stared again at the strange rock formation with the oddly human shape.

As they reached the drawbridge, the sun was setting in a lurid blaze of orange and purple. They tramped across it and up the hill to the castle, glancing down at the silvery water in the moat, where fluorescent fish swam and white swans with gilt-edged wings glided across its glassy surface. The City lay spread out below, bathed in the sunset glow.

Nick gazed up at the towering walls of the castle, the chains of the drawbridge stretching up to the battlements, the turrets and flags flapping in the evening breeze. The whole castle was bathed in multicoloured lights from some mysterious source, dancing across it in moving patterns. As they reached the great doors of the castle, Nick's heart began to beat a steady tom-tom of anticipation.

The doors were flung open and the two-headed goblin, Skank and Skism, stood before them, arms folded across one massive chest.

'Right, brats!' roared Skank, his voice bouncing off the walls and echoing round the moat. 'This way! Walk in an orderly fashion please. And be quiet!

No chattering, no fidgeting.'

'Welcome to the party, kiddiwinks. Hope you enjoy it!' said Skism, in slightly friendlier tones.

The children were ushered into the great reception hall, where they tripped over each other in their astonishment. Their mouths fell open and their gasps of wonder echoed into a vast space. It felt strangely cold after the warmth outside, like a museum. All around them, tall pillars and arched walls rose to the ceiling, as high as any cathedral, completely covered in gold leaf and inlaid with precious stones. Overhead stretched a huge domed atrium of clear glass, letting the golden light pour down.

The children gawped as they filed up the sweeping marble staircase and shuffled along endless hushed and carpeted passageways, all of them lined with portraits of Magda in various poses. The portraits' eyes seemed to follow them.

Everywhere you looked were massive flower arrangements, vases filled with the exotic blooms from the Queen's legendary royal gardens. The flower heads were massive and so brightly coloured they looked unreal. They had been bred into all sorts of weird and wonderful shapes: dragons, swans, birds. Some had what appeared to be human faces, which smiled and nodded as you walked past. They had an unnerving beauty. You could actually see the plants still growing even though they'd been cut, unfurling their petals and shooting out new leaves.

They finally reached the end of a splendid passage, where two goblin guards stood with their spears crossed on either side of heavily embossed double doors.

Nick was full of anticipation at his first chance to approach the Queen and reveal his identity. Elvina had climbed on top of his head again and was gripping the edge of his hood with such force it felt as though it had been nailed to his head. She was quaking more violently than ever before. After a few grunted commands and exchanges, the goblin guards dropped their spears and flung open the doors to reveal the stateroom. As they were ushered in, Nick gulped for breath.

Huge tapestries woven with luminous gold and silver thread hung on the walls. Magnificent velvet curtains held back with thick gold tasselled cords draped the floor-to-ceiling windows. Carved pillars stood round the room, inlaid with precious stones set in intricate patterns, and a crystal chandelier the size of a small tree hung from the ceiling, reflecting beams of light. There was an enormous fireplace where logs crackled and roaring flames leaped up the chimney. On either side of the fire stood two marble plinths bearing more massive flower arrangements.

The room was lined with tables laden with food of all kinds: pies, jellies, roast chicken legs, glazed fruits, sweetmeats, all gleaming in the firelight. There were dark chocolate gateaux oozing with cream, ice creams and sundaes, cakes and biscuits crammed with fruit and nuts, and tarts full of jam. The saliva rushed into Nick's mouth.

At the end of the stateroom was the Queen herself, seated on a carved gold throne. Tonight she was decked out in a rich red velvet gown, embroidered with diamonds. A cloak made of dazzling gold cloth was draped over her shoulders and a sparkling tiara was perched on her head. She rose as they entered and held out her arms in a regal gesture.

'Welcome, my children! Are you ready to enjoy yourselves?'

The children gaped at her speechlessly.

'Well, are you?' she enquired, holding her hand up to her delicate pointed ear as if waiting for a response. Nick noticed with a thrill that it twitched elegantly.

'Yes, your Majesty!' cried the children in unison.

Suddenly the sinister man from the carriage appeared at Queen Magda's side, as if from nowhere. Nick felt a quiver of unease. He stood next to the throne, hunched and dark like a hooded predator, his thin lips pulled back to reveal sharp pointed teeth. Nick realized with a shudder that this grimace was a smile.

'Haven't you forgotten something?' the man said, in an oily voice with undertones of menace.

The children were momentarily perplexed, then remembered.

'Hail Queen Magda, O Great and Glorious One!' they mumbled rather untidily.

'We will try that again at the end of the party,' the man growled. 'My name is Volpo Volterammerdung and I am the Queen's advisor and Master of Ceremonies. But you can call me Uncle Volpo. Are you ready to begin?'

'Yes, Uncle Volpo!' intoned the children.

A look passed between Magda and Volpo. She flashed the children a brilliant smile, turned to a door and clapped her hands. The sound cracked in the air like a whip. 'Spackle! Skreech! Thrang! Klax! Devo! Flitch! Snark! Come and entertain my young citizens!'

A band of minstrels sounded a fanfare from the balcony above and a team of clowns and jesters burst through the doors and tumbled into the room, shrieking with maniacal laughter. They were all masked, with painted faces and garish, elaborate patterned costumes. They wore three-tailed hats and long pointed shoes, all adorned with jingling bells.

A cry of delight rose up from the children as the entertainers leaped around them, doing cartwheels, somersaults and a variety of astonishing acrobatic displays. Their movements were so fluid and rubbery, they looked as if they didn't have any bones in them at all. The jesters grabbed the children and whirled them around in a frenzy, dancing to the madcap tunes from the minstrels above.

Behind the masks, Nick could see eyes glinting in

the glow of the fire, fierce and cruel like birds of prey. He felt another quiver of fear.

Suddenly Johan grabbed him by the arm and pulled him over to a table. Johan's face was ashen and he was trembling.

'I think we should get out now. I don't like this,' he whispered shakily.

Nick hesitated and started cramming his mouth with chocolates, playing for time.

'There's something I have to do first,' he told Johan, his heart pounding.

Johan swallowed. 'Well, get on with it then.'

The clowns and jesters whirled the younger children round and round, faster and faster, cackling with glee. The children were laughing and shrieking hysterically. Others were falling upon the food, gulping it down ravenously, snatching it off the platters and cramming it into their mouths. They gorged like animals, then returned to their romping, eating while they played.

Magda watched from her throne, smiling benevolently. Volpo surveyed the scene with extreme distaste, his thin lips curled into a sneer, his eyes waiting and watchful. Nick had never tasted anything quite like the food. It melted and exploded in his mouth in a cascade of delicious flavours. Suddenly it didn't seem so urgent to do anything except feast.

'These fruit pies are really good,' he said to Johan with bulging cheeks.

'Never mind the pies, do what you have to do and we'll go!' hissed Johan frantically.

Nick crammed his pockets with as much food as he could lay his hands on. He kept a close watch on Magda, trying to decide on the right moment to approach her. Then he gulped down one final pastry oozing with jam and cream, wiped his mouth, and nodded at Johan.

'OK. I'm doing it now.'

He set off through the gambolling children, towards the throne.

'No, wait! Come back!' Johan called after him. But it was too late.

Nick's heart beat frantically as he drew nearer to the Queen, taking in every line of her lovely face. She had not noticed him yet. With quivering hands he began to loosen the cords of his hood. There was a high pitched squeal.

'It's no good, Elvina. I've got to do it,' he whispered.

Then he stopped. A sense of foreboding filled him as he saw the expression on Magda's face. The gracious smile had vanished, to be replaced by a hard, cold, calculating look. She stood up and walked forward. Then she pulled back her golden cloak. In one stomach-wrenching moment, Nick realized what a horrible mistake he had made in coming here. The ground on which he had built all his hopes had vanished from under his feet.

There was a gaping black hole where her heart

should have been. A yawning window into nothingness, deep and fathomless, like her eyes, which Nick now saw were cold and empty of all human feeling. He could feel Elvina's violent shaking throughout his whole body, and the hairs prickling on the back of his neck.

A dark force was radiating from the black hole, like a whirlwind. Nick could feel it seeping towards him, chilling his bones, like an invisible fog. It swirled around, filling the room with a loud sucking noise. Like a great shadowy snake, the black whirlwind coiled around the other children until it had enveloped them all.

One by one, they stopped playing. Nick watched in helpless horror as the laughter faded on their lips and they fell silent. The lights in their eyes went out and the smiles died on their faces. They sank to the floor on their knees and bowed their heads.

Numb with terror, he waited for the creeping blackness to surround him – but for some reason it didn't. *Why had it not come to claim him?* He looked at Johan, and saw with despair that his friend was also sinking to his knees with a blank, glazed look on his face.

'Hail Queen Magda, O Great and Glorious One!' the children chanted in unison.

A smile of triumph spread over Magda's face. She began to glow with a new energy and her beauty seemed more radiant than ever. Nick felt as though his feet had taken root in the floor. His heart somersaulted in his chest as though it wanted to run away, but his body couldn't follow it.

He looked around at the kneeling, obedient children, suddenly robbed of their childhood and drained of their youthful energy. Icy fingers of fear gripped his stomach as he realized he was in the presence of pure evil. And he had walked right into the trap. Why had he ignored the alarm bells in his head, the nagging voice of doubt? Why had he hidden the truth from himself? And more important than anything else, why had he not been affected?

Suddenly he felt the burning hot beam of Magda's gaze. He tried not to look into those black, empty eyes.

'Why are you not kneeling in homage?' she hissed venomously.

Nick nearly retched with shock. He jumped, and before he could stop it, his hood fell down and revealed his ears. Magda let out a rattling gasp and stared at Nick in astonishment, her eyes ablaze.

'The elfin brat!' she screamed. 'At last! He's here! Get him!'

The room erupted. The costumes and masks of the jesters fell away to reveal hideous demons underneath, their faces putrid green and their eyes glowing like burning coals. They had clawed talons as long as knitting needles and yellow fangs jutting out from red lips, curled into horrible grimaces. Suddenly the room was full of howling wolves, pouring in from all sides.

172

Nick looked around wildly as the monsters swarmed towards him, shrieking and howling. Skank and Skism thundered across the floor, bellowing in rage, the other goblin guards lumbering in their wake.

Nick's eyes came to rest on the fireplace – his only possible escape. He dashed towards it, feeling the demons' hot talons tearing at him, and the sharp teeth of the wolves snapping at his ankles.

He was nearly at the fireplace when Volpo materialized before him, hunched and threatening, a wolf about to pounce. An evil smile stretched his lips into a horrible leer. He brought his bony hands out from under his cloak. There was a sharp hissing sound. Ten shiny steel talons unsheathed from the ends of his fingers, glinting in the firelight.

Escape and Exile

Volpo advanced upon Nickolai, making low guttural sounds in his throat, his steel talons outstretched. His hooded lids blinked and suddenly his eyes changed; they became black, vertical slits in sulphur yellow irises, the eyes of a wild animal. Nick shuddered.

'You might as well give in now and save us all a lot of trouble, young man,' said the creature, in a kindly voice that didn't match his appearance. A thrill of revulsion ran down Nick's spine. 'Uncle Volpo knows best.'

The rest of the monsters had closed around Nick in a circle. In the fireplace, the flames roared and leaped and crackled. He was trapped. His mind raced frantically, turning over several hundred possibilities per second.

'OK,' he said suddenly. 'I'll do whatever you say.' He held out his hands and allowed his shoulders to slump in apparent defeat.

'Good boy!' said Volpo coaxingly, moving forward.

For one fleeting second, there was a clear path to the

fireplace, a minuscule chance of escape. Nick seized the moment; he shot towards the massive opening and hurled himself into it.

The flames scorched his face and arms in an agonizing rush, but he dived through them and began to climb the chimney, scrabbling furiously at the sooty sides, hauling himself upwards with the strength born of fear and desperation. He felt the intense heat of the flames licking around his feet, the smoke pouring into his throat and choking him. He scrambled higher, the howling of the demons and wolves echoing in his ears from below.

Velvet lay dying on a bed of dried leaves. She had been placed in a hollow scooped out by the hooves of the reindeer in the clearing. The whole tribe knelt in a circle, gazing down at her frail old body in sorrow and respect. She was the ancient matriarch of the tribe and had lived longer than any of the flying reindeer before her. Her muzzle was now completely grey and her antlers had become like withered branches. She lay on her side, her gnarled old limbs stretched out limply and her breath coming in shallow gasps.

Rudolph wept quietly at his mother's side and the other young reindeer sniffled and sobbed.

'Why does she have to die?' wailed Rudolph miserably.

'Because she is many, many twelvemoons old,' whispered Comet, 'and no one can last for ever. It is her time to return to Arkfel, and we must let her go.'

Lancer slumped his head on his front hooves and let out a long, snuddering sigh. 'I wish I had not been so impatient with her sometimes, when she whiffled on about superstitious things. She was right, much of the time . . . she knew things we did not.'

Comet rubbed her head against his. 'She understands. She is old and wise. She knows you have a tribe to look after and you have to be sensible and think about everyday things.'

Velvet's eyes flickered open. They were cloudy and had a faraway look, as though they saw somewhere beyond the forest. She lifted her old head and looked at Comet and Lancer.

'The flying power,' she croaked, with enormous effort. 'You must conserve it now. Hold on to every last drop. The Two Legs who came to us all those years ago . . .'

She stopped, panting and exhausted. Rudolph broke into fresh sobs. He had been the one who had missed Nick the most when he had disappeared from their lives; the Two Legs had always ridden on his back. Comet had explained that something had changed in the boy's life.

She had returned only once after that night and hovered in the sky above, waiting for him to appear on the roof. When he didn't, she understood that his nightly visits had been discovered and he was keeping away to protect them, to conceal their existence from his fellow humans.

'All things come to an end,' she had told the sniffling young reindeer at the time. 'He is from a different world. Maybe one day when he is older he will come back and see us.'

Now Velvet was struggling, with all that was left of her strength, to tell them something about him that she obviously felt important. They leaned closer, listening as she lifted her head to speak again.

'The Two Legs boy,' she gasped painfully, 'he will return . . . he will need you. You must hold yourself in readiness to help him. It is the will of Arkfel.'

Then her head fell back and her laboured breathing stopped. Her body went still and quiet. A chorus of moans and sobs broke out amongst the reindeer, and a large tear rolled down Lancer's cheek and fell on to the snow.

Then they all stood up. With their teeth they began to pile fallen branches over the hollow to protect her body from wolves. They stood around the grave in a circle and said a silent prayer to Arkfel to keep her safe.

Then they walked slowly away across the snow, back to their cave.

The chimney was suffocating. The heat and smoke enveloped Nick, pouring into his eyes and filling his lungs. He struggled on, bracing his hands and feet against the burning, sooty walls, trying to ignore the pain as they seared his palms, trying to shut out the howling as it echoed up the chimney.

Don't look down! Just keep climbing! His brain sent urgent survival messages into his legs and arms and they obeyed, scrabbling fiercely to haul him higher. He glanced up and saw a circle of sky above him, an artificial blue with twinkling stars. He felt a claw scratching at his ankle and cried out in shock.

Frantically he renewed his efforts until at last he reached the top of the chimney and scrambled out. He was a mess – covered in soot, hands and feet scorched and burned. Surprisingly, his red robe was undamaged. But there was no time to think. He began to run across the strange uneven roof, dotted with turrets and domes, and noticed with a start that its surface was coal black, not gold.

From this high vantage point on the castle's battlements, he had an aerial view of the whole of Doransk; a twinkling fairyland stretching away on all sides, enclosed in its great bubble and sealed off at its outer edges by the city walls. Beyond the walls lay the dark and snowy wastes of the outside world.

Nick glanced down and gulped, overcome by giddiness. It was a very long way down. The moat surrounding the castle was a thin ribbon. The goblin guards patrolling the grounds were tiny figures down below.

A spasm of terror shot through him as he heard ear-splitting shrieks behind him. The demons were

Nick glanced down and gulped, overcome by giddiness.
It was a very long way down.

pouring out of the top of the chimney, their red eyes glowing, their mouths stretched open in horrible grimaces of rage. Their unearthly howls echoed across the still night air as they swooped towards him.

Nick looked down at the yawning drop below. He had no choice. The demons were closer now, rushing towards him like a hurricane. One of the chains of the drawbridge was bolted on to the wall of the castle, some way below him to the left.

Nick steeled himself in readiness, then launched himself off the edge of the roof into the void, aiming for the drawbridge chain. The warm night air rushed past his cheeks as he plunged downwards, just managing to grab on to the chain with the tips of his fingers. Fastening his hand round it, he hung there for a few moments, legs windmilling wildly. Then he swung his body over, wrapped himself round the chain and slid down it like a monkey, gasping in pain as the metal bolts tore at his hands.

There was a horrible noise from above; a loud banshee screeching and a flapping of wings. Nick looked up and saw that the demons had unfurled enormous leathery wings. As Nick reached the bottom of the chain and was about to jump on to the drawbridge and run across, he heard a rumbling, clanking noise. He was jerked upwards. The drawbridge was being taken up, with him clinging to it, legs dangling wildly in mid air.

Goblin shouts rang out all around him and he could

hear Magda's voice screaming above the clamour. The shrieking of the demons grew closer; the dry crackling of their wings filled his ears as they hurtled through the air towards him, ready to snatch him off the drawbridge like a tiny bird on a rock face.

Without a moment's hesitation, he let go of the chain and dropped into the moat, gasping as he landed with a splash in the icy water. He sank like a stone into its depths, then struggled to the surface, panting for air as he broke through. The demons were swooping towards him with their teeth bared and their claws outstretched.

'Don't kill him!' he heard Madga screech in the background. 'Bring him back here! I need him alive until the time is right!'

Nick began to swim furiously over to the bank. The demons were closing in on all sides, divebombing him, screaming in fury – but as they neared the water they recoiled and swooped upwards again.

Yes! Water! They were obviously afraid of it! Nick ducked to avoid them as they lunged at him again and again, trying to snatch him out. Then he began taunting them, trying to lure them in, until one or two of them lost control and plunged into the water. They let out shrieks of agony and began to fizzle and smoke, thrashing their hideous limbs and gurgling horribly. They writhed in their death throes, sputtering and hissing away into nothing, like dried leaves in a vat of boiling oil, leaving only a trail of evil-smelling bubbles behind them as they sank beneath the surface. The other demons hovered above, screeching in helpless fury.

Overhead the drawbridge rumbled back down and the shouts of goblins rang out as they thundered across.

Something was pecking Nick's face, and there were loud honking noises in his ears. In seconds, he was surrounded by the gilded swans. A ring of angry white faces surrounded him, long necks arching as they lunged at him savagely, tearing at his clothes with their beaks.

Time to get back under the water.

Nickolai took a deep breath, plunged beneath the surface and began swimming towards the bank. The water was dark and murky, a forest of black muddy reeds. He struggled through, pushing the reeds aside. Not far now, and he would reach the other side of the moat.

Suddenly, a row of bulbous, luminous eyes loomed at him out of the murk. He stopped, confronting the moat's fluorescent fish as they gawped at him, streams of bubbles flowing from their loose, fishy mouths. His heart lurched in horror at the sight of their savage, razor-sharp teeth.

There was a violent movement as they attacked him from all sides, their scaly bodies flashing silver. Their monstrous faces came at him again and again, drawing back and charging forward, nipping at his arms, legs and face. Nick thrashed around wildly, fighting the creatures off and pulling himself towards the bank. He could feel their sharp teeth biting into his flesh as he swam with a strength he never knew he had.

With a last spurt of effort, he kicked out wildly, pulled himself towards the bank and dragged himself out, slumping exhausted and breathless on the grass. He was some way down from the drawbridge gates. He looked at himself; he was covered with bites and bleeding gashes. The fish gathered at the bank, their open mouths and sharp teeth still snapping at him, like carp clamouring for bread in a pond. Then he heard more shouts and saw that the goblins had spotted him.

'After him!' screeched Magda's voice from above.

Nick leaped up and ran on trembling legs towards an avenue that opened on to the castle forecourt. There were thundering feet behind him from the pursuing goblins, shouting and bellowing. He dived into the avenue and hurtled past crowds of strolling people, who halted and stared in astonishment.

'Stop him!' bawled Skank.

'Don't let him get away!' yelled Skism.

The people tried to close ranks but Nick barrelled into them, scattering them in all directions. He raced on down the avenue until he saw a side street lined with glittering silvery buildings. A tall man made a grab for him and he ducked, then sprinted down the side street, his feet slithering on the shiny pavements.

A gang of goblins was rounding the corner ahead.

Skidding to a halt, Nick looked behind him. More

goblins were approaching from the other end of the avenue. He saw a gateway leading into the courtyard of a grand house, with light pouring out of its windows. Dashing through the entrance, he searched feverishly for a door or a passage he could escape through. But there was none. The shouts of the goblins drew nearer.

Once again he was trapped.

Nick's ears began to twitch violently in terror. Suddenly he felt a force coming from them, the same force he had felt that day in Norsk, when Finn had been dragging him along by a rope. It was much stronger now, overwhelming and unstoppable, as though it was drawing on something outside him. Letting it flow through him, he heard a loud crunching noise from below; a crack opened up at his feet, revealing a dark shaft stretching downwards into inky blackness. It was just big enough for him. In seconds the goblins would be inside the courtyard, surrounding him where he stood, cornered and helpless.

There was nothing else for it. Nick hurled himself into the crack and found himself sliding with enormous speed into darkness. The chute wound down, spiralling deeper and deeper into the earth, until he landed with a thump on a hard surface and lost consciousness.

Up in the courtyard there was a heavy thud, like the crunch of stone doors slamming shut, and the crack closed up, leaving no trace of evidence on the smooth paved surface.

The goblins rushed into the courtyard and looked around. It was empty. Their mouths gaped open stupidly and they blinked like idiots. Skank and Skism lumbered into the courtyard and stood there breathlessly.

'Where is 'e, then?'

'Dunno,' said one of the goblins. 'He's gawn. Disappeared into thin air.'

Skank's head twisted round violently and glared at Skism. 'This is all your fault!'

'What d'you mean you let him go!' roared Magda. Her beautiful face was twisted into a mask of fury.

Skank and Skism cowered before the throne in the stateroom, both heads hanging in shame, a two-headed dog cringing before its master. The elite goblin force stood around them in a huddle, arms hanging loosely at their sides, bald heads shining in the firelight as they stared at the floor like naughty children. Magda towered over them all with her blazing eyes and Volpo stood impassively at her side, tense and watchful.

'It was 'is fault!' snarled Skank, his head shooting up and swivelling round to glare furiously at Skism. ' 'E wanted to go a different way from me!'

'Did not!' retorted Skism. 'We went the way you said! You never listen to me!'

'That's 'cos you ain't worth listening to, you bumbling idiot, you kept confusing fings!'

'Did not! You definitely said—'

Skism was cut off as a loud crack split the air and a thunderbolt shot out from Magda's long red fingernail. It bounced off their heads and banged them together violently. They both grunted in shock as their heads wobbled on the massive shoulders. Four eyes rolled around in their sockets like pinballs.

'Shut up!' she screeched. 'Where exactly did he disappear?'

'He ran into a courtyard on Silver Street, Majesty, and when we went in after 'im 'e was gawn.'

'Disappeared!' added Skism unnecessarily.

'Well he must be somewhere,' hissed Magda. 'He must have found a hidden passage or something. Did you search the house?'

'Turned it upside down,' said Skank, who had evidently found this process enjoyable.

Magda sent out another bolt of lightning, which crackled around the goblins and made them recoil. 'Order a citywide search!' she stormed. 'Every house, every street, every shop, and every hut in the immigrant compounds! I must find him. He's got to be somewhere in the City! And if I don't get results . . .' She sent out another thunderbolt of such force it knocked the goblins' feet from under them and slammed them on to their knees, cowering in terror. '. . . I can always send you back down into the Vortex!'

A collective moan of horror went round the goblins.

'Yes, your Majesty!' they said in unison, before

scrambling up and lumbering out of the room. The door slammed behind them.

There was an ominous silence. Magda turned to face Volpo. His bony hands plucked nervously at his cloak and his dark eyes watched her carefully. She undulated towards him with a look that made his hair stand up in spikes.

'Do not worry, Majesty,' Volpo stammered, backing away. 'We will find him. He cannot go far. There is no escape from this City. We will find him and hold him captive until—'

He was cut off as Magda sent a snake of fizzling fire into his body, making him fall to the ground and curl up in agony. He writhed and twisted on the floor, gasping for breath as the fire coiled through his organs, blazing a trail of pain.

'Idiot!' she screeched. 'He finally comes here, like we knew he would, then when we've got him, you let him escape!'

Volpo struggled to speak, his voice coming out in a strained whisper. 'Alas, it seems the boy has some spirit, like his mother. And the fairy seems to be protecting him somehow. But at least you have him here in the City. He can't escape. And his Light Fairy will not leave him. So when we catch him, we will catch her too.'

Magda released the snake of fire and his body slumped. He gasped in relief and continued, 'And then all you have to do is keep him captive till Winter

Solstice Eve. You will be able to take the creature and he will perish without her.'

'And my power will be complete?'

'Yes, Majesty. The full matrix. Our long-term expansion plans will be able to proceed unhindered.'

'You'd better be right,' Magda snapped. 'If that Light Fairy escapes, my future hangs in the balance. And it'll all be your fault. Now get those wolves out there! I want the City watched day and night.'

Volpo shakily pulled himself upright and let out a low, growling whistle. A torrent of dark shapes filled the room, howling eerily. Then the doors flew open and the swirling mass swept through them like a tornado.

Zak and Anneka waited in the doorway of their hut. Footsteps were coming down the alleyway. They watched as the children filed past, returning from the party under goblin escort. Their faces were solemn and serious and they remained silent, marching along in orderly lines. No more straggling, jumping, skipping or chattering laughter. At the front was Johan, his face now a closed book. Rosa and Kristoff came forward to meet him.

'Did you have a good time, love?' asked Rosa.

'Yes, Mother,' replied Johan primly. 'It was most interesting. Queen Magda is indeed a great and glorious monarch.'

The parents glanced at each other, then started leading Johan away.

'How about finishing that game of chess then?' Kristoff asked. 'Or if you're tired, maybe some reading. We still haven't finished *The Tales of Skaggerak*.'

Johan looked at his father in disdain. 'No, Father, I no longer wish to read childish fairy stories.'

'Oh. A quick game of cards then?' said Kristoff hopefully.

'No thank you. I only wish to study the official texts of Doransk.' Johan held up a red leather volume. All the other children were carrying similar books, and Queen Magda dolls, which they clasped reverently.

Kristoff's face drained of its colour, as though somebody had just died. He put his arm round his son's shoulder and the little family walked back towards their hut.

'I can't bear it,' said Anneka as she watched them go. 'I think that was the saddest thing I've ever seen.'

'Aktuk,' Zak muttered in agreement. 'They sent their son up to the castle and got a stranger back. But where's Nicku?'

The two of them craned their necks. The last of the children had filed past and there was no sign of him. Then they heard clanking noises as a posse of goblins marched towards them, carrying heavy chains and padlocks.

'Extra security procedures! Curfew!' boomed a goblin. 'Dangerous criminal on the loose!'

Zak and Anneka stared at each other. A slow smile spread across Anneka's face.

'He's escaped!' she whispered incredulously.

Nick's eyes opened and met with darkness, lit only by a dim blue glow. Wincing in pain, he sat up and felt around. He was on a hard, freezing floor. He shivered. Wherever he was, it was cold, damp and silent, except for the slow *drip drip* of running water echoing all around him.

There was a loud squeak and a flash of light. Elvina burst into view and buzzed around Nick's face, lighting up the gloom. In the dim light shed by the fairy, he could make out a long dark tunnel. What was this place? It must be some underground cavern beneath the city. And there was no way out. He was trapped down here, all alone, without his friends – friends who probably weren't speaking to him now anyway.

Suddenly Nick became aware of something in his pocket, digging into him. He felt inside and brought out a pendant on a thong. Elvina hovered around, shedding light on to the object in his hand. Nick squinted at it in the gloom.

It was Zak's Tupilak. He must have somehow slipped it into Nick's pocket last night. Zak had lent him his precious talisman, hoping to protect him. Even though he wasn't talking to him.

Nick felt a pang of remorse. His friends did care after all. He examined the crude carved figure, with its hideous, painted green face and fierce black eyes, and the jagged white chips of teeth in the red gaping mouth. A small quiver of recognition ran through him. It was familiar, very familiar. Where had he seen that face before?

It hit him like a thunderbolt. It was exactly the same as the horrible image that had flashed in front of his eyes at the procession; the image that had come to him the first time he had seen Magda. Zak's Inuit intuition had somehow guessed at the truth and expressed it in the form of his totem.

Shivers ran up and down Nick's spine. Finally, he understood. He was looking at Queen Magda's true nature, the monster behind the beautiful mask.

Suddenly Elvina began spiralling down the tunnel. She wanted him to follow her. He struggled to his feet, grunting in pain, and limped after her. His whole body ached and hurt. There were cuts, burns, bruises and bleeding gashes all over him. On and on Elvina flew, occasionally stopping to wait for him, beckoning him on. The labyrinth wound endlessly, twisting and turning through caves and grottos that opened out into each other, crisscrossed by tunnels and passageways. Everything was covered in a thick layer of ice and encrusted with icicles. It seemed to stretch beneath the City for ever.

Finally, Nick followed Elvina into a huge, vaulted, cathedral-like cavern, lined with tall pillared stalagmites and stalactites. It was full of strange rock formations, a whole crowd of them, standing around like statues frozen in mid motion. Dotted all around the cavern stood large rectangular blocks covered in icicles, and over in a corner was something tall and square, raised on a higher level. A jagged scar scored the floor and scattered lumps of coal lay around in heaps.

Nickolai stared hopelessly at the desolate scene. What was he going to do now? He was all alone, trapped down here for ever. His chest tightened unbearably. All the feelings he'd been forced to hold back since he'd seen Magda's black and empty heart burst out of him in a torrent of grief. He slumped down against one of the lumps of rock in despair.

'It's no good, is it, Elvina?' he whispered. 'I'll never find the Elfin Kingdom. I'll never find my family, or my parents. It's all over for me.'

Elvina buzzed round the cavern, weaving in and out of the rock formations and making loud, meaningful noises. But Nick was too distressed to take any notice of what she was trying to tell him.

Climate of Fear

The Golden City was in turmoil. Skank and Skism led the army of goblins as they brutally ransacked every corner of the City and searched every home, their two heads issuing conflicting orders and quarrelling constantly. The streets echoed with the sound of marching feet as goblin patrols stomped back and forth, looking for the fugitive. The statues' watchful eyes glittered more intently than ever, and wolves prowled the metropolis day and night, their yellow eyes flicking to and fro, never missing a thing. Pictures of Nick were posted all over the city, with notices underneath saying:

WANTED, DANGEROUS CRIMINAL!
1,000 GOLD MAGGOTS REWARD.

The statue Tannoy system blared out regular news bulletins and proclamations, urging people to keep a close look out for a boy with pointed ears, yellow hair and a red hooded robe.

Everyone was under suspicion. Mistrust lingered in the air, and greed brought the worst out in many citizens as the ransom for turning Nick in climbed higher and higher. They began telling tales on each other, or presenting themselves at Goblin High Command, claiming to have information. Children were encouraged to inform on their parents, or anybody else they suspected. Magda was turning her citizens into the worst kind of human beings.

Joachim, Lotta, Louisa, Zak and Anneka had been promptly taken down to the Detention Centre, under suspicion because Nick had been with them. They were relentlessly interrogated by Volpo, subjected to his piercing hypnotic gaze, but even he could see they knew nothing of Nick's whereabouts. They had finally been released and kept under hut arrest.

After two weeks, Nick had still not been found and there was no information about him. Magda was beside herself with rage and frustration. She paced her stateroom furiously, followed by an anxious Volpo.

'We've got to do something!' she hissed. 'This is not good enough, Volpo!'

Volpo jerked convulsively, expecting another painful reprimand, but none came; Magda needed his brains at the moment. 'He cannot possibly escape, Majesty,' he ventured nervously. 'The City is completely sealed off.'

'What about the labyrinth?'

Volpo shrugged and spread his bony hands. 'There is no way he can get down there, Majesty. It is impenetrable. Only you have the power to enter it.'

'But he must be hiding somewhere! What about the people he was living with?'

'They have been repeatedly interrogated, Majesty, but have been eliminated from our enquiries. They genuinely have no idea where he is.'

'Are you certain? Have the children been to a welcome party yet?'

Volpo looked unsure. 'I do not know, Majesty. But I can find out.'

Magda paced the floor fretfully, plucking at her cloak with her long red fingernails. 'How can we make the population work harder at finding him for us? We've offered them money. What more can we do?'

Volpo pondered for a moment, then an evil smile spread over his wolf-like face. 'I have the perfect strategy, Majesty. Greed has not worked. Now we need to try fear.' He began prowling up and down, his eyes glowing and his spiky hair standing on end. 'Yes! A brilliant campaign, creating a climate of fear. All masterminded by myself, your loyal and humble servant.'

'Tell me about it,' Magda demanded.

Volpo pulled a small golden trumpet from his robes and held it towards Magda. 'Just repeat my words, Majesty. Let the proclamations begin!'

If it hadn't been for Elvina, Nick would have been hopelessly lost in the labyrinth. The endless maze of tunnels and caves looked pretty much the same, except for the main central cavern. The food he'd managed to salvage from the party, soggy and almost inedible, had run out. He had kept himself alive by eking it out carefully, but now hunger pangs gnawed at his stomach. Luckily his red cloak, still mysteriously unscathed, had kept him warm.

A confusing jumble of thoughts whirled in his head. Was there any hope of stopping the monster that was Queen Magda? If one of his kind was so cruel and evil, what did that say about him? Why was she after him, the only other elf left in the world? What did he have that she wanted? And what was this strange place he was in?

He spent hours wandering around the rock formations, gazing curiously at them, trying to guess at their nature. But the harder he looked, the more they seemed like lifeless rocks. He began to explore the labyrinth and memorize its layout, etching a rough map on the wall with a piece of rock.

Before long he began to hear terrible sounds coming from above. Marching feet, screams of terror and brutal shouts. Booming proclamations echoed from the statues. He could feel mass panic and paranoia seeping down through the layers of ice. With a pang of guilty alarm, it dawned on him that something nasty was going on up there – and it was all about him. The goblins were looking for him, and innocent people were bearing the brunt of the search.

'I can't let this happen, Elvina,' he said anxiously, as the full impact hit him. 'I've got to do something!'

Elvina nodded her head vigorously and whizzed round in circles.

'But what?'

Elvina made a few darting gestures up at the ceiling.

'You mean, find my friends?'

Elvina nodded.

'But how will I get up there?'

Elvina divebombed at his ear and gave it a hard tweak. 'You mean – try and open the ground up again? Like I did before? But on purpose?'

Elvina squeaked and nodded again. Nick thought hard for a moment. 'But how will I find the right place?'

Elvina sighed with exasperation and made an impatient warbling noise. Then she darted down a tunnel, beckoning him to follow her.

At midnight, Finn burst into hut number 21 with a whole gang of goblins.

'You're under arrest!'

A torch blazed mercilessly around the sleeping bodies on the pallet beds. Everyone sat up, blinking and shielding their eyes from the glare.

There was an air of menace about Finn as he strutted into the hut, his feet clipping on the floor and his eyes glinting with the thrill of power. He was wearing steel-tipped boots, a smart new black uniform and an enormous new badge. There was a lot of stamping, saluting and shouting. Finn unrolled a scroll and started reading aloud.

'I am here in my capacity as new Head of Youth Intelligence for Compound Eleven!' he announced, preening like a peacock. 'I am vested with the powers of the Supreme Orders of her Majesty, the great and good Queen Magda, under the new Law and Order Act, to charge you with treason under suspicion of conspiracy with public enemy number one, the Evil Elf Boy, who is plotting to overthrow her Majesty and endanger the state, thereby threatening the peace, harmony and freedom of our glorious realm!' he parroted in pious tones. 'I am therefore empowered to arrest your children and take them away for intensive questioning. They will be absent for an indefinite period in the Youth Detention Centre.'

A cry of horror went round the hut.

'No!' shrieked Lotta, clutching Louisa to her bosom.

'You are under suspicion,' continued Finn, staring coldly at Zak and Anneka, 'because you have failed to respond appropriately to the Queen's most gracious and bountiful invitation to attend one of her special welcome parties for new young citizens of the state. This would indicate an anti-Doransk attitude.'

There was a tense silence as parents and children looked at each other.

'I said you should have gone,' whispered Lotta. 'Now look what a mess we're in.'

'However, should you change your minds and respond to the invitation, the arrest warrant will be withdrawn forthwith,' finished Finn triumphantly.

At last, Anneka's shoulders slumped in defeat and her face emptied. 'All right, Mother, if it's come to this, we'll go. We have no choice now, do we?'

Nick had been following Elvina for some time now, keeping his gaze fixed firmly on the glowing light flitting ahead of him. He had stumbled along endless, winding tunnels, snaking around in loops and crisscrossing each other, and passed through numerous caves, all opening out into each other like Chinese boxes. He was beginning to wonder if Elvina was as lost as he was. Maybe he would never find his way out of this giant underground maze, and end up perished and frozen like the stalactites and stalagmites around him.

Suddenly Elvina stopped and began quivering violently, making swift darting movements at a spot high up in the wall.

It was time for Nick to put his powers to the test, to see if he could do it. *What if he couldn't?* He pushed the treacherous thought away and gathered up his willpower, preparing to make his first conscious attempt to open the rocks. Taking a deep breath, he concentrated hard, trying to imagine himself at the centre of the universe, with all its forces revolving around him. At first nothing. *It wasn't going to work.* He shook his head to chase the doubts away, then tried again, holding himself as still as a statue.

Slowly, he began to feel the gigantic force from the core of the earth rising up and swirling around him like a strong current in the sea. He relaxed and opened his mind, letting the force flow into him, filling him up with its strange, unearthly power. It was an indescribable feeling, a sensation of being in control and yet at the same time completely helpless.

His ears began to twitch. *No! Stop! You're not supposed to do that till I tell you!* he cried inwardly, gritting his teeth and making a superhuman effort to keep them still. He must have complete command over them, or the connection with the power might be broken. When he felt he had them under control, he began to lever them, like someone turning the handles of a rusty wheel, trying to gather up the force flowing through him and channel it out again.

His heart leaped in his chest.

A low rumbling came from deep within the earth. The ground began to shake and tremble. The vibrations grew stronger until they became a shuddering roar, echoing around the tunnel. Nick felt them booming through him like a tidal wave, up into his brain. His mind grasped the force and directed it at the point in the wall where Elvina was hovering . . . there was a loud crack . . . and an opening appeared.

Nick's heart sank in dismay. It was only a sliver,

barely wide enough to let a mosquito through. He had to make it bigger! He began to tremble with the effort as he tried to force the crack open wider by sheer willpower. Painfully slowly, the crack creaked and groaned and stretched into a hole just wide enough for him to squeeze through, revealing a sloping shaft leading up to the surface. A faint glimmer of false moonlight shone down through the darkness.

The rumbling stopped and everything went quiet and still again.

Nick felt a surge of elation and triumph pass through him. 'I did it!' he gasped. 'I actually made the rocks move!'

Elvina squeaked her approval and flitted into the shaft, beckoning him to follow. He took a running leap and scrambled in after her. The sides of the shaft were slippery, but it was narrow enough for him to brace himself with his hands and knees. Slowly, he hauled himself to the top, and finally poked his head out of the crack he had made in the ground. After several days in the cold, dank tunnels, the warm air hit him like a blast from an oven. He had come out in Central Compound Square; the crack was hidden underneath the food counters.

'Clever Elvina,' he whispered. 'You've picked just the right spot.'

He saw a loaf of bread lying on the ground nearby, fallen from the counter. *Food!* It was grubby and stale, but he hadn't eaten for three days. He snatched it off the ground and began to tear at it ravenously, with the desperation of a starved animal.

He was about to venture out, when he heard pounding feet. He ducked as a posse of goblins marched past, their clumsy boots thumping next to his nose. The square was empty and silent for a moment. Tucking the half-eaten loaf in his pocket, he slipped quietly from under the counters and scuttled across the square into the shadows, then tiptoed along the rows of alleyways till he came to number 73.

He turned the corner and froze.

Several dark shadowy shapes prowled along the alleyway further down, sniffing and swinging their heads to and fro. *Wolves!* He stepped back into the shadows and flattened himself against the wall. If they saw him he was finished. He waited, his heart hammering against his ribs, so loudly he was sure it would be heard. The wolves loitered, raising their heads and flicking their ears alertly. Had they sensed him? Nick held himself still, trying to imagine himself not there.

After a few agonizing moments, the wolves slunk down the alley, peeled off in different directions and disappeared. Nick darted forward and made his way to hut 21. With trembling fingers, he began to try and break the heavy padlock with a piece of rock. But it was no good – he would have to smash it with such force he would make too much noise and alert the whole compound.

Elvina whizzed out of his front and flitted down the side of the hut to the window. It had been left open a crack. She flew in. Nick went up to the window and crouched underneath it, waiting. A few moments later, Zak's brown face appeared. It creased into a wide grin when he saw Nick.

'Nicku!' he whispered. 'I knew you'd come!'

Anneka's pale face appeared beside him and her hand flew to her mouth, stifling a shriek of surprise.

'Help me get this window open,' said Zak urgently.

They heaved at the window, trying not to make any sound, until they had wrenched it off its hinges. Zak climbed out and landed nimbly on his feet beside Nick. Anneka scrambled out after him.

'You've come just in the nick of time,' hissed Anneka. 'We were being forced to go to the next children's party, tomorrow.'

'Over my dead body!' Nick whispered fiercely. 'Come on, I've found somewhere to hide. They'll never find us, 'cos only I can get down there. Follow me.'

They turned to go, then froze as a tiny voice piped up behind them. 'Where are you going?'

Louisa's face was at the window.

'Shh!' whispered Anneka. 'Go back to bed.'

'Shan't. I'll scream if you go without me,' Louisa said conversationally, enjoying her moment of power. Her mouth opened into a round pink O.

Anneka shot over to the window in two seconds

203

flat. With angry resignation, she reached up and yanked Louisa out headfirst. 'All right, madam! But one peep out of you and you're dogmeat!'

They tiptoed between the huts and emerged into the alleyway. 'Come on. Follow me!' whispered Nick. He began to scuttle off, the others following him. Then they stopped dead.

A river of dark shadowy shapes suddenly poured out from the narrow passages between the huts. They came from all sides, out of nowhere. The wolves prowled towards them, growling under their breath. Their teeth were bared and their yellow eyes glowed horribly in the dark. The children stifled gasps of terror and huddled together.

They were hemmed in; completely trapped.

What Lies Beneath

'Stay still,' hissed Nick. He braced himself, every muscle tensed, his mind racing. He would get them out of there if it killed him. There was no way Magda was taking his friends away.

The wolves circled them, crawling forward and quivering on their haunches, ready to pounce. A desperate thought came to Nick.

'Go, Vina!' he whispered. Elvina quaked under his tunic, shivering in terror. He tried again. 'Please! It's our only chance!'

He felt her trembling, then suddenly she tensed herself in readiness. With a tiny war cry of a squeak, she buzzed out of his front and dived at the wolves. They jerked around as she teased them, zooming at them and then flitting away, their scrawny heads lunging forward again and again as they snarled and snapped at her. Her glowing shape flitted off down the alleyway and the wolves bounded after her in pursuit. Everyone heaved a sigh of relief, then . . .

'Oi! 'Ooo goes there!' boomed a rough voice. Skank

and Skism were barrelling towards them, surrounded by goblins. A greasy leer spread over Skank's fat face as he saw them. He and Skism lumbered to a collective halt. Skank put his hand on his hip and cocked his head on one side. Skism, not to be outdone, did the same. It was an odd sight.

'Ahhh! Sweet! The little elfin scum come back to save 'is little friends.' Skank's smile hardened into a sneer. 'Right, you 'orrible brats, let's be 'avin' yer!'

'Yurr!' agreed Skism.

Nick backed away, pulling the others, but it was no good; the goblins closed in, rattling their chains. Suddenly Nick remembered. *The day in the marketplace! They couldn't resist food!* He pulled the stale crust out of his pocket and hurled it on the ground. The goblins stopped in their tracks and stumbled over each other in disarray, their ham-like fists hanging at their sides as they gawped at the pathetic scrap of food, mesmerized by it. Loops of spittle drooled out of their slobbering mouths and splatted on to the ground.

'Don't even fink abart it!' roared Skank.

'Nar!' agreed Skism.

The goblins blinked at their joint boss with glazed eyes. Then greed won the battle in their befuddled brains. They fell upon the crust like a pack of hungry dogs, growling and snarling, foaming at the mouth, their chainmail grating as they fought.

It was not a pleasant sight.

'Get up off the floor, you 'orrible gobbos!' bellowed

Skank. There was a loud crack as his whip lashed down, but the goblins ignored him and carried on fighting, oblivious to the blows.

Nick saw his chance. 'Right, now! Head for the square!' he whispered. The children turned and ran as fast as they could down the alleyway, leaving the bellowing, squabbling goblins behind.

As they dashed into the square, Nick jerked his head towards the serving counters. 'Under there!' he called out, leading the way. They all dived under the cover of the counters and crouched there, catching their breath.

'What now?' gasped Zak.

'I've got a secret escape route!' whispered Nick, loping on all fours towards the crack. The others followed him and gasped when they saw the yawning black crevice in the ground.

'You mean, we've got to go down there?' whispered Zak disbelievingly.

'Course we have, you twit,' said Anneka scornfully.

'But Inuits never go below ground!' spluttered Zak. 'It's not natural!'

Nick felt a surge of irritation. 'If you don't go down there now we'll be done for.'

Zak carried on staring at the hole, too terrified to move. Nick finally lost patience and shoved him into the crack. He disappeared quickly, yelping in fright as he tumbled headfirst into the darkness.

'Wimp,' snorted Anneka, grabbing Louisa and jumping into the crack without a moment's hesitation.

'Wheeeeeeee!' squealed Louisa as they hurtled down the chute, leaving a faint echo behind them.

Nick glanced round for Elvina. Where was she? He couldn't leave her behind! To his relief she appeared like a streak of lightning and shot down his front. He heard pounding feet and panting yelps approaching fast as he jumped into the crack, just as wolves and goblins poured into the square from all sides. The compound was in uproar.

As he plummeted down the shaft he concentrated hard, trying to force the rocks behind him back together. There was a rumbling, scraping noise from above and the crack shut, just as a wolf began to sniff around under the counters.

'So you saw it? You actually saw the creature?' Magda's eyes were boring a hole into Volpo.

'Yes,' he whispered, edging away from the throne. His head had almost shrunk into his shoulders. 'My wolves chased it, but it kept evading them. They are notoriously elusive creatures, these Light Fairies.'

'And the elfin brat?' Magda said, disturbingly calm.

Volpo, Skank and Skism cowered in front of her.

'With the – er, other children, Majesty,' mumbled Skank, his piggy eyes looking everywhere but at the Queen.

'*What* other children?' hissed Magda in a low and dangerous voice.

'The ones that escaped with him, Majesty,' said Skism helpfully. 'It was the food see, the goblins just can't res*mmphhh* . . .'

Skank had clapped his hand over Skism's mouth. He smiled at Magda nervously. 'Take no notice of my colleague, Majesty. 'E's an idiot.'

There was an ominous silence. Madga began to glow with rage, like a volcano about to erupt. Then—

'You let him go again!' she shrieked, at such a high pitch that the huge crystal chandelier shattered and fell on to the floor with a deafening crash, showering them with splinters of glass.

Volpo backed away, babbling in terror. 'We will find them, Majesty, I will redouble the search!'

The muscles on Magda's neck stood out like ropes. 'You'd better. Or you'll be sorry!'

She sent out a bolt of lightning at Volpo, Skank and Skism, who keeled over like playing cards and fell flat on their backs. Magda crunched across the broken glass and stood over them.

'If I don't get results soon,' she screeched, 'you know where you will be going!' She pointed at the bowels of the earth where an answering rumble made her servants quake with terror.

They were huddled around a small fire, cobbled together from lumps of coal left lying in the cavern, its crackling flames spreading a comforting glow over them. Nick had just finished telling his friends everything he'd seen up at the castle. Zak and Anneka were staring at him in shocked silence. The blood had drained from Anneka's face. She gazed blankly at the fire for a moment, then closed her eyes as if she could shut out the horrible images Nick had just conjured up.

'I don't believe it,' she whispered at last. 'I don't believe anybody could be that cruel. I thought she just hypnotized them.'

'No, it's a thousand times worse than that,' said Nick, swallowing hard. His throat had closed up, almost choking him, as he'd relived those moments. 'It's not a trance. They're not going to snap out of it. She takes their childhood away. That's why they come back from the parties behaving like little grown-ups. Maybe it's permanent. Maybe they'll never be children ever again.'

Zak shuddered, and Anneka gazed down at her sister, fast asleep on her lap. Louisa looked like a cherub; her breathing made her blond curls gently rise and fall. 'I would rather die than let her do that to Louisa,' Anneka said in a fierce whisper. 'I'm glad she came with us now.' She hugged the child close.

Zak, who had not said a word since Nick told them his story, began mumbling incantations as if to ward off evil spirits. He fumbled at his neck for his Tupilak and froze in panic when he found it gone. Nick took it out of his pocket and placed it carefully in Zak's hand. Zak pulled himself together.

'Aktuk! This is the demon I sensed up here. This is what Queen Magda looks like underneath. Her beauty is just an illusion, a mask. She's feeding on children like a parasite, using their youth to keep herself young and beautiful.'

Anneka and Nick nodded slowly, still trying to take in the enormity of it.

'Thanks for lending me your talisman, Zak,' said Nick. 'I needed to know you were still thinking of me. And it helped me realize the truth.'

Anneka was looking at Nick with a puzzled frown on her face. 'Hang on a minute! How come it didn't work on you? You're still normal. Our Nickolai.'

Nick shrugged. 'You think that hasn't crossed my mind already? The simple answer is, I don't know. Maybe it's because I'm an elf too. Or maybe something is protecting me.'

Elvina, who had been perched on Nick's shoulder preening her wings, gave an indignant squeak and began circling his head in a frenzy of irritation. But Nick didn't notice. He was remembering what it all meant for him.

'I wish I'd never been born,' he groaned, staring into the fire. It had cost him a lot to admit to himself that his friends had been right and he had been wrong. And even more to come to terms with the fact that he was an elf, like Magda. The thought that they came from the same race filled him with self-loathing. It was like a dream where you find you've been a dung beetle all your life. He would rather be dead than like the Queen.

Anneka put a comforting hand on Nick's shoulder. 'Hey! Don't talk like that.'

Nick shook her arm off and pulled his hood tightly over his ears. 'How can you bear to touch me? One of her kind? A race of vile, predatory monsters?'

'Don't talk blubberish!' snorted Zak. 'It's only her that's a monster. And all that stuff about the other elves is lies. They weren't evil. She just twists the truth round.'

But Nick couldn't stop the wave of despair that engulfed him. 'Now I'll never know who my real mother is, I'll never find my family and my people. Or my real home.' His shoulders slumped in defeat. 'I really hoped to find them here.'

Zak slapped the miserable Nick heartily on the back. 'Listen, chavuk, you've still got us. Now, are you going to stop feeling sorry for yourself and think about a survival plan? Or are you just going to keep moaning and groaning like a whale on a harpoon? You're not the only one with problems.'

Nick felt suddenly ashamed. Zak was right. He should be thinking about the others. He was suddenly filled with a new resolve. He sat up straight, a look of determination in his eyes.

'We have to save the other kids! I may not have been able to find my own family, but at least I can help other families.'

'That's a lovely thought, Nick, but how are we going to do it?' Anneka asked, ever practical.

'Tell everyone!' cried Nick earnestly, 'tell all the grown-ups! Warn them, stop them sending their kids to the parties.'

Zak snorted. 'Do you really think they'll listen to us? We're just kids, and you're public enemy number one.'

Nick was silenced for a moment.

'Why don't we just escape from here and go down south?' Zak continued. 'Alert everyone there?'

'You're joking!' said Anneka. 'I'm not leaving my parents! It's all right for you, yours aren't stuck here.'

Zak looked at Nick. 'There's nothing to keep *you* here, Nicku. Let's go down south and see what we can do.'

'Absolutely not!' Nick stormed, standing up and clenching his fists. 'There is no way I'm going to leave this place.'

'Face it, Nicku,' Zak said patiently, 'you're not going to find your family.'

'I might do,' Nick retorted. 'And anyway, that's not the point. I can't leave everyone in the lurch. I can't leave all these kids here, at the mercy of that –' he struggled for words – 'creature. I want to stay here and try to do something.'

Zak subsided into moody silence. They all sat for a while, staring gloomily into the fire, brooding over the hopelessness of the situation. Then Anneka squared her shoulders.

'Well, let's be practical. First things first. We're pretty safe hidden down here, for the time being, until we think of a plan. But we need to eat.'

Operation Elf Boy

The sunshine was so bright it was like a blow to the head. Nick blinked and adjusted his eyes. Then he let out a low whistle. Elvina had done it again, brought them out in a perfect spot for a foraging trip – an alleyway leading on to the marketplace. A tall, narrow strip of colour, noise and frenzied activity, like a moving stained-glass window, filled the far end of the alley. Nick elbowed his way out of the crack in the ground and rolled over to make room for Zak, who heaved himself out with a stream of Inuit curses.

'Great bears alive, Nicku! First you drag me along a load of tunnels, then you do some weird ground-shaking shaman thing that scares the life out of me, and then you make me climb a practically vertical shaft for hours on end! What d'you think I am?'

'Shhhh!' hissed Nick, his eyes flicking around for any sign of wolves. He twitched his ears and made the shaft close up with a scraping noise. Zak stared at the smooth surface where only seconds ago there had been a gaping hole.

'Flying fishbones! I wish I could do that!'

Nick winked at him.' 'S easy when you know how. I want Anneka and Louisa to be safe until we get back.'

He pulled his hood tight around his head and began loping along the alley, Zak prowling behind him. They reached the end and peered around the corner, staying out of sight.

The din of the market blasted their senses. The colours were aggressively bright and the shouts of the traders clashed in the air. The market stalls stretched along both sides of the narrow streets. Zak grabbed his arm and pointed.

'Look! Just what we need!'

Right in front of them was a fancy dress stall, displaying all kinds of flamboyant outfits: garish masks and carnival costumes, high fashion ladies' gowns with glittery decorations, courtiers' costumes with flowing capes and wide-brimmed hats stuck with jaunty feathers, jesters' outfits with pointy caps and curly-toed shoes, all in the brightest possible colours. They winked at each other and scuttled unseen under the stall.

Ten minutes later, two festive-looking masked jesters, one shorter than the other, began working their way down the market, mingling perfectly with the crowds.

The stalls stretched endlessly up and down the street, piled high with a mind-boggling display of merchandise: bright silks, satins, lace, ribbons and braiding; flashy paste earrings like clock pendulums and necklaces that could weigh down a carthorse; stalls full of garish paintings, gilt mirrors, gaudy goblets, vulgar vases, lurid lampshades and fake crystal chandeliers. There were no toys anywhere, except for a stall which sold official Queen Magda dolls, along with flags, commemorative plates, ceremonial goblets, mugs, posters, statuettes – all adorned with her image. In a place where childhood didn't exist, there was no need for toys and dolls.

A nearby gold Magda statue erupted into a proclamation.

'Red alert! Keep your eyes and ears open for the Evil Elf Boy,' Magda's voice rasped through the air. 'He is extremely dangerous. If you see a boy aged about twelve or thirteen with pointed ears, in a red cloak, do not, repeat *not*, attempt to go near him, and call the nearest goblin guard immediately. This boy is extremely dangerous. Three further children have disappeared from Compound Eleven. We have reason to believe they are in league with the Evil Elf Boy. These children are a danger to the state and are undermining our glorious realm. There is a reward of ten thousand gold maggots for anyone who can give us information leading to their arrest. I thank you in advance for your cooperation, my loyal subjects.'

The announcement finished clunkily. A sense of outrage at the gross injustice of it slammed into Nick, swiftly followed by a mounting panic. He was a wanted criminal. A hunted boy. From now on, disguises would be essential every time they came up to the surface.

He felt Zak plucking urgently at his sleeve. A poster was being slapped on to a wall by a goblin. There, staring back at them, were their own crudely sketched faces. The headline underneath screamed at them like a siren.

THE EVIL ELF BOY AND HIS ACCOMPLICES

And underneath, another headline:

10,000 GOLD MAGGOTS REWARD

'Who'd have thought,' muttered two women as they passed by. 'Little children like that, so evil. What is the world coming to?'

Nick had to restrain himself from shaking the truth into them. As they made their way towards the food stalls, appetizing aromas drifted across the steamy air. Saliva poured into Nick's mouth as he remembered how hungry he was. The stalls were groaning with delicious-looking food: pies and fruit, chickens and game hanging upside down from hooks, loaves piled high and mountains of cheeses. The two boys scuttled under a stall and made their way along the tunnels underneath the tables, swiping things surreptitiously when no one was looking.

They were just counting up their loot – two chickens, a slab of cheese, a haul of apples and some small logs – when a familiar bawling voice rang out across the marketplace.

'Come on, you lucky people! Chop chop! This way! No straggling please!'

They peered out from under the stall. Skank and Skism were leading an intake of immigrants through the market. The new arrivals looked weary, but their faces were full of hope and excitement. The children straggled along, eyes as wide as saucers. A jester cavorted up to them with a shriek of demented laughter and began juggling some coloured balls, making the children gasp. Then he bent down and snubbed one of them on the nose.

'What d'you think of that, then? I'll show you more tricks if you like! Come up to the next children's welcome party at the castle. Queen Magda wants to meet all you lovely kids! Loads of food, loads of fun! Six p.m. tomorrow night! See you there!'

'Oh come on! Do you really think we're going to be able to kidnap children from a procession in broad daylight and get away with it?' asked Anneka, through a mouthful of bread and cheese.

'With a goblin escort?' added Zak.

'It won't be daylight. It'll be evening,' Nick said shortly.

'Still light though.'

They were back in the cavern sharing the food around the fire, now blazing with logs stolen from the market.

'Well I still want to go to a party,' said Louisa

defiantly. 'You can swap me for one of the other children.'

'Certainly not,' snapped Anneka. 'She'd turn you into an awful little grown-up and you wouldn't have any more fun.'

Louisa glared back at her in mutiny. Nick stood up and wandered around, gnawing at his chicken leg, staring moodily at the stalagmites. He had to get his friends to understand this idea that had been slowly forming in his mind. A big idea, so ambitious he hardly dared think about it.

'It's risky, Nicku. We could get captured.'

Nick threw his chicken bone impatiently on the ground. 'We have to take that risk. I can't let it happen to them. Would you have liked it if I'd let it happen to you?'

Anneka looked away and Zak suddenly became very interested in the leather thongs round his sealskin boots.

'No, of course not,' mumbled Anneka.

'So. We have to try and save them. 'Cos if we don't . . .' Nick fixed them with a steely look. 'Childhood will become a thing of the past. We'll be the only kids left in the world. We'll be stuck down here for ever and starve to death. Do you want that?'

Zak and Anneka slowly shook their heads.

Nick clapped his hands triumphantly. 'Right then! Operation Elf Boy starts tomorrow. At sunset!'

★   ★   ★

Nick and Zak, dressed in their jester outfits, lurked at the entrance to an alleyway just off the main avenue leading to the castle. The street basked peacefully in the evening sun and not many people were about.

They didn't have to wait long for the evening procession to pass by. The sound of shuffling feet approached and a familiar raucous voice rang through the air.

'Come on, you 'orrible little brats! Chop chop! The Queen is waiting.'

Nick and Zak shrank out of sight as Skank and Skism rounded the corner at the head of a group of children of all ages. Clowns and jesters tumbled along beside them, encouraging them to hurry. Nick waited until the back end of the procession was trailing past, then tensed himself in readiness, his heart thumping against his ribs.

'Now!' he whispered.

They sidled out of the alleyway and began prancing around the children. Zak did a few somersaults and backflips and Nick juggled some lumps of coal, letting out the occasional whoop. The children stopped and stared, letting a gap open up as the front end of the procession wound around the curve of the avenue ahead.

'This way! You're getting left behind!' Nick ushered the slightly baffled children into the alleyway. Anneka and Louisa stood waving and beaming beside the crack in the ground.

'Come on! This is a short cut!' called Anneka encouragingly.

'Party!' squealed Louisa.

Nick and Zak cavorted down the alleyway, beckoning the children on. They dithered like sheep.

'Are you sure this is the right way?' asked a sturdy boy of about seven with tousled blond hair.

'Yes, come on! You'll miss it!'

Nick and Zak tumbled and rolled, leading the children on until they were sure this tail-end of the procession had all come off the avenue. There were about twelve of them in all. Then Nick stiffened as he heard goblin shouts. The children had been found missing!

'Now!' he hissed. He and Zak uncoiled like springs, leaped on the children and bundled them into the gaping hole. Their cries of protest were swallowed up as they plummeted into the darkness, powerless to stop themselves on the slippery sides of the chute.

Nick heaved a sigh of exasperation and looked at the group of children huddled round the fire, eyeing him warily. His ears twitched in irritation and he felt his temper rising. Why wouldn't they listen to him? Why did they not believe him when he told them what was happening at the castle? Didn't they realize he had done them all a big favour?

The seven-year-old boy with the blond hair was glowering at Nick. 'I don't believe you!' he said flatly.

'My mum says Queen Magda is good and kind and loves children. She would never do anything like that.'

'Aktuk! Your mum is a gullible grown-up,' Zak retorted. 'She's swallowed all that blubberish like a codfish taking the bait.'

'And you're dangerous criminals!' said a princessy girl of about ten, who had 'Know-all' written all over her. 'We've seen the posters. You're that Evil Elf Boy, an enemy of the state. Your ancestors tried to overthrow the Queen in the old days. You're from a bad lot! We're going to tell on you! Soon as we get out!'

Nick made a superhuman effort to control his temper. 'That is a load of old rubbish. You're stupid if you believe it. She's the one who's evil. And there's no way you can get out,' he added coldly. 'I'm the only one who can make escape routes up to the surface. If you try and run away you'll just get lost in the tunnels. And you'll die of starvation and cold.'

The children fell silent at this. Nick watched their faces, giving them time for the information to sink in.

'Well, I think he's right,' piped up a girl of about eleven, with an open, honest face. 'We shouldn't just swallow everything we're told. Haven't you noticed how different the kids are here? The ones who've been up to the castle? They don't know how to play!'

The other children thought about this. Nick felt a little surge of hope.

'And I'm glad I got rescued,' the girl continued

stoutly, 'because I don't want to turn out like them. They're no fun.'

Anneka, Nick and Zak smiled at her in gratitude. At last an ally.

'What do you want with us?' the princessy girl asked suspiciously.

'We want you to join us,' said Nick simply.

'But I want to go back to my parents!' wailed a frail-looking girl who'd been snivelling quietly ever since she'd arrived.

'You'll be reunited with them when we've sorted out this mess. But first we need your help.'

'Help with what?' said the blond boy.

Nick took a deep breath and launched into explaining his grand plan, striding around the cavern and waving his arms about. When he'd finished, he looked at them all in triumph.

The kidnapped children were staring at him as though he were a madman.

'You'll never do it,' the princessy girl snorted. 'What with all those goblins and wolves and statues about. And anyway, it's all wrong!'

Anneka leaped to Nick's rescue. 'Well, I think it's a brilliant plan. And it might even be fun!'

'You call that fun?' The princessy girl looked aghast. 'It sounds downright dangerous! Mission impossible.'

Suddenly Nick felt something squirming around in the region of his chest. Elvina flew out of his clothes in a flurry of protest, fluffing her wings. In the gloom of the labyrinth, she seemed to glow more brightly than ever. She did a lap round the children, squeaking at them angrily as though she was trying to talk some sense into them. Nick allowed himself a smug smile as their jaws dropped open. They watched the glowing shape in astonishment as Elvina swooped and dived playfully around their heads.

'What's that?' one of the children gasped.

'That,' said Nick, trying very hard to keep the triumphant note out of his voice, 'is a fairy. A real one. And when you've got her on your side, anything seems possible.'

The throng fell back to make way for Magda as she swept magnificently into the ballroom. In the riot of colour she was the most splendid of all, in a royal blue satin gown trimmed with gold brocade. The tight bodice, sewn with thousands of seed pearls, emphasized her tiny waist. The skilfully draped folds of the skirt gave her an exaggerated hourglass shape. The puffed sleeves, slashed to show red silk underneath, showed off her ivory arms to perfection. On her head was a tall, golden crown studded with glittering jewels, and beneath it, her long lustrous black hair flowed around her shoulders.

A hush fell over the courtiers as Magda inclined her head graciously and glided through them. There was a rippling movement as the men bowed low and the women swept deep curtseys. Hands reached out to touch the hem of her skirts as she passed. The minstrels on the balcony struck up a tune and a beak-faced balladeer began to sing a sonnet in praise of her beauty. Her eyes were like stars, apparently; her hair a river of dark fire, her skin like purest alabaster (he'd had some trouble finding a word to rhyme with that), and so on and so forth.

Volpo padded along behind Magda like a faithful dog as she made her stately progress towards the throne. His dark eyes roved over the crowd and his cloak billowed around him like a black cloud. Magda swept on to the raised platform in one fluid movement and settled herself on her throne in a rustle of silks. The courtiers began to form a queue to pay her homage. Madga sighed in deep satisfaction as she held out her hand to be kissed. It was always so gratifying to hold these soirees after the children's parties. She felt so alive and her beauty seemed to shine more brightly than ever.

As the courtiers approached her and knelt humbly at her feet, Magda noticed, with a twinge of alarm, a slight hesitation amongst some of them. People were looking at her with mildly puzzled expressions as they drew near. There was the tiniest flinching movement as they bent to kiss her hand, a flicker of surprise in their eyes as they gazed into her face. She sensed a tremor of unease at her side and shot a glance at Volpo, who was skulking by the throne. As her eyes met his, he plucked at his robe and twitched nervously.

She stood up abruptly.

The music broke off. The young balladeer's reedy voice faltered, then trailed away. Everyone stared. Without a word, Magda swept out of the room, followed by Volpo.

'The Queen is unwell,' he told the assembly hurriedly, before limping off behind her as she swept through the doors and stormed along the corridors; the pain in his body always got worse when she was angry.

'Majesty!' he called softly. 'Do not be alarmed. I'm sure it is only temporary.' He stopped to peer anxiously at one of her portraits and stifled a whine of alarm.

Inside the luxurious bedchamber, Magda flung herself down at her dressing table. She snatched up a hand mirror and a flaming candlestick and studied her reflection. Her face froze.

Was it a trick of the light? Or were there tiny lines around her eyes? Was the skin of her face drooping ever so slightly? Was that the smallest hint of the beginnings of *jowls*? Were those rings appearing on her neck? And was that – horrors – a grey hair, nestled in amongst her dark lustrous locks?

Lurking behind her, Volpo jumped as she let out a piercing shriek. There was a loud smash and a tinkling of glass as she hurled the mirror on the floor and whirled on him, her eyes blazing. A paralysing trail of pain seared up and down his spine, making him go rigid; his hands pawed helplessly at the air in front of him and his steel talons shot out with a metallic hiss, in a reflex reaction he couldn't control.

'What is the meaning of this?' Magda whispered, pointing at her face.

Volpo stammered the first thing that came into his head. 'Why, Majesty, they are only laughter lines!'

'I'm not laughing,' she said through gritted teeth.

'You, you look enchanting as always. And your face has – more character?'

'Damn character! I do not want character!' Magda bawled. 'I want perfection! I'm supposed to be eternally young! Immortal! What's going on?'

Volpo's eyes slid around in their sockets as though they were trying to escape. 'There was less than the usual quota of children at the last party, Majesty,' he finally admitted. 'Erm, it appears some of them disappeared on the way. You need at least thirty for the full rejuvenating effect.'

The crippling pain in Volpo's spine increased, bringing him to the floor in a crumpled heap. Magda smiled pleasantly and spoke in a friendly voice that made his blood run cold.

'The Vortex beckons, Uncle Volpo. Unless you remedy this situation – fast.'

Ministry of Fun

'Are you sure we're doing the right thing?' whispered Anneka.

Nick looked over at the gloomy huddle round the fire. There were now over twenty children, all captured from the new intakes as they passed through the market, or on the way to the Queen's parties. He sighed. It wasn't easy convincing children who had just arrived in a strange new place, only to be kidnapped and wrenched away from their parents, that this was the best thing for them. Louisa's games of tag around the rock formations, chasing Elvina as she flitted teasingly out of their grasp, had cheered them up for a while, but the novelty soon wore off. They drooped about, barely eating the food offered them, eyeing their hosts with mistrust.

'What they need is toys to play with,' Nick decided. 'And proper games. Something to keep them occupied, take their minds off things.'

But doubts were beginning to crowd into Nick's mind. Was he really doing the right thing, taking children away from their parents? Surely yes, if he was saving them from a fate worse than death. And this was the only weapon they had. If they wavered now, the whole plan would fall apart.

The market raids continued. Zak and Nick made daily forays to the surface in a variety of disguises, from lavish courtiers' costumes to labourers' overalls. They collected food, fuel and blankets, materials for making toys – and more children.

The hunt for the Evil Elf Boy was stepped up and the headlines on the posters screamed louder than ever. The reward for information leading to his arrest climbed higher and higher. More pictures of kidnapped children appeared every day. An atmosphere of fear hung over the city and a persistent wailing started up in the compounds as mothers lamented their missing children.

One day in the market, another of Magda's proclamations boomed out through the air.

'I have very sad news for you, my people,' she began, against a background of whining violins. 'It is with great regret that I have to tell you that, due to urgent matters of state, I am unable to make any public appearances at this time. The scourge of the Evil Elf Boy has brought terrible times upon us. Rest assured, we are doing all we can. Once this evil has been stamped out, I will of course resume my daily processions, which I am sure you must all miss sorely. Goodbye for now, my loyal subjects.'

The market erupted into a buzz of speculation.

Nick grabbed Zak's arm. 'D'you see what this means? Our plan is working! She doesn't have so many victims now. The effects must be starting to show! Her beauty is fading and she's beginning to look like the monster underneath. She can't come out!'

But Nick's triumph was shortlived. A few minutes later there was a commotion at the other end of the marketplace. The great golden gates swung open and a stream of goblin soldiers poured through, pulling a convoy of large, barred wagons. At first Nick thought they contained livestock. He expected to see horned heads and hear the bleating of goats and the clucking of chickens. Then he gasped in shock.

A forest of human arms poked out from the bars. New immigrant families were crammed into the travelling cages like animals, crying out and shouting in protest. As the ghastly convoy passed by, the bewildered faces of small children stared back at Nick; for a split second, his eyes met those of a small girl the same age as Louisa. The expression on her face made him want to leap forward and drag her through the bars.

At the head of the procession marched Skank and Skism. Skank looked grim and his face was set in a scowl. Skism wore an uncertain frown.

'Make way for the new intake!' bawled Skank at the crowds as they fell back to let the wagons pass.

'No need for alarm,' said Skism apologetically to the

crowds. 'Security measure. Protectin' new intake children from Evil Elf Boy!'

Skank pressed his ugly snout up close against Skism's identical nose. 'Shurrup, you moron! We do not, repeat *not*, need to s'plain nuffink to no one.'

'Do you need any more proof than that?' Nick declared with grim triumph. He was standing on one of the rectangular blocks in the cavern, his red robe tied around him with different coloured thongs and a jaunty red bandana on his head. There were now over fifty children in the underground colony, ranging in age from three to thirteen. They sat in a crowd round the fire listening to Nick's description of the caged wagons, a bunch of scruffy urchins wearing a variety of bandanas, their grubby faces smeared with tribal markings. The most recent arrivals sat at the front, looking white-faced and bewildered.

'That's how desperate she's getting!' Nick continued. 'Capturing travellers from outside the City gates and dragging them in by force, so she can keep up her supply of victims. She'll stop at nothing to keep herself young and beautiful.'

The newer recruits began to whisper amongst themselves. They were beginning to look as though they believed him. Encouraged, Nick went on.

'So. That means we can't rescue any more children before they go up to the castle and get turned into little adults by that monster.' The ragged bunch of urchins gave a collective shudder. 'You all had a lucky escape. But it's not too late for the others either. I want to give them their childhood back. The childhood she stole.'

The children stared at him in puzzlement. 'How are you going to do that?' piped a girl with freckles.

Nick jumped down from the rock, winking at Zak and Anneka, and began striding around the cavern. 'We're going to teach them how to be children again. We're going to turn this dismal place into an underground play centre, where kids can come and be themselves. And you lot are going to help me do it!'

The first 'refugees' stood before Nick and his gang in the central cavern, eyeing him suspiciously. It had been relatively easy to kidnap them from the Daycare procession. In their stolen goblin guard disguises, Zak and Nick had looked convincing enough. They took the children on a detour, then pushed them down a shaft in the ground.

When the children realized what had happened, they were outraged. The hostile look in their eyes was quite different from the bewildered look of the kids who'd been kidnapped before falling prey to Magda. Their arms were folded across their chests, and they glared at Nick with challenging eyes, as though they were adults and he a naughty child.

'This is disgraceful!' spluttered one of the children.

'You will be punished. Take us back immediately and stop this foolish nonsense!'

The boy who spoke was about ten. Nick realized with a shock that it was Johan.

'Hey, Johan!' he exclaimed, his eyes alight. 'It's me, Nickolai!' He had to restrain himself from running over and throwing his arms round him.

Johan just gave him a blank stare, without a flicker of recognition. 'All I know is that you're the Evil Elf Boy, enemy of the state. I suggest you do as we say!'

'Oh, Johan!' wailed Louisa. 'Don't you know us?'

'It's no good, Louisa,' said Anneka sadly, putting an arm round her sister. 'He's beyond our reach.'

Nick had a sour taste in his mouth. This was not going to be easy. He turned to the colony children, ranged behind him. '*Now* do you see what I mean?' he said bitterly. 'That's what we saved you from.' They stared back at him in silent understanding.

'Why don't you stop all this nonsense, young man, and return us to our compounds?' said a wispy girl of about seven.

The words were chilling on the lips of someone so young. Louisa strode up to the girl and poked her on the shoulder. 'What's wrong with you?' she demanded. 'You sound stupid talking like that. Act your age, you stuck-up snooty-face.'

The girl glared at Louisa with withering scorn. 'I will not even honour that with a reply.'

Anneka whispered in Nick's ear. 'Time to put your plan into action.'

Nick strode over to a huge curtain which had been draped from ceiling to floor, concealing most of the cavern. 'Right, it's time you learned to be children again,' he said. 'Welcome to the Ministry of Fun!' And with a flourish he ripped away the curtain to reveal what lay behind.

The cavern had been turned into toy heaven. It was a wonderland decked out with playthings of every description. Every possible toy, game, amusement and diversion was there, all laid out in a fantastic display; the whole scene was lit by candles and lanterns and all the rock formations were draped with brightly coloured cloth and decorations made from scraps.

Nick looked at his collection with immense pride. Over the last few weeks the underground cavern had been awash with activity; they had assembled a vast collection of scraps and odds and ends from the marketplace and created some quite extraordinary things out of very ordinary objects.

'So? What are we supposed to do?' asked the seven-year-old girl, shrugging indifferently.

'They're toys,' Nick said patiently. 'We want you to play with them.'

'Don't be ridiculous,' snorted Johan dismissively. 'We've all grown out of that sort of thing.'

'Yes, it's very childish,' said the seven-year-old.

The children continued to gaze blankly at the huge

selection of toys as though they were nothing more than lumps of clay. Nick gulped in disappointment. After all their hard work over the weeks, it was like being slapped in the face.

Anneka nodded at the colony children. They moved forward and led the new arrivals over to the toys, picking them up and showing them how they worked. But the newly rescued children just stared with glazed eyes, bored and unimpressed.

Nick slumped down on the floor with his head in his hands. Elvina was quivering under his tunic. Maybe she could sense his sadness. He had felt so sure he could help these children reclaim their childhood.

'Aktuk, they're like a bunch of dead codfish,' muttered Zak.

'It's no good,' said Anneka bleakly. 'I think they've lost it – permanently. I was afraid of this.'

But suddenly, Elvina buzzed out of the front of Nick's tunic. With a loud squeak of triumph, she divebombed towards the toys and began to flit amongst them, touching all of them in turn. She was glowing so brightly she looked as though she would explode with the energy that was coursing through her.

As she touched the toys they twitched and jumped – and came alive. The model houses lit up from within and tiny fires began to glow in their grates. The people inside began to move around, going about their miniature domestic tasks, stoking fires and preparing food. Spirals of smoke began to chug out of their

*As she touched the toys they twitched and
jumped – and came alive.*

chimneys. The tiny model husky dogs began to bark and bay and pull the sleighs along, trotting around in circles and weaving in and out of each other, whipped on by their minute drivers. The carousels began to play tinkly music and whirl around. The toy soldiers began to march up and down in formation, their feet pattering on the ice floor, the sergeant major at their head bawling out orders in a tinny little voice.

The Light Fairy dolls, all based on Elvina, began to glow and buzz and squeak, flapping their gossamer wings, rising into the air and whizzing around in crazy loops. The dolls twitched into life and began to move their arms and legs. Then they stood up and began to walk daintily around on the icy floor, talking in tiny babbling voices.

But the most breathtaking turn of all was the reindeer. Nick had spent the most time and care in making them, an exact replica of his friends in the forest. They shook their carved antlers, pawed the ground with their miniature hooves, cantered forward and rose steadily into the air. They flew around the cavern in graceful formation and circled above the heads of the astonished children. Then they roared past Nick's nose, as if to remind him of his days in the forest.

As the cavern filled with animated toys, the effect on the new arrivals was earthshattering. All of them sat motionless, gawping at the fantastical display, their mouths open and their eyes nearly popping out of their heads. And slowly, very slowly, the faces of the children they had rescued came back to life, like people waking from a coma.

Nick looked hopefully over at Johan. He was blinking and shaking his head as if he had water in his ears. He caught sight of Nick and his face lit up.

'Hey, Nick! What's been going on? Where are we?'

Years later, the children would remember those days and nights in the glittering cavern as the best time of their lives. Every night Elvina would put on her spectacular display, and every day the children helped Nick make more extraordinary and inventive things so they could watch Elvina bring them alive.

The turbo-powered steam engine was born, with a funnel that puffed out smoke. A menagerie of Arctic animals roamed across a miniature ice floe that took off and flew around the cavern. A fir tree came to life and grew in front of their eyes, then began to sparkle with decorations that suddenly appeared on its branches. A galaxy of planets spun round in their orbits, comets and meteors shooting across their paths.

They made a scale model of Doransk, which came alive and began to throng with tiny people. Mini Magda statues boomed out ridiculous proclamations against the great Queen and armies of goblins marched around, a miniature two-headed Skank and Skism at their head, bawling out conflicting orders that brought about terrible disarray.

Every night Elvina devised some new trick or display to delight everyone and reduce them to helpless giggles. During the day there were toboggan races, games of tag and hide and seek, and endless other amusements. There were everyday duties that kept the colony ticking over as well: the catering corps, the fire-making corps, the night watch and the day watch; the market corps, who went up to the surface with Zak and Nick on daily raids to gather provisions; and most importantly, the elite corps, who went to rescue the children whose childhoods had been stolen away.

Before long the colony population was bulging. The tunnels echoed day and night with laughter. Nick's vision, the Ministry of Fun, had become a reality, the most fantastic underground hideout any child could possibly imagine.

But there was still something missing for Nick.

One night, after dinner, he told the whole colony that he had an announcement to make. He stood on top of one of the rectangular blocks and gazed around at his ragamuffin tribe of urchins.

'I want to rescue Finn.'

Cracks

A gasp of astonishment echoed round the cavern, and Anneka nearly choked on her chicken bone. According to the reports from the rescued children, Finn was now Head of Youth Intelligence for all the compounds. His uniform was weighed down with even more badges and medals, and he had his own goblin guard, a small private army with whom he strutted around the compounds day and night, stamping, saluting and bellowing out orders.

'What do you want to rescue him for?' Anneka said in disgust.

Nick felt a prickle of annoyance. 'Because he's the top dog, of course. He controls all the children. If we can get him and convert him, we can use him to rescue the rest of them.'

'Are you sure it's not because you want to prove to yourself you can win him over?' Anneka looked at Nick with searching blue eyes. 'Show everyone how strong and persuasive you are?'

Nick brushed aside this uncomfortable thought.

'No, of course not!' he protested. 'I'm thinking of everyone here. Can't you see what a logical idea it is?'

Zak shook his head. 'How are we going to pull it off, Nicku? He's surrounded by his own goblins now.'

'Not at night, he's not,' said Johan, who always came down on Nick's side. 'Him and that snobby mum and dad of his finally moved out to the Orion Quarter. He goes home at the end of the day to his posh new house and the goblins go back to their quarters at Goblin High Command.'

'See?' said Nick triumphantly. 'Easy peasy!'

Anneka still looked worried. 'It's a mad idea, Nick,' she said. 'It's far too risky. And I've never trusted him. Why not just concentrate on the kids we've got?'

'No,' said Nick doggedly. 'We still have our mission. I want to rescue every single child in this City. Because then, and only then, can we get the adults on our side and rise up against Magda together.'

Through the gauzy black veil Magda was now forced to wear, she saw with satisfaction that Volpo could hardly stand. She began drumming her gnarled fingers impatiently on the carved gold armrest of her throne, her eyes sweeping the stateroom, ready and waiting for her next batch of young guests.

There was a babble of voices outside in the corridor and a pathetically small collection of children was shown into the room by Skank and Skism. There were only about half a dozen of them.

'Is that all?' Magda demanded, as they straggled forward.

Skank's piggy red eyes blinked evasively. 'It's all we could get, Majesty.'

'There ain't so many emigrants coming into the city now,' said Skism helpfully. 'They've 'eard all the rumours about the kidnappin's. Goin' back 'ome before we can get 'em into the wagons, scarperin' like there's no tomorrer . . .'

He faltered and trailed away. Magda made a superhuman effort to control her rage as Volpo limped forward painfully.

'It will have to do,' Volpo muttered through clenched teeth. 'We will be remedying the situation soon. Won't we, Majesty?'

She gave him a thin smile that froze the blood in his veins. 'I certainly hope so, Volpo, for your sake.' She turned to the children and put on a silky voice. 'Hello, children! My darling little new subjects! Welcome to my palace. Come in, come in!'

They stood in a huddle, reluctant to come forward, eyeing her nervously. The figure veiled in black wasn't at all what they expected. Where was the beautiful Queen they had heard about?

'Don't be afraid,' she wheedled. 'And cheer up! You're here to have a good time. Look at all this lovely food!' She waved a frail arm at the lavish feast laid out on the tables. It glistened at them, garish and gooey. 'And you're going to have lots of party games!' She clapped her hands and trilled in a voice of false gaiety, 'Spackle! Skreech! Thrang! Klax! Devo! Flitch! Snark! Come and entertain my guests.'

There was a drumroll and a fanfare; the doors burst open and the clowns and jesters tumbled into the room.

The City lay drowsing in the artificial evening sun. A golden haze hovered over the gleaming spires. The park was beautiful, fronted by an elegant crescent of gilded houses; one or two smartly dressed people strolled across the lurid green lawns, dotted with trees bearing extravagant, heavy blossoms, and laid out with flowerbeds containing exotic plants. The blooms nodded their huge heads and lazily scanned the gardens. Peacocks strutted around, pecking idly at the ground, occasionally stopping to preen their magnificent plumage.

Nick wondered uneasily if this was all part of the surveillance system. A splendid Magda statue stood in the middle of the park, surrounded by sparkling fountains. Its head rotated slowly, turning a full three hundred and sixty degrees. It was now covered in a gauzy black veil which swished in the air as it moved.

'Look at that!' Zak whispered to Nick. 'Even the statues are veiled. She must be in a bad way.'

Nick and Zak hauled themselves out of the crack, hidden under the cover of a clump of trees near the gates, and waited for the statue's head to turn the other way. Then they stood up and smoothed down their lavish outfits. Tonight, they were dressed as courtiers going to a masked ball. Nick was wearing a green velvet doublet and cloak, and a huge cavalier-style hat with a massive red feather. Zak was in blue velvet and a wide brimmed black hat that hid his face. They were both wearing glittery masks.

'Well, here we are. The Orion Quarter. I think that's his house over there. Number eighteen.' Nick pointed to a grand, gilded house just opposite the park gates, whose windows glinted in the evening light. 'Finn should be coming home soon.'

They sauntered casually over to the gates, looking around in the vague manner of people who are lost. They loitered and watched and waited, waving their arms languidly and bowing to passers-by.

Soon they heard approaching feet, and Finn strutted round the corner, surrounded by his goblin guard. His chest glittered with badges and his head was held high. They marched up to the grand steps of Finn's house, where there was some stamping, saluting and garbled shouting before the goblins spun clumsily on their heels and marched off, relieved of their duties for the day. Finn turned to go into his house.

Nick and Zak strolled through the gates across the street, acting the noble courtiers. 'Hey there, young man!' called Nick, in the deepest voice he could muster.

They both swept an elaborate bow to Finn, making curly hand movements.

'Sorry to trouble you, young sir,' drawled Nick in a lazy, aristocratic voice. 'Lord Nickinsky here. And this is my fellow courtier, Lord Zakinskov.'

Finn straightened up and saluted them smartly. 'Good evening, gentlemen. It is always a pleasure to meet the closest consorts of our wonderful monarch. Hail Queen Magda, O Great and Glorious One!'

'Hail Queen Magda, O Great and Glorious One!' echoed Nick and Zak.

'And what a fabulous monarch she is!' added Nick for good measure. 'We're new up at the court. Can you tell us the way back to the castle? We're due at a masked ball at seven o'clock, but we seem to have lost our way. You look like a sensible young man who knows his way around.'

'Of course, gentlemen,' Finn said, puffing up his chest importantly and pointing down the street. 'If you go down there and turn left—'

But he was cut off as Zak shoved a large sack over his head and trussed it up with ropes. The two of them started dragging the sack across the street and through the gates of the park. Finn was kicking and screaming like a pack of wild ferrets. 'Let me out of here! I order you to let me go! I am Head of Youth Intelligence!'

Between them, they dragged the heaving, squalling sack into the cover of the trees by the gates. At once, the surveillance system was alerted. The statue's head started swivelling, the flowers began to bob around crazily and the peacocks came scurrying across the grass towards them.

'Get us out of here!' Zak hissed as he tried to keep the sack under control. It was thrashing around violently, and Finn was swearing horribly. Nick screwed all his concentration together and twitched his ears in desperation. The ground stayed stubbornly shut. *Obey me!* he screamed silently, as he heard tearing noises coming from the sack and muffled shouts of rage from within.

There was a low rumble and the smooth green grass opened up neatly. They tumbled into it, sack and all, and hurtled downwards into the blackness. When the peacocks got to the clump of trees, all they found was an empty patch of ground.

'You'll never get away with this!' Finn stormed. He tapped his badges importantly. 'Do you know who I am? I am Head of Youth Intelligence! As soon I get out I will report you directly to Queen Magda and—'

Nick interrupted him with a loud roar of laughter. 'Not likely! You're trapped. There is no way you can get out.'

'So what?' retorted Finn. 'They will come and find me when they realize I'm missing.'

'Think you're that important to her, do you?' Anneka snorted. She was eyeing Finn with intense dislike. 'If you do you're a total twerp.'

'You will regret speaking to the Head of Youth Intelligence with such disrespect,' said Finn severely. 'Of course they will miss me. And you will all be brought to justice, and punished for daring to challenge the Great and Glorious One!'

A long, mocking chorus went round the children. 'Eeeeeeyooooouuuuuuu!'

Then they all burst into fits of giggles. Finn glared at them with impotent fury. Despite himself, Nick felt just a little bit sorry for him.

Finn's cold blue eyes swept round the scruffy bunch of urchins, with their grimy, painted faces, their bandanas and their tattered clothes. Then he gave them a look of pure contempt.

'Look at you all. A bunch of no-hopers! You and your parents will never amount to anything. But us – well – we are already established in the Orion Quarter. Invited to all the best parties. And my father has a place assured at court! That's what happens to people who work hard and abide by the rules.'

Zak snorted dismissively. 'Codcakes! Do you really think all that snooty stuff impresses us?'

'That's just the sort of rubbish I'd expect from a piece of Inuit scum like you,' Finn hissed. 'What do you lot know about making your way in the world? You Inuits are good-for-nothing layabouts who just loaf about all day digging holes in the ice.'

Zak hurled himself at Finn like a cannonball, his hands clamped around Finn's throat. The two of them rolled over and over on the ice floor, a bundle of flying fists and strangled yelps. Nick rushed over and wrenched them apart.

'Stop it, you two!' he cried angrily. 'Don't you dare insult my comrade like that, Finn. You're one of us now and you'd better get used to it. And now – I want to show you something. Something that's beyond your tiny little mind. 'Cos you don't realize what's happened to you, Finn. You're a stranger.'

Nick tapped his front and Elvina flew out with an indignant squeak. Finn stared at her, his face showing dim recognition. 'I remember her!' he said suddenly. 'Buzzy, insect thing . . . somewhere . . . else . . . before we came here.' He trailed off vaguely, as old memories began to stir.

Nick felt a surge of hope. Maybe there was a chance Finn could be reclaimed after all. They all watched as Elvina did her usual star turn, flitting around the toys. One by one the toys began to come to life, springing into action, until the cavern was a riot of noise and movement.

Nick held his breath, hoping against hope that Elvina's magic would work. Finn looked at the toys warily, mistrustful of his own eyes at first. Then, as the reindeer and the fairies began to whizz around him, a new light crept slowly into his eyes. His face came alive and a smile of wonder began to spread across his face. He turned his head and looked at Nick and Anneka as though he was seeing them again for the first time since they had last met in Norsk. A surge of relief and elation washed over Nick.

'Nick?' Finn said. 'Anneka? Where the heck have you been? I've missed you!'

Magda was in deep trouble. Her beauty problems were getting beyond serious. She sat in front of her mirror, watching in helpless horror as wiry grey hairs pushed their way out of her head, so fast you could hear them rustling. Her hands were curling into claws before her very eyes. She could not even bear to look at her face.

Volpo stood hunched behind her. Magda's eyes met his in the mirror and for the first time, he saw her fear.

'Help me, Volpo,' she whispered in a dry, crackly voice, like a snake slithering through grass.

A heady feeling of power crept over Volpo. He had made Magda everything she was today. He had masterminded the whole scheme in every detail; their far-ranging plans for the future had all been his brainchild. And yet she had punished him mercilessly every time something went wrong, to the point where he could hardly walk. Now his pain was subsiding, as her fear mounted.

He straightened up. 'We have done everything we can to find the missing children, Majesty,' he said smoothly, 'but so far the elfin brat has outwitted us. However, do not fear. I have a very cunning plan in place. It will flush him out of hiding.'

Magda's black eyes lit up and glowed in their wrinkled sockets. 'Tell me!' she hissed.

Volpo held up a finger. 'Not yet. You must trust me on this. But rest assured, we will find him and make a public example of him. We shall broadcast to the world that he has been caught, and on Winter Solstice Eve, as already planned, he shall be publicly executed and you will take control of the Fairy. All the world will believe that the danger from the Evil Elf Boy is over and they will come pouring back to the City in their droves. With their children, of course.'

Magda quivered with relief and closed her eyes.

'Then we will be able to restore your beauty. And you will go on to expand your empire as planned.' Volpo's lips pulled back to show his pointed teeth. It was meant to be a reassuring smile, but it came out as a ghastly grimace. 'Also, Majesty,' he continued in a silky voice, 'there is another piece of the jigsaw that I have long been turning over in my mind. It could increase your powers beyond your wildest dreams.'

Magda trembled violently at the thought, her loose skin wobbling. 'Oh yes! Tell me!' she whispered urgently.

A wolfish leer spread across Volpo's face. 'All in good time, Majesty. But first I want your assurance that the torments will stop. And that I can rule alongside you as your consort. Think what a strange and wonderful pair we will make. How my ugliness will set off your exquisite beauty!'

Magda jerked in fury and her eyes flared at him. Then she glanced back at her reflection and her shoulders slumped in defeat. 'Very well. Just get on with it.'

'Not until you promise me solemnly,' Volpo insisted. 'And if you don't carry out your promise, my services will no longer be at your disposal. You will have no surveillance or broadcast system. Remember, I control all of it.'

'Yes, yes,' said Magda impatiently. 'I promise. Now tell me your plan.'

Nick was overjoyed at the conversion of Finn. It was wonderful to see his old friend back again, restored to his former tearaway self. Finn had thrown himself into colony life, revelling in the anarchy of the underground gang, at the fact that they were flying in the face of authority and breaking all the rules. He was outraged and horrified when Nick told him what he'd seen at the children's party and swore to help in the fight against this terrible tyranny. He was a past master at thieving and became indispensable during the market raids. He joined in all the games with gusto and helped Nick stage daily toboggan races around the icy tunnels. In no time he had become a leading light of the colony.

But Nick noticed that Zak and Anneka didn't seem to share his joy. Anneka still glanced at Finn suspiciously and Zak seemed wary of him, even though Finn went out of his way to be friendly.

'Why did I ever think it was cool to be Street Monitor? Or Head of Youth Intelligence!' Finn scoffed one night over supper, gulping his food down noisily. The whole colony was assembled round the campfire. 'Sad or what? It's much more fun down here.'

'That's the general idea,' said Anneka sourly.

'So are you going to help us in the next stage of the plan?' Nick asked.

He outlined his strategy to Finn. He was to go up to the Daycare Centre and pose as his old self. He would say he had been off sick and had returned. He would be like an undercover agent, with a double identity. Using his authority as Head of Youth Intelligence, he would tell all the converted children to follow him and lead them to a specially arranged place where Nick would open the ground and bring them all down to the cavern.

When all the children in the City had been rounded up and returned to their former selves, they would go to the adults and tell them the truth about Magda. They would demand that her Majesty show herself to her people, unveiled. After seeing her as she really was, Nick felt sure that everyone would leave the City and tell the rest of the world.

After dinner, Anneka took Nick aside. She looked worried. 'Do you really trust Finn on his own up there?'

'Of course!' said Nick. 'Look how well he's converted back.'

'Well, I don't trust him,' Anneka said flatly. 'I never have. He's two-faced.'

Nick brushed away her doubts. 'He's one of us now. And it's our only hope for the rest of the children.'

The next day, Nick, Zak and Finn came out to the surface in a handy courtyard just off one of the main squares. Finn had dressed up in his old uniform.

'What a twit I looked in this lot!' he muttered scornfully, looking down at himself. He winked broadly at the others and gave them a mock salute. 'See you later. Right here in this courtyard, six o'clock sharp. I'll bring as many as I can.' Then he clicked his heels and marched purposefully off down the street towards the Goblin Daycare centre.

It was about an hour later that the proclamations began. Nick and Zak were eyeing a string of sausages hanging from a stall in the food market when every statue in the city boomed out the same message, at the same time.

'I have a very important announcement to make!' Magda's voice rang out across the City. 'Any child who brings me *accurate* information leading to the whereabouts of the Evil Elf Boy will be richly rewarded. He or she will be made my heir, Crown Prince or Princess of Doransk!' A fanfare of trumpets accompanied this statement. 'The lucky royal child will rule, along with me and my consort, Lord Volpo, over all my City, and eventually my empire. Their parents will be given titles and the highest offices in the land. My heir will be given a life of luxury and untold privileges and shall have everything he or she wants. My heir shall lack for nothing!'

Alarm bells began jangling in Nick's head. He turned to Zak and their eyes met under their wide-brimmed hats.

'He wouldn't . . .' Nick began uncertainly.

Zak shrugged. 'I don't know, Nicku. Who knows what the wind brings? You said we could trust him. And it was your idea to send him on this mission. We'll just have to hope for the best.'

They hung about in the market for the rest of the day, avoiding wolves and goblins, scavenging supplies and trying not to listen to the proclamations, which boomed out every half hour with monotonous regularity.

Towards the end of the afternoon, the proclamations stopped. A dull calm seemed to steal over the city. Nick felt strange and uncomfortable, a feeling of having left a piece of himself somewhere. At six o'clock, they made their way back to the courtyard and waited.

And waited.

By the time the artificial sun had gone down in a blaze of glory and the shiny false moon had risen in the sky, Finn still hadn't returned with the children. Nick felt a cold dread creep over him. Where was he? Why hadn't he come back? Maybe he had been captured by the goblins. Yes, that must be it.

They waited a while longer, until Zak insisted they go back to the cavern. Anneka was strangely silent when they told her Finn hadn't returned. She took Louisa off to organize a treasure hunt; it was as though she knew that time was running out, that this would be their last game.

An atmosphere of foreboding settled over the colony that night, and dinner was a solemn and gloomy affair. Nick tried to cheer them up, telling them that Finn had simply got held up and captured. He would find a way to carry out their plan. He had been converted. He could be trusted. His companions just looked at him sadly.

That night, Nick stayed awake at the campfire, keeping watch with Anneka and Zak. He felt numb and awkward and the uncomfortable silence grew.

'I've got you all into this,' he burst out suddenly. 'We should have just left things the way they were. It was too risky a plan. Now we don't know where Finn is! He might have betrayed us, even without meaning to. They could be torturing him for information.'

'That'd be good,' grunted Zak.

Anneka smiled wanly at Nick. 'We had to do something, however risky. We couldn't just go on like this for ever. We all need to go back to our families some time.'

Nick nodded and felt a lump rising in his throat. He remembered how he had come here to find his family. He looked around at the cavern and thought, for a fleeting second, that he saw a face on one of the rock formations. Then it was gone.

It was after midnight when Nickolai heard the steady, insistent thumping. At first it came from a long way off and only he could feel the slight tremor in the ground. He held himself very still, his ears twitching to pick up the vibrations, his heart hammering in his chest. It was coming from all directions.

Thump thump thump.

Persistent and regular. Louder and louder. Closer and closer. The unmistakeable sound of pounding goblin feet, hundreds of them. Terror gripped Nick so tight he could hardly breathe. Then Zak and Anneka woke with a start. Without any need for words, they drew together and held hands. The thumping got closer.

One by one, the other children woke. Whimpering in alarm, they scuttled across and clustered together round the fire, clinging to each other for comfort. The pounding feet were very near now.

Then the pounding stopped. There was a horrible, unnerving silence.

With a deafening crash of steel-tipped boots, hundreds of goblin soldiers poured into the cavern from the tunnel entrances all around it. Wolves followed at their heels, wheeling around like currents in a dark stream, prowling around the children and surrounding them. Skank and Skism stomped up and stood in front of the cowering children, folding their beefy arms over their shared chest. Skank for once said nothing, but his red eyes roamed over them nastily. Skism looked away, and for a second Nick thought he saw pity in his face.

There was a deathly hush as a small party of people came into the cavern. A wizened old woman hobbled forward, using a stick to support herself. She wore a heavy black veil that covered her head and shoulders. The only sign that she was Queen was the crown that perched precariously on her head. Volpo slunk along beside her. His dark eyes raked over the children and he grinned at them wolfishly.

On the Queen's other side swaggered a boy with black hair and cold blue eyes. He was wearing a royal blue velvet cloak lined with silk and trimmed with fur. Under the cloak was a black military uniform, gleaming with brass buttons and dripping with medals, and on his head was a gold crown, an exact replica of Magda's.

'Hello, children,' said Magda sweetly. 'Meet the new Crown Prince of Doransk.'

Finn smirked at them in triumph.

'Hello, children,' said Magda sweetly. 'Meet the new
Crown Prince of Doransk.'

Facing the Enemy

Finn stuck out his chin arrogantly and looked round with such a smug expression that Nick felt physically sick. A hot rush of anger filled him.

'You . . . you . . .' he whispered, unable to find a word strong enough. Finn just widened his eyes mockingly and returned Nick's gaze with a cold blue stare.

Shame and misery engulfed Nickolai. He'd thought Finn could be trusted. How stupid was he, to think that he could take on a force as strong as Magda? Volpo's eyes gleamed at him, and Nick saw again the vertical black slits in the yellow eyes. With a hiss the steel talons unsheathed. Volpo smiled at the children, showing his pointed teeth.

'Uncle Volpo is watching you, children,' he said, in his sly, creeping voice. 'So I trust you are not thinking of doing anything foolish?'

There was a warning growl from his wolves, who slunk around him, ready to pounce.

Nick looked at his gang of rebel urchins, wretched,

defeated and utterly petrified. The smaller children were whimpering and crying, and the older ones gazed at him helplessly. Zak and Anneka's devastated expressions were worse than anything Magda could do to him. He had given them hope and now all was lost.

A red mist blurred his vision as his rage boiled over. He didn't care what she did to him; all that mattered was that he take his revenge on her, expose her for what she was. He lunged forward and grabbed at Magda's veil. 'Show us your face, you evil old crone!' he yelled. 'Let everyone see what you really are!'

He was knocked back by a force so strong that he felt a violent spasm shoot down his spine. Several goblins pounced on him and held him in an iron grip.

'I know what you've been doing,' Nick gasped, struggling fiercely and gritting his teeth against the agonizing pain. 'You've been stealing childhood to keep yourself young and beautiful! It's vile! It's all a mask, a horrible fake!'

Nick had never felt such overwhelming anger in his life. His whole body was shaking violently. His hood fell down, revealing his ears. Magda's eyes narrowed as she saw them. He began twitching them frantically, hoping to use their powers against the witch, but the answering rumble was arrested immediately as she held up her gnarled hands.

There was silence, then a low cackle escaped from under her veil.

'Puny boy,' she whispered. 'Think your powers are any match for mine?'

Nick could feel her eyes burning into him. 'Who are you?' he spat. 'You're supposed to be an elf too, but something went horribly wrong, didn't it? I'm ashamed to be one of your kind! You've given our race a bad name!'

A low hiss of laughter made Magda's veil puff out. 'Not as bad as the one I've given you, dear. The Evil Elf Boy. The brat who dared to challenge me, whose villainous ancestors tried to overthrow me. A bad chip off a bad block.'

'That's a monstrous lie,' bellowed Nick. '*You* overthrew *them*!'

Magda chuckled softly. 'Dear boy. You are so young and naïve. The truth can be twisted any way I want.'

'Where are my people?' yelled Nick, beside himself with rage, hardly registering the pain as she sent another agonizing bolt of fire through his limbs. 'What did you do to them? Where is the old Elfin Kingdom, my real home? Because that tasteless pile of junk up there certainly isn't it!'

Magda waved her wizened arm around the cavern. 'Silly boy! It's all around you,' she said mockingly. 'Those great lumps of square rock were their sleighs. So careless of them to just abandon them there, don't you think? And those are your people – what's left of them.'

Nick's head swam as he stared at the lifeless rock

formations dotted around the caverns. Suddenly it all became clear, as though he was looking at them for the first time. It hadn't been his imagination after all. The rocks were frozen elves. All shapes and sizes, clustered together in groups. Mothers. Fathers. Children. Families. *Elfin* families. You could see their outlines, so encrusted with icicles they were almost unrecognizable. He and his friends had lived amongst them for months, played around them, taken shelter under them. His people.

'What did you do to them all?' he whispered.

'They have been turned back into the lifeless rocks from which they came,' she hissed venomously. The gnarled and mottled hand that held the stick began to tremble. 'They deserved it. They cast me out. Down into the Vortex, where all my youth and beauty vanished. Where the forces did terrible things to me. Things which I did not deserve.'

'I think you'll find you did!' Nick snapped, ignoring the fresh wave of pain that swept over him. 'Why did they cast you out? Tell me! What did you do?'

The veil twitched convulsively and a low snarl came from under it.

'They were jealous. I knew things they didn't. Only I had the courage to exploit the forces to the full. They had no imagination! They sickened me, with their virtuous ways and their sweetness and light. I despised them! So I came back and took control of what was mine. It was for their own good!'

Zak stepped forward, black eyes gleaming fiercely. 'And what about *my* people?' he roared. 'Was it for their own good too? You drove them away from their lands. Some of them starved. You tore my family apart! You deserve to look like an old hag!'

Magda sent a bolt straight into Zak's stomach. He gasped and fell to the floor in agony.

'That's what happens to children who show disrespect to her Majesty,' drawled Finn. 'Inuit scum.'

A nasty silence followed. To Nick's alarm, Louisa piped up.

'You're not a very nice lady,' she observed loudly. 'I'm glad I didn't come to one of your parties after all.'

Magda turned slowly towards the child.

'Don't hurt her!' shrieked Anneka, throwing herself over Louisa and knocking her sister to the floor. She let out a cry of agony as a searing pain hit her between the shoulder blades. The other children gasped in horror.

'Leave them alone!' cried Nick hoarsely. 'I'll do anything you want. But there's just one more thing I want to know. Where's my mother? And my father? Are they here?'

'Ah yes, your mother,' Magda purred. 'I'll take you to her. Come!'

There was a rattling noise as the goblins brought out their chains and began to shackle the children together. Skank and Skism locked Nick into a huge set of manacles and placed an iron collar around his neck that sat heavily on his shoulders.

'Are we ready?' cried Magda brightly, as though she was taking them all on a school outing. She turned and pointed a clawed finger up at the domed roof. There was a cracking noise and a hole opened up, revealing the lurid moon hanging over the square above; then a gentle hiss as a massive, coal-black stairway unrolled out of thin air, stretching down to the cavern floor. A cold feeling crept over Nick as he realized how awesome her powers were. She had conjured the stairway out of nowhere.

'This way children!' she cried gaily.

'Come on, elfin scum,' said Skank roughly, pushing Nick forward. 'And don't try no funny business.'

'It's best if you do as you're told, awright?' whispered Skism in his other ear. 'Then you won't get 'urt.'

Nick stumbled up the staircase, his head bowed from the weight of the iron collar. The goblins hustled the children up the staircase behind him. As they emerged into Golden Square, a gust of warm air hit them in a stifling wave. Everything was silent and deserted. The fake stones in the pavement glittered in the false moonlight and the fountains tinkled eerily as the hole in the ground closed up behind them with a gentle thud. The square was barricaded, every street leading into it blocked off by ropes. Goblin sentries stood at each corner.

Magda threw her wizened arm at the rock

formation Nick had noticed the first day they passed through. The one they had been unable to destroy. A slender, lone figure, leaning forward, its arms outstretched as if trying to reach something. A faint echo rang through his mind.

'*Nickolai!*' . . .

It was his mother. Nick's mouth went dry.

'There she is,' Magda said breezily. 'Your mother. One of these annoyingly plucky types. Ella, I think her name was. Full of herself, because she'd just won the Winter Solstice Sleigh Race. She tried to escape with you and reached the surface, but the wolves chased her and caught up. Unfortunately you got away. Carried off by a bird of prey, I was told.' She shot a venomous glance at Volpo.

Comet, thought Nick. If it were not for her . . . Then a new thought struck him. 'So why did I not turn to stone? Like my mother and all the other elves?'

Magda shot Volpo another nasty glance through her veil. 'Yes that was extremely . . . inconvenient. The answer to that has been with you all the time. Show him, Volpo.'

Squirming violently under Nick's tunic, Elvina stifled a squeak of terror as Volpo unsheathed his steel talons with a metallic rasp. They flashed in the moonlight as he tore the front of Nick's tunic open, and the Fairy was revealed, cowering against Nick's chest.

A sharp hiss escaped from under Magda's veil.

'There she is at last! Your little fluorescent friend. She managed to stay with you, somehow. That is what kept you alive. And your mother, because she was holding you so close – until she tripped and dropped you. This little creature of yours has been a thorn in my side ever since. But that's all about to end. Tell him, Volpo.'

Volpo folded his hands under his cloak and cocked his head on one side like a schoolmaster.

'It's like this, Nickolai,' he explained. 'Every elf had their own Light Fairy: their constant companion and spirit force. It protected them and stayed with them. The Light Fairies created the Kingdom, transformed the rocks into elves and kept them alive. But when an elf's Light Fairy is taken away I'm afraid . . .' he coughed delicately, '. . . he turns back into stone.'

The last piece of the jigsaw fell into place; the full extent of what Magda had done that terrible night hit Nick like a sledgehammer. In the same instant, he realized how Elvina had been able to restore the reindeer's flying power. It had all come from the Lights.

'You took the Lights and the Light Fairies and destroyed my people, didn't you?' he whispered. 'Then you used the Power of the Lights to make all this gold. You built this City to lure people up here so you could prey on their children!'

Magda cackled loudly in the shocked silence. 'Well done! Very clever of you to work it all out. Shame you're not on my side. However, one tiny ray of Light escaped – with you, Nickolai. Your little friend here.

And I've been looking for her ever since. Without her my power matrix is not complete and I can't carry out my long-term plans.'

Nick clutched frantically at Elvina. He felt her fluttering inside his closed palm. 'I won't let you have her! She won't leave me!' he screamed.

Magda tutted. 'That's where you're wrong,' she sighed. 'Because tomorrow night – on Winter Solstice Eve, when the forces are at their strongest – I will take her from you, and you will not be able to stop me. You will turn back into stone, and I will absorb her. Then my power will be complete. I will be able to make more gold than anyone could possibly dream of – mountains of it! – and I will spread my City over the entire globe, so that as all the children in the world are born, I will be there to take their youth. I will live for ever, and childhood will be a thing of the past!'

She cackled with triumph, then let out a long wheezy sigh of satisfaction. 'Don't worry, dear. They won't miss it.'

Nick became aware of a restless stirring behind him. A stamping of feet began to shake the ground, and a great roar of anger and defiance went up from the colony children. Their voices joined up in a swelling chorus that rose into the air.

'Freedom! Freedom! Freedom! Freedom!'

The chorus grew louder, echoing around the whole City. The goblins lashed at the children with their whips, but they ignored the blows and continued chanting and stamping until the noise became deafening. Nick felt tears of pride pricking his eyes. Even in the face of this awesome power, his friends had the courage to demonstrate their defiance.

'Shall I 'ave 'em restrained Majesty?' asked Skank hopefully.

'No need,' Magda glowered. 'They will be silenced soon.'

Suddenly, there was a further commotion. On all sides of the square, crowds of adults had gathered. They had heard their children, come out of their homes and surged down the City streets towards the noise. Hundreds of them were thronging around the barricades, shouting, shoving and straining against the ropes. The goblins pushed them back and a new roar of protest rose up.

'We want our children! Give us our children back!'

Volpo sidled up to Magda, brought the tiny golden trumpet out of the folds of his robes and passed it to her. The chanting and shouting died down as Magda spoke into the trumpet, her message booming out of statues around the city.

'My loyal citizens! Thanks to the valiant efforts of my servants and supporters, your children have now been rescued from the Evil Elf Boy. They are shaken but unharmed, and will be returned to you later this evening. All is now well in the glorious realm of Doransk. Thank you for your continuing support and loyalty, and for your patience in what has been a long and difficult search. Please return to your homes and wait for my staff to bring your children to you. Tomorrow night, at midnight, here in Golden Square, you will witness the public execution of the Evil Elf Boy, and then we will all be free from this terrible menace that has been threatening our peace and stability. Thank you and goodnight.'

Within minutes, the adults had been escorted away from the square, back down the streets. Magda's veil quivered in anticipation as she turned back to the children.

'Time for my beauty treatment,' she trilled. Nick felt a cold dread descend on him. He knew what she was about to do.

'Leave them alone!' he shouted, struggling against his manacles like a crazed animal. The children were still chanting, louder than ever, raising their fists and jumping up and down with excitement.

'Freedom! Freedom! Freedom!'

Nick watched in helpless horror as Magda slowly pulled back her robe, to reveal the black and empty hole where her heart should have been.

Childhood's End

The dark whirlwind unfurled and snaked towards the children. To Nick's fierce pride, their chanting never faltered.

'Freedom! Freedom! Free . . . dom . . . free . . .' Their voices trailed away and they fell still and silent, their faces blank and the light gone from their eyes. Anneka's hands dropped to her sides and Zak's shoulders slumped as he let his Tupilak drop to the ground. Even Louisa quietened down. A silence fell as the colony children were transformed in moments from a band of rebel urchins into serious little adults. They looked at each other, then formed into lines, watching Magda expectantly.

Nick became aware of a soft, slithering noise beside him. He looked round and gasped. The wizened old crone was transforming. Her whole body seemed to be stretching and straightening as though pulled up by a string. Her figure filled out into stately curves. With a rustling sound the long, shiny black hair was growing again, tumbling down her back; her gnarled claws softened and turned back into dainty white hands. The stick fell to the ground with a clatter as she threw off her veil to reveal her supernaturally beautiful self, completely restored and revived, dressed in a robe of gleaming gold which clung to her figure and fell to the ground in folds. She was decked out with heavy jewels. Her eyes shone and her teeth sparkled as she flashed Nick a brilliant smile.

'That's better!' she said, in a much younger sounding voice.

Volpo knelt before her and presented her crown. It glittered in the moonlight as Magda took it and raised her white arms to place it on her head. Then she turned to the children, who were gazing at her reverently.

'Well?' she demanded. 'And what do you have to say to your Queen?'

As one, the children knelt down in front of her and bowed their heads. 'Hail to the good and beautiful Queen Magda, O Great and Glorious One!' they chanted obediently.

'And what about me?' said Finn expectantly, revelling in his new found royal status. They all swivelled on their knees towards Finn and bowed their heads.

'Hail, O Great and Glorious Crown Prince of Doransk!'

Finn looked as though he would burst with pride. But his face fell when he saw Magda.

'Do not ever think to supplant me, Finn!' she said sharply. 'You are only a puppet prince, here to do my bidding. I will be watching you. My loyal servant Volpo is, and always will be my advisor.' Volpo shot her a warning look from under his heavy brows. 'And is soon to be my – er – consort,' she added.

Finn swiftly rearranged his features in an expression of respect and obedience. 'Of course, Majesty,' he said hurriedly. 'You are Queen of Everything. In the whole wide world. My parents and I are here only to serve you and carry out your every wish.'

Nick couldn't help feeling pleasure at seeing Finn discomfited.

'I wish you to escort the children back home, to be reunited with their parents,' Magda commanded Finn. 'And take the shackles off. There is no need for them now.'

Finn bowed low. 'Of course, Majesty. O Great and Glorious One.'

The children stood meekly, with no apparent desire to run away, as the goblins removed the shackles. Finn stood in front of them in a commanding manner, clicking the heels of his steel-tipped boots and throwing back his cloak with a flourish. The row of medals on his uniform glinted in the moonlight.

'Right, you little plebs. Form up! Chop chop,' he drawled.

The children shuffled round obediently and assembled into neat rows behind Finn, marching along in perfect formation with goblins on either side. Zak, Anneka and Louisa passed Nick without a flicker of recognition. He could scarcely bear it. Dimly, he noticed that Zak's Tupilak was no longer on the ground, where he had dropped it. The procession disappeared round the corner and the square fell silent.

Magda smiled serenely at Nick. He wished she would just strike him dead, right there.

'So,' she said. 'One last night. How would you like to spend it with your mother? Hmm? Because this time tomorrow, you will be turned to stone, just like her. Might as well get used to the idea, eh?'

Skank and Skism gripped Nick's arms and shackled him tightly to his mother's statue. Goblin sentries were posted all around him in a circle and wolves prowled around the perimeter of the square. There was no escape.

'Good night, Nickolai. Sweet dreams.' Magda snapped her fingers. There was a hissing of wheels and a soft panting noise as her golden carriage appeared in the square, drawn silently by a familiar team of black, shadowy wolves. The carriage door swung open and some little gold steps unrolled. Magda glided elegantly up into the carriage as if she was walking on air, Volpo slinking in after her.

'See you tomorrow,' she said breezily, like a teenage girl making a date. 'At midnight.'

And with a regal wave of her hand, the carriage swept out of the square.

Nick was left alone with the ring of goblins all around him. Skank and Skism stood menacingly close, their shared bulk outlined against the night sky.

'Any last requests?' said Skism, almost sounding apologetic.

Skank's head swung round and glared at him. 'What you on abart?' he snarled. 'You blinkin' moron! He don't deserve no last requests. He's a traitor!'

Out of the corner of his eye, Nick noticed his red cloak lying nearby on the ground in a crumpled heap. It must have fallen off him. It was the only thing left from his childhood.

Skism saw him looking at it. Suddenly the goblin's hand, the left one that belonged to him, pointed at the sky.

'Look!'

Skank's head spun round to look. 'Wot?'

'It's a full moon tonight!' said Skism enthusiastically, reaching his long, ape-like left arm down and sweeping up the cloak. He threw it towards Nick in a surprisingly nimble movement. By the time Skank's head had turned back to glare at Skism, Nick had grabbed the cloak and bundled it round himself.

'So flamin' wot?' spat Skank. 'It's a full moon ev'ry blimmin' night, 'cos that's how our Queen fixes it. What are you, some kind of girly? Come on, let's 'ave a swift drink at the Queen's Ears before closing time.'

'Aooow! Can't we go to the Minstrel's Tavern?'

'Nar! So just shut it, dogbrain. I'm the boss round 'ere, remember?'

'But we always go to the Queen's Ears,' whined Skism. 'I 'ate the pork scratchin's they do there. Why can't we go to the Tavern for a change?'

' 'Cos what I say goes. And it's your round.'

'Again?' Skism looked outraged. It was always his round.

Nick stared after the gross goblin as it clumped off across the square, its two heads twisting and bobbing about as they squabbled. He wrapped his cloak around himself and smelled its familiar, comforting smell. He opened his hand and released Elvina, who had been crouched inside his closed palm. Now she fluttered out and buzzed round his face.

Nick stared at her in awe, looking at her properly for the first time. She had been with him all his life. Warning him of danger. Guiding him through the labyrinth. Helping them come out to the surface in just the right places, where they would be concealed from view. And then her star turn with the toys, the miracle that had helped him win back the lost children.

She was the lynchpin to everything. The whole Elfin Kingdom would not have come into being without Elvina and her people. Magda could not complete her plans without her. The whole future of the world rested on her. And he hadn't realized how important she was – until now. He had taken her for granted.

'Sorry I didn't appreciate you before, Elvina,' he whispered. The tiny fairy flew up to sit on his shoulder and squeaked sorrowfully at him. Then she flitted up and sat on the shoulder of his mother's statue. He gazed upwards, wondering what his mother had looked like when she was alive. Was she beautiful? She must have been. And incredibly brave, to try and escape with him. But all he saw now was impassive rock.

'What was she like, Elvina? Was she pretty? Can you remember?' he whispered.

Elvina flitted down and nestled under his chin. Her wings brushed his cheeks comfortingly.

'This is our last night together,' Nick whispered. 'Thanks for looking after me all my life.'

Elvina let out a long mournful chirrup. Nick leaned back against the rock and gave in to his grief.

All over the City, parents waited anxiously in the doorways of their homes, watching for their returning offspring. They had been delivered from the clutches of the Evil Elf Boy, unharmed. An atmosphere of restrained rejoicing and excitement hung in the air. As the procession marched past, parents recognized their children and claimed them joyfully, flinging their arms round them and hugging them tight with tears pouring out of their eyes.

Then they drew back to look at their children in puzzlement. Their eyes were different, somehow blank and expressionless. Instead of greeting them with hugs and kisses, they looked at their parents blankly and spoke in formal tones.

'Good evening, Mother and Father. It's nice to be home. May I come in now? There is much work to be done tomorrow, in the service of our Great and Glorious Realm.'

Strange and stilted greetings like this were repeated all over the City, to the bemusement of the parents. What had Elf Boy done to them? They wanted their real children back, not these unnatural creatures.

Down in Compound Eleven, Joachim and Lotta waited outside hut 21, along with the other parents whose children had gone missing. They had been released from the Detention Centre without explanation. They had heard the proclamations. Now they too awaited the return of their children.

As soon as Joachim saw them approaching, he knew something was wrong. Their eyes were dead, their faces blank. Finn marched at the head of the procession, looking splendid in his cloak and crown. He held up his hand and halted outside the door of hut 21.

'Child citizens Hildebrand – and the Inuit scum. Returning to hut 21, Row 73, Compound Eleven,' he said, waving a scroll at the goblins.

Anneka, Louisa and Zak stepped obediently out of the ranks and marched towards the door. Lotta threw herself at Louisa and Anneka. 'My babies! Oh my babies! You've come back!' She covered them with kisses and wetted them with her tears. Louisa clung to her mother briefly and then pulled back and looked up at her.

'Hello, Mother. It's very nice to be home,' she said formally.

Anneka looked at her parents and for a second Joachim thought he saw a brief flicker in her eyes. 'Good evening, Mother. Good evening, Father. It is very nice to be safe and sound, back at home, and out of the evil clutches of the Evil Elf Boy.'

Zak kicked her on the ankle. 'Don't overdo it,' he hissed under his breath.

They went into the hut and closed the door behind them. The children widened their eyes warningly at Lotta and Joachim and put their fingers to their lips. A silent understanding passed between them all. Then they drew together and clung to each other, trying to stifle their sobs of relief.

Breakfast in Compound Eleven the next morning was a subdued affair. The children filed obediently past the catering goblins for their tin plates of sloppy porridge and sat bolt upright at the tables, eating daintily and occasionally telling their parents off for bad table manners. The parents' faces wore a variety of expressions: some confused and puzzled, others sad and resigned. Anneka, Zak and Louisa sat at their table with Lotta and Joachim, keeping their eyes carefully downcast. Johan sat nearby with Kristoff and Rosa.

'What a relief to have you all back!' said Rosa,

beaming uncertainly around the table. The children ignored her, but Joachim and Lotta smiled back briefly.

The meal was interrupted as Finn marched in to Central Compound Square accompanied by his personal goblin guard. Over his uniform he was wearing a black velvet cloak trimmed with gold and lined with red satin. On his head was his gold crown. He looked every inch the young monarch. He unfurled an official looking scroll and cleared his throat.

'Good morning citizens of Compound Eleven.'

He raised one eyebrow. There was a scraping noise as all the children rose obediently and bowed.

'Good morning Crown Prince Finn, O Great and Glorious Son of Doransk!'

The parents stood up and falteringly repeated the mantra, then bowed clumsily. A smile of satisfaction spread across Finn's arrogant young face, and he began to read from the scroll. 'I have come here this morning, in my capacity as newly appointed Crown Prince of Doransk, to issue your instructions for the public execution of the Evil Elf Boy tonight.' He gave a delicate cough. 'A regrettable but necessary procedure which I hope will swiftly be followed by a much more joyous occasion – my coronation!'

He looked round expectantly.

'Hail to thee, Crown Prince Finn, O Great and Glorious Son of Doransk!'

Finn smirked. 'By my royal order you will assemble

in an orderly queue at the gates at precisely twenty-three hundred hours. You will then be escorted through the City to Golden Square where you will witness the execution. But first, it has been decreed that the Evil Elf Boy is to be punished and humiliated before the people of Doransk. In our position as extremely royal heir to the Kingdom, we feel it would be a fitting chastisement if he were paraded through the streets of the City in chains for all to see, to be whipped and jeered and taunted by the crowds, as a warning to any young citizens who would dare to challenge our Great and Glorious Queen.'

Gasps of shock from the assembled adults rang round the square. The children remained passive and blank-faced, except for Anneka, Zak, Louisa and Johan, who exchanged brief, horrified glances.

'As Crown Prince of Doransk, I have been vested with far-reaching powers by the Queen herself. She has insisted that all children attend this event, as a powerful lesson. Children under the age of sixteen will assemble at the compound gates at eleven o'clock this morning. This will be a parade worth watching.'

Snapping the scroll shut, Finn clicked his steel-tipped boots and saluted. 'Hail Queen Magda, O Great and Glorious One! And me of course!'

'Hail Queen Magda, O Great and Glorious One! And you of course!'

Make-believe

Nick had spent a long and lonely night, dozing fitfully under the rock formation that had once been his mother. Elvina had fallen asleep wedged in the top of his left ear. He woke as the bright orange sunrise spread across the sky, to see the goblins slumped against each other on the ground, snoring loudly, their fat stomachs rising and falling gently and dribble slobbering out of their mouths on to their chainmail. The foul stench of their breath wafted across to him and he nearly retched. Several wolves prowled around nearby, watching him closely.

Weak with hunger, he tried to sit up – and winced in pain. His neck was rubbed raw from the iron collar and the chains lay heavy on his limbs. He dozed off again, until he heard marching feet approaching from a distance. Closer and closer it came, until Nick saw Finn, Skank and Skism, and a whole army of goblins bearing down on him across the square. Behind them was a convoy of children, hundreds of them, marching in perfect lines like a column of ants, their eyes staring straight ahead. And at the front marched his friends, the colony rebels, now stony-faced strangers.

Finn stood over Nick and sneered. 'Morning, Elf Boy. Had a good night? Nice chat with Mummy?'

Nick gathered up all the spit in his mouth and aimed it at Finn's face, where it landed smack between his eyes. Finn recoiled and gasped in disbelief, opening and closing his mouth like a goldfish.

'Come to gloat, have you?' Nick spat. 'The Queen's lap dog, showing off his new-found powers? Can't get them for himself, so he has to lie and cheat and betray his friends!'

Finn's face was pinched into fury as he wiped away the spittle. 'H-how dare you?' he spluttered.

'Your Royal Highness, this is an outrage!' Anneka said severely. 'Even in the face of his defeat he dares to insult you. I suggest the punishment proceeds immediately!'

Nick's heart froze at the sight of his friends staring at him without any trace of emotion.

The other children started up a chant. 'Punish him! Punish him!' Their cries rose in the still morning air.

'Right, sonny boy!' bellowed Skank, twitching his whip threateningly. 'It's payback time!'

People were pouring into the square to watch the spectacle. The chanting grew louder as Nick was unchained from the statue and dragged to his feet. He felt a sharp pain as Skank's whip lashed him across the shoulder. A cheer went up as he gritted his teeth against the pain, determined not to show any weakness. The goblins grunted and heaved as they dragged him across the square, and blows rained down on him from Skank's whip. As the procession reached the edge of the square, Finn bawled at the goblins to stop, before turning to Anneka, who stood on his right.

'We must decide on the best route,' Anneka urged loudly. 'Everyone in the City must see this. Every man, woman and child.'

Nick looked dully at Zak. To his amazement, he saw a tiny flicker at the corner of Zak's eye. Was that the faintest hint of a wink? He noticed that Zak was fingering his Tupilak, which was now back in its place, hanging round his neck. He must have picked it up from the ground himself. But why, if he'd been affected like all the rest?

Zak turned to Skank and Skism and made a quick, respectful bow to Skank, pointedly ignoring Skism.

'Tell me, my Lord Skank,' he said formally, 'what is the best route, that takes in the whole City? As Chief of Police, you must know the City inside out.'

Skank waggled his head and stroked his chin thoughtfully. 'I would say, down Golden Mile, then along by the castle moat, and back up the p'rimeter road, the same way wot the Queen goes on 'er state processions.'

'Now 'ang on a minute,' Skism blustered, annoyed at being ignored. 'You say that, but it's the long way round and we'd miss a lot of the residential streets. We need to snake through the 'ole city down the serpentine route.' Then he glanced at Zak and tapped his half of the shared chest. 'And by the way, sonny, I'm also the Chief of Police. The other 'arf of it.'

There was a short, unpleasant silence. Skank jerked round violently to glare at Skism, pressing his snout aggressively into Skism's face.

'For the last time, shut it, gob-face!' Skank roared, spraying flecks of spittle in Skism's eye. 'I told you, I'm the boss round 'ere. Queen Magda appointed *me* Chief of Police, not you. So wot I say goes! You just keep your trap shut because you're a moron and I'm the one with the brain, right?'

The two ugly faces stayed pressed together, snorting like bulls, nostrils flaring, beady eyes boring into each other. Nick glanced at Zak and this time, saw a definite wink. All his doubts vanished.

'Hey Skism!' he called jauntily. 'Are you going to let Skank keep bullying you like this? You're the smarter one. Tell him to back off and let you have a say in things.'

Both heads swivelled round and stared at Nick. Skism's face wore a thoughtful expression; Skank's, one of sheer fury.

'Shut it, you pointy-eared scumbag. You stay out of this,' snarled Skank.

' 'E's right!' said Skism indignantly. 'You are a bully! And I ain't putting up wiv it no more! I'm not stupid!

In fact I'm cleverer than you. 'Ooo is it reads out the *Doransk Daily Sun* to you every morning 'cos you'se illi— illo— can't read? And the instructions on the operating mechanism for the City gates? I think it's time we sorted this out goo— *mph*!'

Skank's beefy hand clamped heavily over Skism's mouth, then Skank let out a bellow of pain as Skism bit into his hand. Skism's hand came up and shoved two sausage-like fingers up Skank's nostrils, pushing his face away.

Nick had to stop himself from laughing out loud. Grunts and gasps and horrible bellows echoed round the square as the two-headed goblin wrestled with itself. Skank's leg kicked Skism's leg from under him – a pointless and self-destructive exercise which brought them both crashing to the ground. The grotesque two-headed figure began to roll over and over, its legs thrashing and its beefy arms grappling fiercely. Stifled shrieks and horrible gurgling sounds came out of its slobbering mouths. The square was in uproar as people burst in from all sides, gathering from all over the City.

No one was looking at Nick. He glanced at his friends, half afraid of what he would see. Zak was struggling to keep the corners of his mouth straight and Anneka's eyes were dancing with amusement. Johan's shoulders were shaking with laughter, and Louisa was hiding her face in her sister's skirts. Relief flooded through him. His oldest friends were still themselves.

Grunts and gasps and horrible bellows echoed around the square . . .

'We'll guard the prisoner, Crown Prince!' Anneka called out showily to Finn, who was staring transfixed at Skank and Skism. He didn't appear to hear her.

'Come on, let's get you out of here,' whispered Zak as they closed round him.

'What about these chains?' Nick whispered out of the corner of his mouth.

The chains lay in a heavy coil, trailing towards a goblin guard. He had dropped his end, too busy gawping at the grisly spectacle. Hanging on a belt round his waist was a large key on a ring.

'Go Louisa!' whispered Anneka.

Louisa scuttled over and gently eased the key off the ring, then darted back and handed it over. Anneka snatched it and quickly unlocked the padlock on Nick's iron collar. The shackles and chains slid off with a rasping noise, which nobody heard above the din.

'Open the ground now, Nick,' Anneka whispered urgently. 'Magda'll be here any minute!'

Nick closed his eyes and concentrated hard, trying to block out the chaos around him. No one noticed the shaking of the earth, or the crack that opened in the ground. No one saw Nick, Anneka and Louisa disappear through it, before it closed up and sealed them out of view.

But people did notice when Zak and Johan raced off and ran amok in the square, zigzagging through the crowds and taunting the goblins, jumping up and down, thumbing their noses and making a variety of rude gestures.

'Neee— er! Big fat goblins! Bet you can't catch us!'

The goblins tore their eyes away from the macabre vision of their boss strangling himself and stared at them stupidly, unsure what to do without supervision. Finn suddenly caught sight of the jeering boys.

'Hey, come back you little plebs!' he screamed. He turned to the goblins. 'What are you waiting for, you cretins? I order you to go and catch them!'

He was distracted again as he heard two loud thunks nearby; Skank and Skism's heads hit the ground simultaneously and fell still.

The icy cold air hit Nick, Anneka and Louisa as they plummeted down the shaft and landed in a heap at the bottom. They picked themselves up and looked around, shivering. They were back in the central cavern.

Nick looked at his friends. 'That was pretty good acting back there. You were all brilliant! You even had me convinced for a moment.'

Anneka smiled modestly, brushing herself and Louisa down. 'All my idea, of course.'

'I'm good at pretend games,' said Louisa proudly.

'I just want to know one thing,' Nick said. 'How come you Norsk lot all stayed the same? How come you didn't get – de-childed, when Magda did her whirlwind thing?'

Louisa reached up and put her arms round his neck. ' 'Cos we love you, Nicklai.'

'There's your answer,' said Anneka. 'We're your oldest friends. We believe in you. It's the magic. If you truly believe in it, then no one can take your childhood away.'

Nick felt a lump in his throat. 'No one's ever said anything like that to me before.'

'Well, I'm saying it now,' said Anneka briskly. She gave an embarrassed cough and clapped her hands. 'What now? We haven't much time. Zak and Johan are up there, creating a distraction. But they won't be able to hold them off for long. I said we'd meet them in the marketplace.'

Nick came to with a jolt. It was all down to him now. His mind raced over a thousand possibilities. How on earth could he overcome Magda's awesome powers? How could he unmask her and show the world what she truly was? There must be someone that could help him.

The solution hit him like a thunderbolt. 'OK, I've got a plan.' He took a deep breath. 'We're going to visit some friends of mine. They're the only ones who've got the kind of powers we need.'

'Who are they?'

Nick hesitated. He was going to have to break a promise he'd made when he was eight. But it was their only chance.

'Where are these people?'

'In the forest, near Norsk. And they're not exactly people.'

Anneka stared at Nick as if he was mad. 'The forest? Don't be daft! We've got to get there and back before midnight tonight. It took us months to get up here. We'll never do it.'

Nick started striding around the great blocks of rock, trying to imagine them as they had once been – elfin sleighs, racing round the tunnels, powered by some invisible force he couldn't begin to understand. And then he remembered. Magda had mentioned that his mother had won the Winter Solstice Sleigh Race. One of these blocks must be her sleigh. Which one?

Nick noticed that they were all pointing the same way, as though they had all come from the same direction. One of them was ahead of the others, and looked askew, as though it had skidded to a halt. He walked over and put his hands on it, trying to sense the vibrations coming from it. It wasn't just a lump of rock. This had been his mother's sleigh. He knew it, somewhere deep inside him.

'Stand back!' he ordered.

He closed his eyes and summoned the forces. Feeling the eddies swirling around him, he twitched his ears, directing them at the sleigh. After what seemed like an eternity there was a low rumble, a cracking sound . . . and slowly, the encrusted ice crumbled away from the great block and slid to the floor in a heap of dust. They gasped in amazement.

In front of them stood the most beautiful sleigh they had ever seen. It was covered in coloured patterns and carved decorations, with rows of tiny sleigh bells hanging in loops all around it. It was unlike any sleigh Nick had ever seen, with its air of magic and mystery, a relic of something ancient and unexplainable. How had the elves powered these things?

It was suddenly, blindingly obvious. Nick jerked his head at Anneka and Louisa. 'Get in.'

Anneka shook her head disbelievingly. 'What is this, pretend sleigh rides?'

'Can't we have a real sleigh ride?' said Louisa eagerly.

'Yes. Get in!' Nick repeated. He climbed into the driver's seat, and Anneka and Louisa clambered in beside him.

Spotting something shiny lying in the bottom of the sleigh, Nick bent and picked up a tall goblet-shaped object made of crystal. It was encrusted with icicles. He knocked them off and wiped it with his sleeve. In the faint glow of the fire still burning in the cavern, it twinkled and caught the light. 'It's some kind of trophy,' Nick murmured in awe, staring at it.

'Oh great, a cup,' Anneka snorted. 'That'll come in really handy.'

Elvina darted out of Nick's front and hovered around the cup, lighting it up. Swirling, coloured patterns began to play across its surface. Nick saw an inscription on the side in strange loopy writing, very scratchy and faint. He squinted as he tried to read it.

'Come on! What does it say?' asked Anneka impatiently.

Nick read it out slowly. 'It says – the Winter Solstice Cup. Presented to the winners of the Winter Solstice Sleigh Race, Ella Grishkin and her son –' he paused – 'her son, Nickolai.'

Anneka's eyes met his. Nobody said anything for a minute. Then they all jumped in shock as they heard a distant howling of wolves, echoing down the tunnels. Nick jerked himself out of his reverie. 'We'd better go!'

'Excuse me?' Anneka stared at him in disbelief. 'How are you intending to drive this thing? I don't see any huskies.'

Nick sighed and looked at her. 'You said you believed in me, Anneka. Just trust me.' He gathered up the reins and shook them experimentally. They made an eerie jingling noise that echoed round the cavern. 'You'd better hang on tight,' he told them. 'I've never done this before.'

Magic Flight

Nick closed his mind to the howling in the background and waited for the power to build up. He felt it flow through him. He began to move his ears around, trying to gather up the force and direct it along the reins and into the sleigh.

At first, nothing.

Then he felt a wild tingling down his arms and the reins jumped. The sleigh bells jingled loudly as the energy shivered through them like an electric current. Beside him, Anneka and Louisa gasped. He could feel their tension and excitement coming across to him in waves. *Yes! It was working!*

He made a Herculean effort to push more energy into the reins. Slowly, he felt it seeping through, but it was sluggish. *Come on, come on!* There was a sudden release, like water spurting into a pipe, and the sleigh jolted forward.

Then it stopped. The howling grew louder.

'Come on Nick!' Anneka urged him. 'You can do it!'

Nick tried again, pouring every last bit of his willpower into it. The sleigh lurched and juddered, shot forward again – and took off at top speed, zooming over the surface just above the ground. Nick felt a thrill of exhilaration.

'Look out!'

Nick opened his eyes and saw that they were shooting across the cavern straight towards the wall. Crikey, it really was working! He yanked the reins over and the sleigh swerved violently. He aimed it straight at the nearest tunnel opening. Then he gasped in dismay.

A crowd of yellow eyes burned in the gloom as a pack of wolves poured down the tunnel towards them. *Just keep going!* The sleigh crashed straight through, strafing the wolves' heads and scattering the creatures into howling disarray. More wolves came bounding along behind them, and they too tumbled and rolled over, yelping as the ice blades cut across them. Some tried to leap on to the sleigh, but they were thrown off and left behind as the craft picked up speed and flew along the tunnel at breakneck pace. Within moments they had left the creatures behind. Louisa and Anneka cheered.

'Where next?' shouted Anneka.

'Erm . . . dunno yet!' Nick gasped, fixing his eyes on the tunnel ahead and trying to keep the power pulsing down into the sleigh. The wind whistled past his ears and he felt a great thrill surge through him as the sleigh raced along, powered by the energy that he had harnessed.

Louisa and Anneka whooped with excitement and Elvina crept to the top of his tunic and peered out at the view as it flashed past. She gave a loud and indignant squeak and disappeared at once.

'Faster, faster!' squealed Louisa, shrieking with glee on her sister's lap. The wind blew her blond curls about and her eyes were alight.

But their exhilaration was shortlived; a chorus of howls carried along the tunnel, coming from behind. Nick glanced back and saw more yellow eyes glowing in the dark, moving swiftly towards them.

He twitched his ears hard, trying to squeeze more energy out of the air. Another shock of power burst through him and down into the sleigh. With a violent jolt it boosted into top gear, streaking through the tunnel at lightning speed, reducing everything to a blur. The tunnel twisted and turned in dizzying bends and Nick struggled to navigate the sharp corners without crashing into the sides.

'I'm going to try and break out now!' he shouted. 'Hold on tight!'

There was a wall straight ahead of them, where the tunnel split two ways. As they hurtled towards it, Nick directed the forces at the solid ice, trying to power the sleigh and open the rocks at the same time. The familiar rumblings began around them. The wall rushed closer, but remained solid and impassable. *Come on, come on! Open up!* Any moment now and there would be head-on collision. Nick calculated the seconds before impact . . .

Ten . . . nine . . . eight . . .

There was a loud cracking noise and a gap began to open in the wall . . . it wasn't wide enough . . . Nick forced it open with his mind . . .

Seven . . . six . . . five . . .

Another deafening crack and the hole gaped wider. The rocks around them shuddered violently and the girls let out a shriek of terror.

Four . . . three . . . two . . .

The crack suddenly burst apart into a gaping chasm. The sleigh shot straight into it and zoomed up the long, sloping shaft. Nick guided the sleigh, keeping the reins straight. He glimpsed daylight up ahead, framed by the opening to the surface. A few seconds later, the sleigh burst out of the ground with a wild jingle of bells.

They had come out in the middle of the marketplace. The sleigh rocketed through the narrow street, overturning stalls and scattering shoppers. Apples, chickens, eggs, lampshades, clocks, mirrors, Queen Magda dolls – merchandise of every description was hurled in all directions. There were screams and shouts as people flung themselves out of the way.

'Can you see the others?' Nick shouted above the din.

'There!' shouted Anneka, pointing at two masked jesters leaping and cavorting amongst a small crowd.

Nick was confused. 'But they're Magda's demon clowns!'

Anneka shook her head. 'While you were talking to Magda in the cavern, I managed to swipe some fancy dress disguises. I thought they might come in handy.'

Nick glanced at Anneka in amazement. She really was a smart girl. He steered the sleigh towards the crowd, trying to slow down by moving his ears backwards and pulling on the reins.

'Get ready to jump on!' shouted Anneka to the two jesters.

As the sleigh roared past, the jesters leaped on and piled into the back. One of them nearly fell off and had to be hauled back in. Nick steered the sleigh down the narrow winding street until the golden gates rose up in front of them. He was going to have to ram them. Then he groaned in horror.

A posse of goblins had heaved into view and stood directly in front of the gates, arms folded.

'Just keep going!' Anneka shouted.

Nick squeezed all his energy together, twitched his ears and pointed them at the gates, ready to force them open. But this was solid gold, not rock and ice. Was it going to work?

The ground began to shake.

The solid wall of gold flew towards them.

The goblins hurled themselves out of the way at the

last moment, like great fat walruses diving into a pool.

At the point of impact, both sets of gates flew open and the sleigh burst into the real world outside.

The cold Arctic air took their breath away, and the blackness of the Arctic winter closed in. Above them, the sky opened up, with real stars twinkling in its depths and a real silver moon shining down. The fires of the emigrants camped outside the City lit up the gloom. Stray dogs yelped and scattered. The travellers fell back in amazement as the sleigh flashed past and zoomed across the snow, while the passengers let out loud cheers and whoops and hugged each other.

'Go, Nicku!'

'Which way now?' said Anneka breathlessly. She glanced at the moon climbing steadily in the sky. 'It's getting on for midnight!'

'We're heading south!' shouted Nick above the swishing sound of the sleigh blades cutting across the ice. He looked at the stars for guidance. Straight ahead on the horizon lay the Southern Star. The landscape stretched around them, an endless wasteland of snow and ice, and the compass inside him told him that he was on course. Then Anneka clutched his arm and let out a shriek of alarm.

'They're coming after us, Nick!'

Behind them, hundreds of wolves were pouring out of the City gates and moving like swift dark shadows across the snow. Nick shook the reins and the sleigh sped forward. They mounted crest after crest, hurtled down endless slopes and troughs, while the wolves kept up a relentless pace behind them, bounding along like lightning. Their howls echoed eerily across the vast, empty silence and their scrawny shapes poured over ridge after ridge like a dark river.

We must keep going! Nick thought in desperation. *We must keep ahead of them.* He found to his amazement that there seemed to be unlimited reserves of power to draw on, as long as he kept up his concentration.

They finally reached the shores of the Great Frozen Sea, skimming across its jagged surface for miles, still pursued by the wolves. Then they found themselves shooting towards a great gap where the ice had broken apart.

'I'm going to jump it!' shouted Nick. 'Hang on tight!'

As they neared the edge of the floe, he willed the sleigh into the air. It soared across the gap in a great arc – landed with an almighty thump on the other side – spun round a few times, then Nick regained control and steered the sleigh straight ahead. Looking back, they saw that the wolves were also leaping through the air, a dark mass looming against the sky. Some fell short and landed in the icy cold water, howling and thrashing around until they were sucked beneath the waves. But some of them made it and continued the chase.

'I've never seen wolves like it!' gasped Zak, incredulous. 'They never give up!'

'Just ignore them,' muttered Nick under his breath, keeping his eyes straight ahead.

The ice-bound sea stretched on and on. They crested great solid waves and ridges, until they saw the distant shores of the Southern Rim ahead. The howling of the wolves was closer now.

Suddenly a huge shadow fell across their path. Nick looked up and nearly fainted with shock.

Something huge and dark reared up over them. A massive tail, as tall as a tree, sank back beneath the waves and a huge shiny body stretched out beneath them, pushing under the sleigh and lifting it up. A spout of water shot into the air and there was a loud honking noise, like a ship's foghorn.

'It's a qammiq!' Zak stammered.

'A what?'

'A whale!' Zak gripped the sides of the sleigh. 'Get out of the way!'

Nick willed the sleigh forward and it shot through the air.

'Look! It's helping us!' shouted Anneka, pointing behind them.

The whale's tail was rolling and thrashing around, breaking the ice all around it and lashing out at the wolves, flipping them like a giant hand swatting flies. More than half the remaining wolves struggled and yelped and howled and sank beneath the water, swallowed up under the great frozen blocks.

Nick urged the sleigh on. Gradually the snowy

wastes gave way to the open, scrubby wilderness of the tundra. The last of the wolves continued relentlessly behind them, until Nick saw the jagged outline of the forest on the horizon.

The sleigh sped across the final stretch of snow. The forest grew closer and closer, until they could see into its shadowy depths and the pines towered above them. Nick concentrated hard, moving his ears backwards and pulling gently on the reins. The sleigh slewed to a halt. Half a dozen scrawny shapes were still racing towards them.

'Run like mad towards the trees!' shouted Nick.

They scrambled out and dashed across the short gap into the forest. As they plunged into its thick, welcoming darkness, Nick heard a whispering noise. The pines swayed and shook their branches.

'Welcome back, Elfin Boy . . .' They had remembered him.

The remaining wolves bounded into the forest and surged between the trunks.

'We must get away!' cried Anneka, her voice rising in hysteria.

'No!' Nick shook his head and waited.

There was a loud creaking, and the trees moved. Their great trunks shifted sideways, closed in a solid wall, blocking the wolves out. The creatures howled and yelped and thrashed around, scrabbling to get through, but there wasn't the tiniest sliver of space to let them pass. The forest echoed with their howls of rage until finally, they slunk away – defeated.

'Did I just see what I thought I saw?' Zak breathed incredulously.

Nick nodded. 'Yes. The trees move.'

'So it's true, then? This forest really is magic?' Anneka was enchanted. 'All those stories were real?'

Nick nodded again.

'This is why you got grounded all those years ago, wasn't it? You came here.'

Nick grinned sheepishly.

'You sneak! Why didn't you bring me with you?'

The hurt and angry look in Anneka's eyes gave Nick a twinge of guilt. 'Follow me and you'll see why. Come on.'

The clearing was just as Nick remembered it. The tall pines ringed the open space, the snow heavy on their branches and sparkling on the ground. Not a creature stirred or made a sound in the thick silence that pressed in on them.

'Are there more fairies here?' Louisa asked hopefully.

'No. Something just as good though,' whispered Nick. He looked across at the rocky outcrop, where the crack leading into the cave of the reindeer tribe lay hidden behind the bushes. Anxiety nagged him. He had promised to keep the reindeer's secret safe. But now he had brought other Two Legs here. His heart began a slow drumbeat in his chest at the thought of

303

seeing his friends again after so many years. Would they still be here? Would they remember him, and help him? Or would they turn their backs on him? Had they migrated and flown south? Or worse still, had they perished?

'Just stay hidden in the shadows and don't make a sound,' he instructed his friends. He crunched over to the centre of the clearing and made a noise which to the others sounded like snorting and spluttering. They waited and watched in the frosty silence.

There was a rustling noise and a light pattering of hooves on the snow. One by one, the reindeer trotted into the clearing and stood in a row in front of Nick. First Comet. Then Rudolph. Then Blitzen, Prancer, Dancer and Dasher, weaving restlessly, then Cupid and Vixen, and finally Donder, stumbling slightly.

Nick's heart suddenly felt too big for his chest. The young reindeer were all fully grown now, young adults in their prime, with antlers that had reached their full span. They stood as still as statues, watching him warily. Their eyes darted around and their ears flicked nervously; their breath made clouds in the air. Then Rudolph blinked, pawed at the ground and let out a whinny of joy. He cantered forward, bucking his head wildly and skidded to a halt beside Nick, nuzzling his cheek with his wet nose.

'Nickolai! It *is* you! I knew you'd come back one day!'

Nick threw his arms round Rudolph's neck and

pressed his face into the soft fur, inhaling his warm, comforting animal smell. 'Rudolph! You remembered me! I've missed you so much!'

In moments he was surrounded by the other reindeer, crowding round him from all sides. Laughing, crying, he tried to touch and hold them all.

'And why have you returned, Two Legs?' came a booming voice behind him.

Lancer was standing alone, outlined against the snow. He was still a magnificent stag, with massive antlers and a greying muzzle. He strode into the clearing and stood tall and proud and challenging, the undisputed head of the tribe.

'Please sir,' Nick began humbly, 'I have come to ask for your help.'

'What kind of help?' growled Lancer.

'I need your tribe to take me and my friends back up to the North Pole, and to help me fight the power of the woman – the monster – who stole the Lights from the sky twelve years ago. And it's really, really urgent. We need to get there before midnight!'

A tremor of awe ran round the reindeer, amid hushed cries of 'Arkfel!'

'Leave the forest?' Lancer spluttered. 'Show ourselves to the world? It is out of the question. We cannot betray our existence to the Two Legs. It would break the Reindeer Code. It is a sacred secret – known only to you!'

Nick braced himself. 'Actually sir, it's not just me.'

Lancer stiffened, then let out a bellow of rage; his antlers shook like the branches of a tree in the wind. 'You have more Two Legs with you?' he spluttered in disbelief.

Nick nodded at the others, who stepped forward timidly out of the shadows.

'They're my friends,' he said desperately. 'We have been fighting this evil woman who is taking the heart and soul out of the world. You can trust them.'

Lancer threw back his head and roared. 'You promised! You have betrayed our trust!'

Nick held his nerve. 'But please sir, if you and the tribe help us, you will help to restore the Lights to the sky. Your flying powers will be properly returned, and the world will be brought back to order at last.'

Everyone's eyes were on the magnificent stag, standing sternly in the moonlight. Nick felt a growing sense of agitation. The night was wearing on fast.

Then Comet spoke. 'What is the point of us keeping our existence a secret, Lancer, when the whole reason for it – our flying power – is slowly fading away? There is no more power, since the Lights went from the sky. If we stay hidden away, it will never be restored.' She broke off for a few moments, then continued, more gently than before. 'And remember – your mother told us on her deathbed that Nickolai would return and need our help. She told us to conserve our powers for when he came. She said that Arkfel brought him to us. We are destined to help him rid the world of this monster. It is part of our destiny. It *is* the will of Arkfel. Like it or not, we are part of the world, Lancer, and we must play our part.'

The moon was rising higher in the sky and midnight was approaching. Time was running out. Lancer snorted, dipped his head and swung it around in deep thought. Finally, he stamped his hoof and raised his head proudly.

'You are right, as usual, Comet,' he declared with a sigh. 'Of course we are fated to play a part in a destiny greater than ours. And the flying reindeer tribe *shall* have all its powers restored. We shall be a proud race once again! Once a year, on this night only, I give my permission for the tribe to fly north with Nickolai to help him do whatever he needs to keep Arkfel in the sky!'

The reindeer were sitting on their haunches on the snow, Nickolai and his friends already settled on their backs. Elvina had restored the reindeer's powers once again and now they were ready for flight. Nick glanced at the moon, hanging over them like a great silver clock face. Would they make it in time?

Zak was on Donder's back, looking white-faced with fear. Anneka, who was sitting on Cupid, looked apprehensive but excited. Johan, on Prancer's back, was stroking the beast's neck and whispering quietly into his ear, while Louisa jiggled feverishly on Vixen's back, raring to go. Nick settled himself into the comfortable curve of Rudolph's back. It felt warm and familiar. A thrill ran through him at the thought of riding with him again.

'Erm . . . Nicku . . .' said Zak shakily. 'I suppose this isn't a good time to mention that I don't like heights?'

'No it isn't,' said Nick shortly. 'Just hold on tight to their antlers, grip with your legs and let them do the rest. They'll look after you. Now come on. We have to go!'

Carrying their loads, the reindeer got to their feet and trotted over to the edge of the clearing, where they formed a line. Comet stood at their head, ready to navigate the way. Lancer trotted up in front of them and stood to attention, like a general sending off his troops into battle.

'Good luck, my family. Be brave. Be daring. Do your best. And come back safe. I shall be waiting here.'

He trotted off to the side to give them a clear run across the open space. The anticipation grew as the reindeer began to paw the ground with their hooves. Anneka, Zak and Johan were pale and trembling, their knuckles white as they gripped the reindeer's antlers. Only Louisa looked comfortable.

Suddenly all the reindeer cantered forward, building up speed as they thundered across the clearing, their hooves thudding on the snow and sending up white spray. Faster and faster they went, until they lifted gracefully into the air and took off, tucking their hooves underneath them.

'Wooah! Steady!' Zak screamed. 'Let me off! I want to get down!'

'Just shut up and enjoy it!' Nick called back to him, as Rudolph sailed into the air. Then he gave himself up to the thrill of the flight. All the memories of his childhood, of flying through the forest with the reindeer, came flooding back as the ground fell away beneath them and the reindeer headed straight for the trees.

At the last moment, the pines parted obediently into a wide sweeping avenue. The convoy began to hurtle along the twisting paths on a hectic rollercoaster ride. The trunks flashed past and the snow sparkled on the laden branches of the trees. Nick kept his eyes fixed on Comet's antlered head in front of him, navigating her way through the forest. The wind whistled past his ears and blew his hood down as the avenue opened up to reveal the wide expanse of snowy wasteland beyond. They had reached the edge of the forest.

Nick tightened his grip on Rudolph's antlers as the view spread out below them and the sky opened up above. They rose higher in the air and, with a sudden whoosh, shot into hyper speed, leaving trails of light behind them.

They soared over the Arctic Wastes, eating up the vast distances. After a while they saw the curve of the earth at the North Pole ahead of them. The golden spires of Doransk thrust above the horizon in jagged points, surrounded by a halo of glowing light.

Nick's heartbeat quickened. The fun was over. He steeled himself and called out to Comet. 'Begin the descent. I want us all to fly low over the whole City. Everyone must see you! Especially the children!'

They swooped over the camps outside the City gates. The immigrants looked up and gaped in shock as the extraordinary convoy passed overhead. Nine flying reindeer streaking through the sky, five of them with children on their backs.

They approached the artificial bubble that enclosed Doransk and shot straight through it with a gentle popping sound. The hot steamy air hit them in a wave after the freezing Arctic night. A lurid silver moon hung in the artificial sky and false stars twinkled at them.

As they flew over the golden streets, circling lower and lower, Nick's heart began to hammer. It must be nearly midnight now. He had it all worked out in his mind. *Let the children see the reindeer*. Surely the sight of them would bring their lost childhoods back? Then Magda's spell would be broken, and without the children's youth to keep her beauty intact, she would be unmasked.

Gather everyone in the City together, to see Magda as she really was. Let the reindeer take the Lights from her, so the other illusion – her Golden City – was revealed as a fake. Then, after that, it was up to him to wrestle the magnetic forces away from her, at the stroke of midnight, when they were at their strongest.

Nick's heartbeat quickened. The fun was over.

And her power would be gone. Now Nick thought about it, it seemed like a crazy, impossible plan. But it was their only hope.

They banked round above the City. Nick noticed with a shock that the streets were deserted. Where was everyone? Was Magda expecting him to return? A tremor of disquiet ran down his spine.

Suddenly he felt Rudolph jerk violently beneath him. A powerful force was pulling them all down, drawing them towards Golden Square, like water being sucked into a plughole, a million times stronger than the force of gravity, and impossible to resist.

The Final Reckoning

The children clung on to the reindeer's necks, screaming as they spiralled downwards. The reindeer bellowed in terror and their hooves paddled helplessly in the air. Nick glanced down and saw that Golden Square was jam-packed with people. A space in the middle was left free, cordoned off and patrolled by goblins, where Magda was standing, staring up expectantly, flanked by Volpo and Finn. Within moments they had slammed on to the ground.

The reindeer pitched over, snorting in terror, and the children tumbled off their backs. A posse of goblins dragged them all off the ground, tethered the reindeer together and tied up the children. Nick was shoved in front of Magda, who stared at him impassively, then curved her lips into a malicious smile. 'Thank you for bringing the reindeer to me, Nickolai. Most convenient.' Nick gasped in shock. 'Did you really think your little secret was safe from me?' she sneered. 'I know everything. My wolves spotted your reindeer years ago. Saw your little jaunts in the forest.'

Nick felt a hopeless fury rise up in him. 'What do you want them for?'

'I will be needing them to draw my flying sleigh around the world when I visit every corner of my Golden Empire,' Magda said with satisfaction. 'You see, I plan to control the entire surface of the globe. There will be many darling little children to visit, who will clamour to come to my parties and take rides in my sleigh. These wonderful beasts will make an ideal means of transport to all corners of my realm.'

She gestured at the crowds, who were still gaping at the reindeer. 'I told these people that you had stolen the reindeer from me; that I made you bring them back. They're mine now. Living proof of my goodness and greatness.'

'Hail Queen Magda, O Great and Glorious One!' chanted the children. Nick groaned in despair. The sight of the flying reindeer, which he'd hoped so fervently would do its magic, hadn't worked. He looked at the reindeer who returned his stare mutely. He had unwittingly betrayed his friends, led them into a trap. He boiled over with rage.

'No!' Nick screamed. 'You shan't have them! And you shan't have Elvina!' He swung round to the assembled crowd and pointed a shaking finger at Magda. 'Don't listen to her. She's a liar! Don't you know what she's been doing to your children? She's stealing their childhood to preserve her beauty. That isn't her real face!' He stared wild-eyed at the crowds, who gazed back at him in confusion.

Magda smiled. 'See?' she purred. 'It is me they believe in, me they worship and follow, Nickolai. Only I can give them what they want.'

She took her small golden trumpet from Volpo and her voice rang out from statues across the city. 'My loyal people, the Evil Elf Boy has finally been brought to justice. You are about to witness his execution! His reign of terror is over and we can live in peace at last. But I am a good and kindly Queen. He will not feel a thing, but will simply turn to stone and remain for ever rooted to this spot, a statue standing in this square as a monument to folly, a constant reminder of the wickedness that could have threatened us all.'

Suddenly there was a cry from the crowd. A woman threw herself forward.

'You're wrong!' she cried. 'And he's right. We know what you've been doing to our children. Those of us who have any sense can see it. You're the evil one! It's been you all along!'

It was Lotta, her face blazing with righteous anger. A white-faced Joachim stood next to her, making no attempt to restrain her.

'Arrest that traitor!' bawled Magda. The goblins strode into the crowd and grabbed Lotta.

'Leave Mama alone!' Anneka and Louisa screamed.

Joachim tried to fight off the goblins, clinging to his wife, but then he too was dragged forward. They were tied up and thrown together with Anneka and Louisa.

Suddenly Elvina crawled to the top of Nick's tunic and peeped out timidly. Magda let out a gasp of anticipation. 'Yes! There she is!' she hissed, reaching towards the fairy. 'Soon she'll be mine!'

Elvina let out an angry squeak of protest.

'Go on, Elvina,' Nick cried in desperation. 'If you want to stay with me, you have to be brave. Go and visit the children. It's our last chance!'

He felt her quivering in anticipation, then with a sudden burst of daring, she buzzed out of Nick's front and began zigzagging round the crowds. A collective cry of wonder went up as the glowing shape flitted above their heads.

'There!' shouted Nick. 'That's not one of Magda's fiendish tricks! It's a fairy! A real live fairy and she's mine!'

The crowd gasped as Elvina swooped down and began to circle the children in dizzying loops, touching each one of them in turn. As she flitted past each child's face, strafing their noses as she went, the magic finally began to work. Slowly, the light came back into their eyes as one by one, they snapped out of their spells. They blinked and shook their heads, as though coming out of a deep trance. Then they looked up at their parents.

'Mum? Dad?'

'Where have I been?'

'What's going on?'

All over the square, parents threw their arms around their children and hugged them tight. Then they all jumped as a shrill, unearthly shriek came from Magda.

The most horrible transformation was taking place. The Queen was growing old before their eyes. The youthful beauty began to fade. Her jowls fell and her skin began to wrinkle and fold into heavy creases. Her eyes grew bloodshot and disappeared behind pouches of rotting flesh. Her skin turned green and putrid. There was a rustling noise as wiry grey hairs pushed their way out of her scalp, turning her luxuriant black mane into a matted, grizzled mass. Her body began to shrivel like a dried-up leaf, and her hands turned into gnarled and mottled claws. The dainty, pointed ears drooped and hung down in wrinkled flaps. Her teeth dropped out one by one and fell on to the ground with a dull tinkle, leaving a gaping toothless mouth.

Within seconds, the beautiful, radiant Queen was gone. Magda let out a long howl of agony and clutched at her ruined face. Volpo stood frozen to the spot and Finn was backing away, white-faced with shock and revulsion.

'Look! Now do you believe me!' shouted Nick, pointing at the wizened crone in front of him. 'That's what she's really like! That's what she's been using your children to hide!'

Magda let out a low howl of rage and gave Nick a look of such loathing it made his blood curdle. 'Very clever, Elf Boy,' she spat. 'But I still have the Lights! And the magnetic power! I will punish you for doing this to me. I will destroy you! Look! The hour is here!'

And she pointed a clawed finger at the clock face on the tower of the Doransk City Hall. It was midnight. With a loud, resonant boom, the bell began to toll the hour. The heavy chimes echoed through the hot night air.

One . . . two . . . three . . . four . . .

'Your death knell, Nickolai,' Magda hissed. 'The moment I have been waiting for, when my power will be complete. What you have just done can be undone None of these fools matter. I can dispense with them and start all over again!'

She pulled aside her cloak, revealing the gaping black hole in her chest.

Ten . . . eleven . . . twelve!

The last stroke boomed round the City. Elvina, who was cowering behind Nick's left ear, started squealing in terror.

'No!' screamed Nick. 'Don't take her away from me!'

The whirlwind poured out of Magda and snaked towards him. Nick felt Elvina's tiny fingers clinging to the tip of his ear. Then they lost their grip and she was torn away from him and sucked towards the black hole. She whirled around, squealing loudly, then her cries were shut off as she was swallowed into the blackness.

Immediately, Nick felt faint and dizzy. His hands

went numb and a cold, creeping heaviness stole over him. He was slowly turning to stone.

From very far away, he heard Anneka's voice, screaming at him in panic. 'Move your ears, Nick! Wiggle your toes! Anything to stay alive! Fight it!'

Nickolai tried to twitch his ears. It was like trying to get a rusty lock to budge. He tried again and they shifted sluggishly. He tried once more. This time he felt a force coming out of them that gave Magda a sharp jolt and made her gasp.

With an immense effort, Nick turned his eyes to the reindeer. They were quivering violently, pulling together, as though they were drawing a heavy weight backwards. Their antlers were touching, glowing with an inner energy. Sparks fizzled round them and bolts of Light flashed back and forth. They were trying to draw the Lights out of Magda.

The struggle went on for several minutes. The reindeer strained and pulled as Magda's ugly face twisted and her body writhed, trying to hold on to the vast, cosmic energy she had stolen and held for so many years.

She let out a horrible shriek as a massive explosion of brilliant coloured Light burst out of her. It hung suspended for a moment, trembling around the edges, and a swarm of luminous creatures, like a cloud of insects, was released, floating around in a great clustered ball of light and making a loud humming noise. There was an almighty whoosh and the main body of Light swooped upwards. Within seconds, huge curtains of shimmering multi-coloured radiance were dancing across the sky.

The Northern Lights had returned.

Nick stared at them through dimming eyes, the Lights which had brought his people into being. The crowd gasped, pointed and stared. Zak sank to his knees in awe, clasped his hands together and gazed at them like someone worshipping at a shrine.

'Holy Sedna! I can see them, Grandfather! I can see them!' he shouted at the sky. 'Are you up there, Paptik? Can you see them too?'

A tiny shape separated itself from the shimmering ball above the square and flew towards Nick. He tried to snatch at her with his hand, but it felt leaden and heavy. He was still partly stone, only half alive. Elvina flitted around him, chirruping anxiously, and Nick felt the life beginning to flow back into him.

Magda was reaching up towards the Lights, as though she would claw them out of the sky. 'Give them back! I need them! They're mine!'

'No they're not, you witch!' shouted Zak angrily. 'They belong to everyone. You think everything in the world belongs to you! It doesn't!'

Magda pointed a shaking, scaly finger at him, ready to send out a thunderbolt. But she stopped short as a loud creaking came from close by. There were screams and shouts. The golden dome on top of the Doransk City Hall wobbled dangerously – then toppled and fell to the ground with a loud crash and a cloud of black dust. The crowds cowered together to avoid the tumbling masonry as more buildings began to crumble and collapse. The castle on the hill began to fall apart, all the layers of gold leaf and sparkling stones peeling off and vanishing to reveal dense black coal underneath. In dream-like slow motion, the whole edifice came crashing down into the moat. The Magda statues keeled over, breaking into pieces.

Up in the sky, the artificial moon throbbed brightly, exploded and vanished. The false stars flashed on and off, like faulty fairy lights, then fizzled and went out one by one. With a sickening squelch, the protective bubble that enclosed the whole City burst. Instantly the warmth vanished and the cold night air rushed in upon them with an icy blast.

In the space of a few moments, the Golden City of Doransk lay in ruins, turned from gold into coal.

'Look at your Golden City now!' Anneka crowed at Magda. 'The land of promise, your city of dreams! It's just an illusion, created by your sorcery!'

Magda stared at her fallen City. She turned to Nick with a look of such hatred that he could feel its heat scorching him. 'This is all your doing. You've taken everything from me. But we'll go down together!' Suddenly her arm shot out and snatched Elvina from where she perched on Nick's shoulder.

'No! Give her back!' shrieked Nick. But he felt steel bands closing around him. Magda was sucking him towards her like a magnet. Her powers were diminished, but they were still greater than his. Her hideous, twisted face loomed towards him until it filled his vision and the two of them became one, locked together in a coil of magnetic energy. He was entering the very heart of darkness. It seeped into his soul until he became part of it.

'Come with me, Nickolai,' whispered an invisible voice, a voice that seemed to come from inside his own mind. 'Our power is one! We are part of the same energy. Together we can rule the world!'

He couldn't tell now where he ended and Magda began. It was as though they were the same person.

'No!' he screamed. 'I won't let you take me over!'

He commanded his mind to fight her. His brain grappled with the dark feelers that swarmed through it. He must reclaim the forces. As the two of them wrestled fiercely for control over the vast magnetic energies, the earth could take no more. There was a deafening, agonized groan and the ground beneath them opened up into a yawning chasm.

The crowd gasped as the empty caverns of the Elfin Kingdom were revealed and Nick and Magda were sucked down into the crack. The jagged scar in the cavern floor had opened up again, the abyss from which Magda had emerged all those years ago. Flames leaped towards the spinning figures as they plunged into it.

Somehow Nick's hand found Magda's bony fist, still

clutching Elvina. Above the roaring of the Vortex, Nick could hear the Fairy squealing. He tried to prise Magda's claw open, but her talons dug into his palm like hot needles. He would not let Magda take Elvina, even in death. He gritted his teeth in one last effort and pulled the gnarled claw open, closing his hand around Elvina before the flames consumed him.

Behind them, there was an almighty rushing sound. Magda's monsters were pulled down together in one twisting, howling mass. Volpo let out a terrible shriek as his creatures swirled around him. The hungry pit sucked the whirlwind of goblins, demons and wolves into its depths, then closed up with a hissing noise, leaving a smoking scar and a few lumps of steaming coal on the cavern floor.

Immediately, the shimmering ball of Light Fairies swooped down from Golden Square into the cavern; all except one, which remained above the surface, searching for something. A thin film of ice began to form over the hole in the ground, concealing the Elfin Kingdom from view.

Down in Solstice Square, the Light Fairies scattered into a thousand tiny glowing shapes and flew up to the lifeless statues. One by one, the stalagmites and stalactites transformed back into beautiful dainty creatures, with ice blue eyes and pointed ears. The elves blinked and looked around. Then carried on doing exactly what they had been doing the moment they had been frozen, as if nothing had happened. The music started up and the cavern began to ring with the sounds of festivity as they returned to their riotous dancing.

King Vilmar, still sitting on his ice throne, exactly where he'd been when Magda had come back from the Vortex all those years ago, blinked and looked round in puzzlement; he felt confused and disorientated, as though there had been a hiccup in time. His mind tried to snatch at the memories, but it was all a dim and muddled haze. Something had happened. There was a jagged scar in the cavern floor; lumps of smoking coal scattered around it. Signs of occupation. Toys lying about that he had never seen before. He glanced up at the domed roof of the cavern. It seemed thinner than before, the stars twinkling through the ice.

He gasped as a beautiful, four-legged, antlered creature burst through the fragile barrier and flew down into the vaulted space. The music stopped abruptly as the elves gazed up at the reindeer in wonder.

Vilmar stood up. 'Something has happened tonight, my people,' he called out in his quavering voice. 'All is not as it was before.'

They stood and watched in silence as Rudolph landed by the jagged scar on the cavern floor. He bent his head and sniffed at a lump of smouldering coal, burning his nose, and jerked his head back in pain. A tear ran out of his eye, rolled down his cheek and plopped on to the coal, where it smoked and fizzled for a few moments before evaporating into the air.

The Mission Begins

The crowds in what was left of Golden Square milled about in a state of shock. Finn's crown sat askew on his head as he stared at the crack in the ground, the arrogant young monarch replaced by a lost, white-faced, bewildered boy. His face crumpled as his mother rushed over and swept him into her arms.

'I'm here, darling! All those nasty people have gone now. There there . . . everything'll be all right . . .'

Anneka, Zak, Louisa, Lotta and Joachim were huddled together, still looking at the place where Nick had disappeared. Louisa began to cry.

'He's not really dead, is he? He will come back?'

Anneka smiled at her sadly. 'He was very brave. He sacrificed himself so the rest of us could be free. We'll always remember him.'

'I suppose there's only one place for us to go now,' said Joachim, pulling his family together in a bear hug. 'Home.'

Zak was lingering on the edge of their circle. Anneka saw his wistful face and drew him in. 'Come back with us,' she said, slipping her arm through his. 'It'll be a good base for you to go looking for your people.'

'You're very welcome,' said Lotta fondly.

Zak smiled shyly and blushed. He was about to reply when something roared over their heads. The flying shape soared above the square, emitting loud roars of laughter. It circled in crazy loops over the astonished crowd. Sitting astride Rudolph's back, Nickolai did one final, triumphant lap of honour and swooped in to land with a clatter of hooves.

A hush fell. It was a miracle. Impossible. He was completely unharmed. In fact, he had a supernatural glow about him; his face looked older, more grown-up. His red velvet robe was in mint condition, and the white fur that edged it seemed whiter than ever. His hood was down and his ears were twitching with excitement.

Anneka was the first to recover from the shock. 'Nick! Is it really you?' She stumbled towards him.

He jumped off Rudolph's back and swung her round. 'Who else would it be?' A great bubble of laughter was rising up inside him. He let it out in a roar which shook his whole body. After so much horror and sadness, there was a lot of laughing to catch up on. He opened his arms to the crowd.

'I'm back!' he shouted. 'It's me, Nickolai! Aren't you pleased to see me?'

There was a stunned silence, then the whole crowd

erupted into deafening cheers. Hats were flung in the air and everyone surged forward and surrounded him, slapping him on the back.

'Long live the Elf Boy! Long live Nickolai!'

Their chants rose high in the air, echoing around the ruins of the city. Zak pushed through the crowds, white and shocked, and enveloped Nick in a bear hug.

'Sedna's toenails! You are some kind of shaman!'

Nick shrugged modestly and looked at his friends. 'Wouldn't have done it without you guys. I never thought I could do it, but I did! I beat her!'

'But *how*?' breathed Anneka.

'Elvina. She saved me. She protected me down there, kept me alive, stopped me from burning up.'

'Where is she?' asked Zak, looking around.

Nick tapped his chest. 'In here,' he said. 'Somehow, in the Vortex, she became part of me. She's safe now. She'll always be with me. No one'll ever be able to take her away again.'

A trembling female voice came from nearby. 'Nickolai?'

Nick looked round at the voice. An elfin woman stood gazing at him with intense longing. He stared back at her, a hazy memory swimming into his head. The face no child ever forgets.

'Mother?'

Tears filled the elfin woman's blue eyes. 'How long have I been gone? What happened? How old are you? You were a baby when I last saw you.'

Nick felt like crying and laughing at the same time. It was the strangest feeling. He strode over to his mother and folded her in his arms. He realized he was taller than her by half a head. After a few moments, during which neither of them were able to speak, they looked at each other.

'It's a long story. We were separated twelve years ago. I'm thirteen now.'

She gazed at him. 'You've grown so much! You're going to be tall like your father.'

'There's an awful lot happened since then,' Nick said. 'I don't know where to begin.'

Ella suddenly looked stricken. 'You're not a child any more! I missed your childhood. All those years when you were growing up, I wasn't there,' she whispered.

It was too sad to think about.

'I came up here looking for you,' Nick said, swallowing the lump in his throat. 'I was rescued, and these nice people from down south brought me up. We can go back and see them. They'll tell you all about my childhood, what I was like. All the things I did.'

Ella looked at him with tears pouring down her face. Nick put his arm round her and squeezed her shoulders.

'It's all right,' he murmured. 'We can make up for it.'

His mother began to dry her eyes. 'You're right. We should be grateful for what we have now. Tell me everything,' she said firmly. 'Everything that's happened to you since that night in the snow.'

He strode over to his mother and folded her in his arms.

Nick took her hand and gently led her over to a fallen block of masonry. They sat down together and he told her. When he had finished, she looked at him in awe.

'Nickolai, do you realize what this means? You're not an ordinary elf any more. I knew it, that time in the tunnels when you were a baby. I knew you were special.'

Nick snorted. 'Rubbish! I just want to go back home and take up where we left off. Make up for lost time. Once I've said goodbye to my friends, of course.'

'No, Nickolai! You can't do that. You've been into the Vortex and survived. You're immortal now.'

Nick wasn't sure he liked the sound of that. 'You mean I'll always be thirteen years old?'

'No no no, you'll grow old and turn into an old man, but you will live for ever,' his mother told him, clasping his hand tight. 'You've done something tonight that means you have a duty to the world, to the Kingdom, to what you've saved. And you'll be able to carry out your mission for years to come, into eternity. It's your destiny, what you were born to do.'

'And what is this mission?' Nick asked, still bewildered.

'That's for you to decide,' said Ella. 'How can you make sure this never happens again? How can you make sure that childhood stays alive for ever? And how do you think you can carry out this task, for every child born into the world in the future?'

Nick looked at the reindeer, who were now surrounded by adoring children stroking their heads and patting their flanks. He had restored their flying powers. They would do anything for him. And Lancer *had* said that he would let them out every year on Winter Solstice Eve.

He thought of the Elfin Kingdom below, and King Vilmar, and how flabbergasted he had been to learn what had happened. The elves would be eternally grateful to him as well.

He looked over at Zak and Anneka and all his friends, his allies who had helped him, and thought of what he owed them.

He thought of the toys he had made, and how Elvina had brought them alive and helped bring back so much lost childhood.

He thought of the chimneys that had helped him get in and out of so many places.

He moved his ears, and felt the answering call of the magnetic forces, now under his control at the twitch of an ear tip. And suddenly the whole plan fell into place.

But there was one thing he had to tell his mother first.

'Er Mum,' he said awkwardly. 'I've got a small confession to make. I sort of – borrowed the sleigh? Just for a while?'

Ella looked at him sharply. 'Where is it? That's a family heirloom, you know. It's not damaged, is it?'

'It's all right,' Nick assured her. 'I've left it

somewhere, but I can go and pick it up, no problem. 'Cos I'm going to need it. For this mission.'

'Have you decided what to do?'

'Yes.' He stood up. 'I know just what I have to do now. And I'm going to tell everyone, before they all go home.'

The derelict square was now a scene of rejoicing. A carnival atmosphere filled the air as the crowds celebrated their freedom amongst the smoking ruins. The whole scene was covered in a blanket of white snow, since the microclimate bubble had burst and the Arctic weather had rushed back in. Fires had been lit and temporary shelters built. Many people were making plans for the long journey home, pooling their resources. The reindeer were enjoying a new-found celebrity status, flying round the square with children on their backs. The air was ringing with laughter.

Nick strode up to a fallen statue of Magda and clambered on to it. As he stood up to address the crowd, the cheers and whistles rose to a deafening roar that echoed across the Arctic wastes.

'Nickolai! Nickolai! Nickolai!'

Nickolai surveyed them all, a sturdy young man on the brink of adulthood, tall for his thirteen years, his red robe wrapped round him. His blue eyes blazed in the darkness and his pointed ears twitched. Everyone listened intently as he spoke.

'I came here to find my family and my people,' he

began. He looked over at his mother, who smiled back. 'And while I was looking, I found another sort of family. My friends.'

He looked at Zak and Anneka, and all the other colony children who were gathered together in a crowd. They grinned and waved back at him.

'They helped me get rid of the evil we have seen tonight. They helped me find my people and my mother. They helped me restore our Elfin Kingdom. So what I've realized is that, even though I've found my own people, the whole world is my family too. We're all in it together. And the thing that binds us all together is children. We nearly lost that. We nearly lost childhood. I want to make sure that doesn't happen again.'

A huge roar of approval went up at this.

'I want to celebrate this night every year for the rest of time. I want to remind everyone that childhood doesn't last for very long. Once it's gone, you can't get it back. We have to make the most of it while it's there. And what do children like most?'

'Toys!' shouted all the children in the square.

'Well that's good, because I do toys,' said Nick. 'My people are going to help me make them, and bring them to all the children in the world on Winter Solstice Eve every single year. And when you're grown up, I'll do it for your children too. And their children! 'Cos guess what? My mother tells me I'm going to live for ever.'

Another massive cheer went up. Nick waited for it to die down. 'So go home and get back to normal family life,' he continued. 'Wait for me to come next Winter Solstice Eve. Spread the word. And remember, I want all the children in bed, asleep, before I arrive. Or I won't be dropping in on your house.'

The entire gathering exploded into tumultuous applause. Then Nick held up his hand as he remembered something. 'Oh and by the way, can you all please leave something for us to eat? It'll be a long old night. Something for the reindeer, and some of those berry pies, like Lotta makes, would be good.'

'Done!' shouted Lotta. Then she looked round. 'I'll give you all the recipe later.'

Nick's friends gathered round, full of questions.

'It's a great idea, Nick,' Anneka began, 'but how on earth are you going to do it? Get round to every house, in one night? It's impossible!'

Nick sighed and put his arm round her. 'I thought you believed in me? Just trust me on this. You've seen what can be done.'

'He's a shaman,' said Zak wisely. 'He'll find a way, Anneka. Wait and see.'

'How will you get the toys delivered? Will you leave them on the doorsteps like we did back in Norsk?' asked Johan eagerly.

Nick smiled. 'No. I'll find a way into everyone's house. You won't even know I've been.'

'Where will you leave them?' asked Louisa. 'So we know they're from you?'

Nick thought about this. 'I haven't quite worked that one out yet,' he admitted.

Suddenly there was a commotion on the edge of the square. Panting, baying noises carried across the air. The crowd fell back as an old sledge creaked across the snow, weaving amongst the smoking ruins, drawn by a team of husky dogs. It was painted red and hung about with clonking cowbells. And driving it were two old people he hadn't seen for a while, bundled up in furs and wrapped in layers of brightly knitted woollen garments.

It was Joe and Hannah.

Nick felt a wave of affection as the sledge drew to a halt. The old couple climbed out and dusted themselves down. Hannah turned and spoke loudly. 'Has anyone seen a young man called Nickolai?'

'Blond-haired lad, quite well built, blue eyes and – er – pointy ears,' added Joe. 'Should be about thirteen?'

Joe and Hannah hadn't noticed Nick standing on the fallen block of statue. Their eyesight wasn't what it had been.

'Hey, Joe! Hannah!' Nick called. 'I'm here!'

At the sound of Nick's voice, the dogs began to whine and leap in their harnesses. Hannah's face creased into a broad smile. She held her arms out to him.

'Nickolai! What are you doing up there? You'll fall off

335

and hurt yourself. Get down at once.' She looked around at the crumbled ruins. 'And what happened to this place? I thought it was supposed to be a Golden City?'

Nick leaped down, ran up to them and hugged them both in a bear-like embrace. More cheers rang out.

'She insisted on coming up here to find you,' Joe explained. 'Sorry to embarrass you lad, in front of all your friends. But she was missing you terribly. Took us ages.'

'I was worried about you,' said Hannah. 'Wanted to make sure you were all right. Here, I've got something for you.' And she bustled over to the sledge and came back with a sack. She opened it to reveal a bundle of knitted garments.

'Oh no!' said Nick, shaking his head. 'Not the brown thing with the earflaps.'

'No no no dear, threw that away years ago,' Hannah clucked. 'I've brought you some socks. I hear you can get frostbite up here if you don't keep your feet warm.' And she held out a pair of brightly coloured, long woolly socks. 'Knitted them special. Put them on now, Nickolai, before you catch your death of cold.'

Nick grinned and took the bundle of stockings. 'Thanks, Mum. I'm sure they'll come in handy.'

THE END

Epilogue

Every Winter Solstice Eve, a miracle happens at the North Pole.

The moon shines down on the Arctic wastes and the Northern Lights play across the night sky.

At the stroke of midnight, there is a resounding boom, and a crack opens in the ice. A magnificent sleigh shoots up into the sky, drawn by nine flying reindeer and driven by a jolly old man in a rich red velvet robe, lined with white fur. He has pointed ears, pink cheeks, white hair, a long white beard and ice blue eyes which sparkle with merriment. He seems to find everything funny, and his roars of laughter shake his belly and echo through the cold night air.

The sleigh is elaborately festooned with jingling bells and covered with decorations and carvings. In the back is a huge bulging sack, full of toys made down in the Elfin Kingdom, which lies in the vaulted caverns beneath the ice. The sack never seems to be empty.

The sleigh shoots across the sky like a rocket, leaving a trail of Light behind it. Passing over a dark, silent forest, it comes to the very first town. This is always his first stop. It used to be a small settlement, but now it is a city, twinkling with lights. In the grand central square stands a statue of a young man with pointed ears and a fur-edged robe. It is made of white marble which sparkles in the moonlight.

The sleigh circles the twinkling city and slowly comes in towards a small house with a sloping roof.

This year, there are two grey-haired people peering anxiously out of the window of an upstairs bedroom. Behind them, their two grandchildren sleep soundly. Their woolly stockings have been hung on the end of their beds. On their bedside table is a plate of carrots and some berry pies, carefully laid out.

Downstairs, their daughter and her husband are putting the finishing touches to a fir tree, planted in a pot, hung with coloured lights and decorations. The final detail – a fairy sitting on top of the tree, who looks very like Elvina. Great Aunt Louisa is helping them, or rather, telling them what to do.

The grey-haired couple hear the sound of bells and see the sleigh approaching through the sky; they glance at each other and smile. They watch it coming in right over the house, swooping down so close they can almost see their old friend's face. They wait for the thump on the roof and the clattering of hooves, hoping that none of the tiles will be dislodged.

It always comes.

When it does, they know it's time to leave. They

338

glance at their grandchildren, then at the fireplace, still red with glowing embers. Anneka quickly douses the coals. Zak puts his arm round her and they tiptoe quietly out of the room.

ACKNOWLEDGEMENTS

ACKNOWLEDGEMENTS

First of all, I must thank my daughter Isabel Raby, for inspiring me with the idea for this story. She started the whole thing six years ago when, just before Christmas, she wondered who filled Santa's stocking when he was a child. I thought, yeah, good question; what was his childhood like, where did he come from and why does he do what he does every year? I spent the next six years trying to find the answers to all these questions and I hope I have now done this. I would also like to thank my husband Peter Raby, for his unflagging support throughout my entire writing career. Also the rest of my family, Eleanor Raby, Susan Daniel, Georgia Daniel, Ciara Thompson, Anne and Ian Toms and their children and grandchildren – special mentions for Charlotte, Toby and Joshua. Plus Grace Lockett, who first inspired me to write.

Many thanks also to the following people for all the help, support, encouragement and advice they have given me during the long and rocky road of developing this story: Gillian Gordon, Michael Forte, Anna Home O.B.E. and Grainne Marmion at the Children's Film and Television Foundation, Richard Carpenter, Richard Morss, Di Redmond, David Collier, Tessa Sheridan, Naomi Telford at the UK Film Council, Christopher Vogler, Gemma Hirst and Caroline Walsh at David Higham Associates, Rachel Wade, Anne McNeil, Charles Nettleton, Geraldine Stroud, Elisa Offord, Alison Still and all the team at Hodder Children's Books, Andy Gee, Jane Liddiard, Krissy Alice Wood, John and Alex Baker, Jacqui and Robin Stubbs, Ben Heslop, Graham and Hector Lester-George, Pat Harris, Jane Cheney, Pete and Jeanette Sears, all my mates at the Writers' Guild, my dear friend Sophie Spiller for the much-needed diversion therapy during the dark times and finally, She Who Gave me the Wonderful Inspiration for Magda. A great debt of gratitude to all.

RESEARCH NOTES

Arctic Information

The Northern Lights or Aurora Borealis appear in the sky above the Arctic Circle during the winter months. They are not predictable in their patterns.

There are many different ancient folklore theories about them amongst the tribes of the Inuit. Some believed they were the souls of unborn children playing in the sky. Some that they were torches held by the dead to help the living hunt during the long dark winter. Medieval Europeans in southerly latitudes believed they were the fiery glow of battles and conflagrations taking place further north, since the colours appeared red that far south. The Vikings thought they were a reflection in the sky of Vulcan's forge and miners in Alaska thought they were a gaseous form of lightning, or the glow from radium mines.

I like the one about unborn children best. But they were all wrong, of course. The scientific explanation for the Northern Lights is this: the fantastic display is created by an electric discharge in the earth's ionosphere. As solar winds from the sun pass across the curve of the earth in a constant stream, they release an electric current containing solar particles. These solar particles travel along the force lines in the earth's electro-magnetic field, curving down in the centre of the earth, like seams running down into an apple core – above the North Pole. Positive and negative terminals are created, giving rise to polar winds. These winds excite the electrons in oxygen atoms and nitrogen molecules in the atmosphere, which give out energy in the form of visible light, infra red, ultra violet and radio waves. The extraordinary and beautiful colours – mostly pale pink and pale green – come from oxygen and nitrogen atoms.

The more energetic the sun's streaming particles, the taller the curtains of light towering over the earth become and the more active. If there are magnetic storms taking place on the sun, the disturbances are even greater – playing havoc with compasses, radio signals and navigational systems.

Because of all this electro-magnetic activity in the air, the Northern Lights are said to be very sensitive and reactive. Many people say they make a gentle swishing, crackling noise and some Inuit claim that 'the Lights' will respond to a gentle whistling by dipping closer to the earth. The power created by this phenomenon is astonishing and if we could harness it, it could provide a revolutionary source of energy. But I hope we never do. We have done enough to harm this planet already.

So you see, I didn't make it all up, not entirely. The Lights are said to be the most awe-inspiring sight imaginable. They are one of the things I wish to see before I die.

Inuit Information

There are many Inuit tribes who roam the Arctic Circle – Sami, Thule, Yupik, who live in Siberia – and Inupiaq who live in eastern Alaska, Canada and Greenland. Like many people living in inaccessible parts of the globe, they still live in much the same way as they always have. It's a tough life, carving out an existence in this harsh and inhospitable environment, and the Inuit rely on nature to survive. Needless to say, the changes brought about in global ecology have affected the way of life in the Arctic Circle. There is much to learn about them, too much to cover here, so I recommend further reading.

The Inuit have their own alphabet. Some Inuit words:
Muktuk – dried meat
Tupilak – talisman
Inuk – single Inuit person
Sedna – the supreme goddess in Inuit folklore
Inuktitut – Inuit language
Qimmiq – dog
Qamtiik – sled
Tuktu – caribou
Igluigaq – igloo or house
Kamik – sealskin

Other words, such as tuktik, paptik, qammik and aktuk, I have made up, using the general constructions of their language.

True North

What does this mean? Well guess what – there is not just one North Pole, but four! It is hard to pinpoint the precise location of the Pole, because the earth wobbles on its axis as it rotates and orbits round the sun. The average position of the Pole is known as the Geographic North Pole.

Attempts have been made to define the Pole more precisely by arranging it around several more poles, according to different criteria.

In 1985, the North Magnetic Pole, around which the earth's magnetic field and its magnetosphere revolves, was calculated to lie 30 miles east of Edmund Walker island, some 400 miles further northwest of where it was first discovered in 1831.

The North Geomantic Pole – a more theoretical, mathematical version – is calculated to lie about 500 miles east of the North Magnetic Pole, in Greenland.

Finally, there is the Pole of Inaccessibility, or True North, which was mooted by the Victorians. This is where some believe the real North Pole lies – a constantly moving, inaccessible and indefinable place, because of the earth's movements and all the sea and ice. I like to think this is where the Elfin Kingdom lies – at True North.

The caverns I describe have recently been discovered under the Polar Ice cap by explorers and potholers.

Legends behind Saint Nicholas, Santa Claus or Father Christmas

There are many of these. One is the famous Christian saint, Nicholas, who was reputed to live on an island off the coast of Turkey many centuries ago. Like Saint George, he was not in fact a white Christian. Saint Nicholas was Turkish. He was reputed to do great acts of kindness. There is also Woden, a Norse god, who – legend has it – flew around the sky in a wooden sledge delivering gifts to children around the time of the Winter Solstice. Baba, in Italy, was an old woman who delivered gifts to children and left them in shoes, although in some parts they believed baby Jesus delivered them himself. In India the Hindu god of learning, Ganesha, is supposed to bring gifts to children at Yuletide. Like the Noah's Ark story, there are corresponding Santa Claus-type legends in mythologies all over the world. The Christian festival of Christmas, like all our festivals, is grafted on to an old pagan festival; in this case, Candlemas, which also became known as Yuletide. This would always take place in the depths of winter, at the Solstice, to cheer everyone up during the dark months and reassure them that spring and sunshine would return. They were often known as 'needfire' festivals, since the flames of candles and fires reminded people of the missing sun.

It was Coca Cola™ who created the image of Santa Claus as we know him today – the jolly guy in the red outfit. Prince Albert and the Victorians introduced the idea of Christmas trees, Christmas cards, decorations, and reindeer. The Light Fairy idea comes from Inuit mythology, but I think the idea of the fairy on top of the Christmas tree must come from inside all of us.

So all the original myths and legends have become overlaid and expanded in time by many other influences and ideas; there are many races and religions in the world and we must all learn to accept each other. I believe the annual winter festival should be shared by all the children in the world, regardless of race or creed.

I have drawn together all the different myths, legends and customs around Christmas and Santa Claus and put them into one embodiment – a brave, selfless hero who personifies the spirit of kindness that prevails during the festive season which we celebrate all over the world.

It's a shame we can't be like that all the time, isn't it?

So, kids, you're the future. Over to you!

BIBLIOGRAPHY

Flight of the Reindeer, The True Story of Santa Claus and his Christmas Mission, by Robert Sullivan, Macmillan USA, 1996.

Arctic Dreams by Barry Lopez, Charles Scribner's Sons, New York, 1986, Harvill Press, London.

The Writer's Journey, Mythic Structure for Storytellers and Screenwriters by Christopher Vogler, second revised edition, Pan Books, 1999.

What Do We Know About the Inuit? Bryan and Cherry Alexander, Hodder Children's books, 1997.

Many journeys on the internet to websites too numerous to list.